All at once, Klag's senses were assaulted.

The sound of exploding consoles and blaring alarms slammed into his ears. The stench of melted conduits and burning components filled his nostrils. Smoke burned his eyes and coated his tongue.

Rodek was shouting over the din. "Shields down! Structural integrity field at thirty-five percent! Cloak offline! Main power failing!"

From the pilot's console, Leskit said, "I've lost helm control—we're heading into the atmosphere!"

Swallowing down the bitter taste of the smoke—and of defeat—Klag asked, "What is the status of communications systems?"

"Offline!" Kal's voice sounded peculiar, but Klag did not have time to determine why. He was more concerned with the fact that he had left Toq and his team behind on the Elabrej homeworld. *Without us to extract them, they will die on that world. My abysmal luck with first officers continues unabated. A pity—you were a fine warrior, Toq. May you die well.*

"Entering stratosphere," Leskit said.

Klag gritted his teeth. "On screen."

The *Gorkon*'s main viewer switched from the tactical overview to the grayish moon that they had been orbiting—and which now was getting closer by the second.

"All hands prepare for crash landing!"

STAR TREK®
I.K.S. GORKON

BOOK THREE

ENEMY TERRITORY

Keith R.A. DeCandido

**Based on STAR TREK
and STAR TREK: THE NEXT GENERATION®
created by Gene Roddenberry
and STAR TREK: DEEP SPACE NINE®
created by Rick Berman & Michael Piller**

POCKET BOOKS
New York London Toronto Sydney Elabrej

This book is a work of fiction. Names, characters, places and incidents are products of the author's imagination or are used fictitiously. Any resemblance to actual events or locales or persons, living or dead, is entirely coincidental.

An *Original* Publication of POCKET BOOKS

POCKET BOOKS, a division of Simon & Schuster, Inc.
1230 Avenue of the Americas, New York, NY 10020

STAR TREK is a Registered Trademark of
® Paramount Pictures.

This book is published by Pocket Books, a division of Simon & Schuster, Inc., under exclusive license from Paramount Pictures.

ISBN: 1-4165-0014-6

First Pocket Books paperback edition March 2005

10 9 8 7 6 5 4 3 2 1

POCKET and colophon are registered trademarks of Simon & Schuster, Inc.

Cover art by Keith Birdsong

Manufactured in the United States of America

For information regarding special discounts for bulk purchases, please contact Simon & Schuster Special Sales at 1-800-456-6798 or business@simonandschuster.com.

Dedicated to Mittens, 1986–2004
The sweetest cat in the entire world, he also had the heart
of a warrior, doing battle with diabetes and melanoma until
the very end. If there's a place for felines in Sto-Vo-Kor,
he's more than earned it.

HISTORIAN'S NOTE

This novel commences six weeks after Book 2 in this series, *Honor Bound* (except where specifically indicated otherwise), about ten months after "What You Leave Behind," the final episode of *Star Trek: Deep Space Nine*, and approximately three years prior to the feature film *Star Trek Nemesis*. This places it in the middle of the Year of Kahless 1001 on the Klingon calendar and late in the year 2376 on the human calendar.

ENEMY TERRITORY

PROLOGUE

Two months ago . . .

Before the alarm sounded, Shipmaster Vor Ellis had thought it was a good day.

Her reason was simple: The conveyance hadn't exploded.

Ellis woke up every morning grateful that the conveyance hadn't blown up while she slept, and she went to bed every night grateful that the conveyance hadn't blown up during the day. It was a routine that might have been comforting if it related to a different subject.

When the alarm sounded, she had been securing herself into the hammock in her private living sphere. Even had she not been shipmaster, she would have been entitled to a living sphere to herself by virtue of being of the Vor strata.

Letting out a puff of annoyance through her windpipes, she unsecured herself from the hammock with her hindlegs, grabbed the rectangular handholds on the living sphere's wall with her forelegs, and used her midlegs to activate the intercom next to her mouth.

"What's happening?" she asked.

Silence greeted her.

She pressed the stud again, but this time she noticed that the signal wasn't going out. *Damned substandard equipment.*

Irritated, she used all six legs to climb first to her living sphere's entryway, then through the tubes that would eventually lead to the flight sphere. Once she reached the final tube, she let her inertia carry her the rest of the way to the flight sphere, as it was now a straight path. The entryway parted at her approach and she floated into the flight sphere.

All the stations along all parts of the sphere's wall were staffed, each crewperson tethered to the station. She floated to her place at the flight sphere's epicenter and said, "The intercoms aren't working."

The long-suffering voice of Technician Monik said, "The network is down *again*."

First Mate Yer Bialar hissed at the technician—it was not proper for a non-strata to speak out of turn to a Vor—but Ellis waved it off with her left midleg. She had long since grown accustomed to improper behavior from technicians; besides, this far from Elabrej, those sorts of societal strictures often got in the way of the work. It was better to have the information that the network was down—again—than to not be informed because of a custom that served little purpose in a star system billions of units from home.

2

"Why the alarm?" Ellis asked as she settled into the cushioned seat that was suspended at the flight sphere's midpoint, attached to the circumference by several thin tubes.

"We have found something." Second Mate Vor Pitral spoke enthusiastically.

Glaring at her strata-kin, Ellis said, "I swear by Doane's legs, Pitral, if you woke me from my sleep to tell me about another windstorm on the planet—"

"No, Shipmaster!" Pitral said quickly. "This isn't something on the planet."

They had been studying the fourth planet orbiting this star for half an *ungret* now, and while it had proved fascinating, with many indicators that it would be favorable to the terraforming process—which put it one up on the first three planets—Pitral had a scientist's tendency to get overexcited about discoveries that necessitated neither an alarm nor waking the shipmaster from her sleep.

"Although," Pitral added, "we did, in fact, find another windstorm on the small landmass that indicates a faster seasonal change than we'd previously hypothesized—but," he continued, his hindlegs waving back and forth in a gesture of humility, "that is not why the alarm was sounded. We have detected movement within the system."

A section of the flight sphere's wall near Pitral's station lit up. Ellis saw an interpreted image of a scan reading. It appeared to be a disturbance in space of a peculiar—and particular—shape.

Bialar took over from here. "At first, Shipmaster, we

3

thought it to be a natural phenomenon. We could detect no solidity, and it seemed to be drifting. However, at times its shape seems very articulated."

"That alone indicates nothing," Ellis said tersely. "Asteroids can be articulated, after all."

"Of course, Shipmaster." Bialar went on without apology, for which Ellis was grateful. Her response was nothing more than the snappishness of one woken from sleep, and Bialar recognized that. "But then it began to move."

Pitral's display tracked the reading's movement even as the second mate spoke. "Shipmaster, we have studied this star and its orbiting bodies quite thoroughly, as you know—"

Then why do you remind me? This time Ellis was able to keep her sharp retort to herself.

"—and I can assure you that this reading is following no path that can possibly be dictated by any prevailing gravitational forces. It is my opinion that it is moving by means of propulsion."

"I concur in this opinion, Shipmaster," Bialar said. "What's more, its course will take it directly to the fourth's planet's largest moon."

Ellis studied the image on Pitral's display. "So you believe it to be a conveyance?"

"An alien conveyance, yes, Shipmaster," Pitral said quickly.

Again, Bialar hissed, but Ellis actually laughed. "You do realize, Pitral, that some would accuse you of speaking heresy."

For the first time speaking not as an enthusiastic scientist but as a subordinate officer, Pitral said, "Those who would do so, Shipmaster, would do likewise to our very mission."

"So you believe that the clerics are wrong in their assertion that there is no life besides the Elabrej?" Ellis already knew Pitral's answer to this question, but at least part of their mission to explore beyond their own sun was to make contact with any other alien species that might exist in the far reaches of space.

"Of course they are." Quickly, noticing the disapproving midleg waves of several of his crewmates on the flight sphere, Pitral added, "The clerics are wise in many things, but they do not understand the vastness of space."

"We have explored a dozen suns," Ellis said, "yet found no life orbiting any of them. Wouldn't this lend credence to the clerics' view?" Again, Ellis knew the answer, but she wished to gauge the crew's reactions. It was all well and good to talk about such matters in theory, but if this reading was truly an alien conveyance, she needed to be sure that the crew would be ready to accept it and deal with it head-on, not hide behind rigid dogma.

"Shipmaster, we could explore a million times twelve suns and still the number we will have explored would be practically nil—it would be so small a fraction of the stars in the universe as to be mathematically irrelevant. I find it impossible to believe that in all that vastness that Elabrej is the only one that has produced life."

Ellis saw no distress among her crew at that. Some would balk at the clerics being spoken ill of—that was heresy and punishable back home—but none could deny the truth of Pitral's words.

"Good." Ellis then spoke to Bialar. "We shall investigate this reading immediately."

"Navigator, plot a course that will bring us to the reading with greatest speed. Pilot, prepare the conveyance to leave orbit."

Ellis saw Pitral's midlegs waver. "Don't worry, Pitral, we'll return to study your windstorms in due course."

"Thank you, Shipmaster."

"In the meantime, prepare a message to the space center informing them of our diversion." They sent three messages back home per *digret*, and the next wasn't due for some time, but Ellis wanted to make sure that their actions were reported. "And send a continuous feed to them of what we do from here on in."

"I will do what I can, Shipmaster," Pitral said, "but I cannot promise that the feed will be continuous. The equipment is not designed for—"

Waving her hindlegs, Ellis said, "Yes, yes, I know, and the equipment can barely do what it *is* designed for, so asking it to be innovative is being generous. Do the best you can, Pitral."

"Yes, Shipmaster."

"Course is plotted," the navigator said.

The pilot then said, "Ready to execute when launch window opens."

Bialar said, "Proceed, Pilot."

"Defensor, prepare batteries."

Bialar waved her forelegs in surprise at Ellis's order. "Shipmaster, may I recommend that we not adopt a defensive posture?" Bialar's cautious wording amused Ellis. She did not come out and condemn the action, but simply recommended a different one—perfectly within her purview as first mate.

"We are alone out here, Bialar," Ellis said, "without anyone to aid us if we are in need of assistance. Worse, we are in a conveyance that, frankly, is likely to fall apart if a solar wind hits it the wrong way. We proceed from a position of weakness, and that is not one that will serve us well. Besides, these aliens do not approach us as friends, but skulk in shadows like enemies. They attempt to hide themselves from us."

Bialar folded her forelegs in deference. "I withdraw my recommendation, Shipmaster."

"Preparing to leave orbit now," the pilot said.

Indicators flashed on all consoles in the flight sphere, telling everyone to prepare for acceleration. Similar indicators were supposed to flash all over the rest of the conveyance. Ellis hoped they did, as anyone who did not secure themselves in cushions risked being slammed against the sphere walls when the conveyance left orbit.

For those in the flight sphere, they needed to expand the cushions in their tethers, which would protect them from the acceleration.

Ellis was concerned. The conveyance had fine armament, from the batteries that let loose with a spectacular barrage of photonic plasma to the hundreds of missiles armed with explosive warheads located in the weapons sphere. The spheres that made up the conveyance were made of *litrarin*, which was the strongest alloy anyone in the hegemony had created.

Theirs was the first civilian conveyance to be constructed with *litrarin*, which necessitated its being constructed in space, as no conveyance made of *litrarin* could achieve escape velocity, not even with the new engines.

"Shipmaster, the reading is altering velocity!" Pitral cried from his station.

"Navigator, plot its new course," Bialar said quickly.

After a moment, the navigator said, "At its new course and speed, the reading will intercept with us in five *engrets*."

Any doubts that this was an anomaly evaporated. Up until now, Ellis knew it was at least possible that this was a natural phenomenon that was acting bizarrely owing to some aspect of the star system that they had yet to fully understand.

But now the reading was changing course, changing speed, and was doing it as a direct result of stimulus, to wit, Ellis's own conveyance moving toward it. That only happened when driven by intelligence.

Bialar asked, "What are your orders, Shipmaster?"

Ellis's limbs felt as if they had shriveled. Her windpipes were dry, as if she hadn't had water in days instead of the mere hours it had been. And it was all for one simple reason: She didn't know what to do.

While it was true that she did not believe, as the clerics did, that the Elabrej were alone in the universe, it was also true that many Elabrej did, particularly those in positions of authority. As a result, there was no standard procedure for what was happening to her right now. There were no rules that dictated what to do when

8

coming into contact with a conveyance from an alien species because the conventional wisdom was that no such species existed.

All she knew was that she was alone in a sky very far from the one she called home, master of a conveyance that was in danger of falling apart at any moment, facing something that could camouflage its presence in the vacuum of space.

Bialar kicked off from her station and grabbed one of the handles on Ellis's cushioned chair. In a soft voice, she said, "Shipmaster, standard procedure is that we identify ourselves and ask the other conveyance to do the same."

"For an Elabrej conveyance, yes—but how do we ask that to these beings?" Ellis snapped. "All our transmissions are coded—and even if they weren't, do you think they speak Common? Or perhaps we should try sending it in Gorraman—or Vlrinto, perhaps?"

"Shipmaster—"

Not giving the Yer another chance to question her authority, Ellis called out in a louder voice, "Defensor, when will the reading be in range of our batteries?"

"One *engret,* Shipmaster."

"Yer Bialar, you will give the order to fire the *engret* we are in range, is that understood?"

"Shipmaster, this is—"

"You will give the order, or I will remove you from the flight sphere!"

"Of course, Shipmaster." Bialar's words were followed by a loud expulsion from her windpipes. The first mate was not pleased with this turn of events.

In all candor, neither was Ellis, but she had no choice. Her words to Bialar *engrets* earlier were true: They were Elabrej, and they could not be weak.

"In range," the defensor said.

Without hesitating, Bialar said, "Fire all batteries."

Charged particles leapt out from the outermost spheres in the conveyance, arcing toward the reading. The lights in the flight sphere dimmed in response to the drawing of power for the batteries, then came back up.

Close enough to fire also meant close enough for real-time light images. "Switch view to visual spectrum," Ellis said.

Even as the image changed from a vague scan reading to the black of the sky, stars providing their hundreds-of-*ungrets*-old images in the background, Ellis saw the energy strike the reading.

Then, even as the energy died down, a solid image coalesced into a definite shape.

"Doane's limbs," Bialar muttered in awe.

The alien conveyance—for it could hardly be anything else—used a truly bizarre design. It was all angles and rectangles—no spheres in its design at all, which struck Ellis as horribly impractical. Two almost-flat parts jutted out from either side of a central portion.

It took Ellis half an *engret* to find her voice. "Pitral, how—how *big* is that?"

"It's—it's of uneven dimensions. I don't even know how to measure it. But it would appear to be at least four times as large as our convey—"

The defensor interrupted. "Shipmaster, I'm reading a buildup of energy in the alien conveyance!"

He almost needn't have bothered saying so, for Ellis could now see it. Each almost-flat protuberance tapered off into a different-colored endpiece. Those endpieces were now glowing.

Elabrej researchers had spent many *ungrets* developing the technology that would allow their spacefaring conveyances to have a weapon that could supplement—perhaps even supplant—the missiles. Missiles were, after all, expensive and had to be replaced whenever they were used. Energy weapons, though, if a regenerating power source could be applied, would have none of the disadvantages. A weapons sphere full of missiles would have to be restocked constantly. An energy weapon would only need to be installed once.

The difficulty had always been in finding a way to do it that wouldn't drain the conveyance's power completely. When they overcame that difficulty, it was a great breakthrough for the Elabrej Hegemony. It allowed the military to effectively keep the peace among the Four Worlds—and, if the project of which Ellis was a part was successful, beyond.

Never had anyone in the hegemony seen a weapon as powerful as the batteries, though Ellis knew that they were working on something more powerful back home.

Whatever it was that the alien conveyance fired at them now was several orders of magnitude more powerful than the batteries.

The lights again dimmed, but this time they did not come back up. The flight sphere shook madly, thrown about in several directions at once. Then it started tumbling end over end.

That can't possibly happen, unless—

"We're coming apart!" Pitral cried. "The tubes have been fractured! We're—"

Ellis's strata-kin's words were lost to the sound of wrenching metal that screeched through the flight sphere, followed by the explosive pop of the atmosphere being blown into space.

They hide their ships from visibility—their weapons can shatter litrarin—*and I thought to show them that we were strong?*

As the conveyance exploded, Shipmaster Vor Ellis's penultimate thought was that it wasn't as good a day as she thought it had been.

Her last was a prayer to Doane that her disgrace would not damage the Vor strata too badly.

"The alien ship has been destroyed."

Captain Wirrk of the *I.K.S. Kravokh* clenched his fist with approval at his first officer's words. Somehow, these creatures with their ship made up of interconnected ball bearings managed to penetrate a Klingon cloaking device. Then they had the temerity to fire on them.

"Are there any survivors?" he asked his first officer.

Commander Komor turned toward operations. "Report to the captain."

The operations officer, Ensign B'Etloj—a woman young enough to be Wirrk's granddaughter—said, "Reading no life signs. Each of the balls that made up the ship had hull breaches, sir, and they do not appear to have any decent method of sealing those breaches."

Wirrk grinned. "Hardly surprising. What damage have we taken?"

"Cloaking device is offline. Shields have been reduced to twenty percent."

Looking at Komor, Wirrk said, "An impressive weapon."

"Yes, sir."

"Sir," B'Etloj added, "there is something else. The ship was transmitting a directed signal up until it was destroyed."

This pleased Wirrk. "Good. Pilot, track the transmission and plot a course on its vector. I want to see where these creatures came from. Operations, send the transmissions to security—I want a full translation by the time I drink my *raktajino* tomorrow morning."

"Yes, sir."

Wirrk rose from his chair and walked toward his office, gesturing for Komor to come with him. "Not the most glorious addition to our record of battle," he said as Komor also rose and walked with him.

The commander shook his head. "But still a victory."

"I suppose so. It would seem I've lost half my bet."

Frowning, Komor asked, "Sir?"

"Back on Ty'Gokor, when Chancellor Martok gave us this oh-so-glorious assignment to explore the Kavrot Sector, Captain Klag and I made a wager." Wirrk smiled at the memory, now nine weeks in the past, of standing in the amphitheater on Ty'Gokor, and the disappointment that, rather than fighting the Romulans, the Chancellor-class vessels, the cream of the Klingon Defense Force, were instead being sent to map stars. Wirrk had been convinced that no battle would come of it, but Klag, the captain of the *Gorkon*, thought otherwise.

"What," Komor asked, "was the wager?"

"Klag bet a case of '98 bloodwine from the K'reetka vintner that both our vessels would see combat in the Kavrot Sector."

Nodding appreciatively, Komor said, "A fine vintage."

"Yes, but I'd rather have the combat than the bloodwine."

"Sir, I have a report," came a voice from behind him. The door to Wirrk's office had just parted. Both captain and first officer turned to see that the pilot was facing them.

Komor nodded, and the pilot continued: "The range of the transmission is approximately fifty light-years—after that, the signal would degrade. There is only one star within that distance on that vector. We have already designated that system Kavrot *wej'vatlh wa'maH vagh*.

Turning toward B'Etloj, Komor said, "Report."

"We are too far for a long-range scan. It was scanned when we designated it five weeks ago, and determined only that it had four planets. From our present position it is three days away at warp eight. At our current schedule, we would proceed toward it in seven weeks."

Wirrk looked at Komor. "That schedule has been shortened to one hour."

Nodding, Komor walked back to his chair, located to the right of the command chair at the front of the bridge. "Operations, continue scan of the alien ship for the next hour, then prepare a full report on what you find. Pilot, set course for system Kavrot *wej'vatlh wa'maH vagh*. Execute at warp eight one hour from now."

"Also," Wirrk added, "prepare a message to General Talak. Include our record of battle and our course change."

Then he continued into his office. He saw no reason to be on the bridge while they ran scans of a dead ship. That was what he had a first officer for.

Soon enough, we'll trace these craven petaQpu' *to their nest. True, they did not last long in a fight, but they did penetrate the cloak—and their weapon was quite powerful. Perhaps they have other technologies that will be useful to us after we conquer them.*

Wirrk ordered a *raktajino* from the replicator and sat at his desk. *Today was a good day.*

CHAPTER ONE

The salty taste of *gagh* blood filled Toq's tongue as he bit down on the serpent worm that wriggled in his mouth.

It was the first thing he had enjoyed all day.

"What I find most irritating about Kallo is—"

Rodek snarled, the *grapok* sauce that he had put on his *trigak* flying out in all directions. "Not again. You have done nothing but complain about Kallo since she first came on board!"

They sat at the "secondary bridge," the table in the *I.K.S. Gorkon*'s large mess hall that was usually occupied by members of the bridge crew. At the moment, Toq and Rodek, the ship's first and second officers, respectively, were the only ones at the table.

Toq swallowed the *gagh*. "She drives me mad! Every morning, when the shift begins, she has some suggestion for improving operations, or improving the warp engines, or improving the style of making reports, or—"

"I *know* what she does, Toq," Rodek said. "I stand

right next to her on the bridge, just as you did when *you* were operations."

Shaking his head, Toq said, "Yes, but I did not pester Drex or Tereth or Kornan with such minutiae every waking moment."

Leskit, the primary-shift pilot, walked over to the table, carrying a plate of *racht, taknar* gizzards, and some *trigak* of his own. Before sitting, he looked at Rodek. "Is he still carrying on about Kallo?"

In a deep, dangerous voice, Rodek said, "Yes."

Shaking his head, causing the Cardassian neckbones he wore around his neck to rattle, the old pilot sat down. "I was hoping I'd get here late enough that he'd have moved on."

"I fear he will never move on from this topic."

"It is just that—" Toq hesitated. "She vexes me!"

"Women do that, Commander," Leskit said. "It's their function in the universe, to vex men. My suggestion to you is that you either ignore her or bed her."

"I can't ignore her—she *is* the operations officer."

"That just leaves the other option, then. Rodek, give me that *grapok* sauce."

As Rodek gave the container with the condiment to the pilot, Toq said, "The other problem is that her suggestions—" Again Toq hesitated.

"What of them?" Leskit asked, biting down on his gizzards.

Toq shook his head. He hated to admit this out loud. "They're *good*."

"So they're good," Rodek said. "As first officer, isn't

it your responsibility to make use of good suggestions from your inferiors?"

Toq hesitated a third time, which was three more times than he was comfortable with doing so.

Leskit let loose with one of his papery laughs. "I believe, Rodek, that we begin to see the root of the problem."

This confused Toq. "What do you mean, Leskit?"

Rodek added, "I do not understand, either."

Grinning, Leskit said, "She isn't your inferior, is she? What is vexing you, Toq—oh, sorry, *Commander* Toq—is that she is better at the job than *you* were."

Snatching three serpent worms from his bowl, Toq said, "That is absurd."

"Is it?"

"She is just a child!"

Leskit laughed. "*She* is a child? Toq, I have a son who's only slightly less mature than you, much less Ensign Kallo."

Toq chewed on his *gagh*. *Perhaps the old razorbeast is right*, he thought. Toq had been serving on the *Gorkon* since its shakedown cruise nine months earlier, serving first as a bridge officer. He successfully challenged the second officer, an old imbecile named Kegren, and took his post after killing him. After Commander Kornan—the *Gorkon*'s third first officer since its launch—died in battle at San-Tarah, Captain Klag promoted Toq to first officer. Klag had told him that his excellent service to the ship more than made up for his youth.

But I am not that young—and I have earned the respect of my peers. Seeing Leskit's snickering face, he amended the thought slightly. *Still, I have earned my place on this ship. And Kallo has earned hers. So why does she vex me so?*

Before Toq could pursue the thought further, a tall figure approached the secondary bridge. Wearing a version of the Defense Force uniform that left his arms bare, the lieutenant stopped when standing between Leskit and Rodek and folded those arms, which were massive, over his equally massive chest. This was Lokor, the *Gorkon's* chief of security. He stood taller than average, with a fierce mien and long intricately braided hair that extended to the small of his back.

"Commander," he said to Toq, "I would speak with you."

"Join us, Lieutenant." Toq was curious. Lokor never ate in the mess hall. There were those who said he was an agent of Imperial Intelligence, but Toq suspected that Lokor himself started those rumors. But he was also the eyes and ears of the *Gorkon*, and he was the one person besides the captain to whom Toq would never deny an audience. As the lieutenant sat between the pilot and the gunner, Toq said, "Speak."

"I want to assign bodyguards to all the senior officers, and double the captain's guard."

This was not a conversation Toq expected to be having in the mess hall. "Why tell us this here in the open?"

Leskit made a small noise. "Because with all the noise in here, it's impossible to eavesdrop."

"Don't be naïve," Lokor snapped. "This is the most difficult room on the entire ship to secure. No, I came

20

in here because I never do, and because I want it to be known that I wish to increase security."

"You haven't answered my question, Lieutenant," Toq said. "Why?"

"Because if there is a danger to the hierarchy on this ship, I want them to know that I'm aware of them."

Rodek swallowed the last of his *trigak*."You think there is a threat?"

"Yes. For the first time since we launched, I feel that there are those on this vessel who do not wish to serve with Captain Klag."

"It isn't the first time," Rodek said. "There was Vralk."

Toq remembered a conversation he had with Rodek at this very table months earlier, shortly after Vralk—a pilot who served while Leskit was off on the *Rotarran*—made noises about threatening the captain's position.

Lokor barked a laugh. "Vralk was not a threat, he was an insect that I took great pleasure in crushing."

"Wasn't he your kinsman?" Rodek asked.

"That is *why* it was a pleasure." Lokor smiled, a frightening sight. "I'd had to put up with his mewling for far longer than the rest of you." The smile dropped. "But this is not a pusillanimous little *petaQ* with delusions. This is an organized campaign, being led by people who transferred from the *Kreltek*—along with some whose loyalties were strained at San-Tarah."

Toq nodded. Klag had put the *Gorkon* in the position of fighting fellow Klingons at San-Tarah. Most of the crew was behind him, but there were bound to be those who disagreed. One of them, a *bekk* named Grint, had spoken out against the captain's actions on the bridge. *But he died in battle. Still, there may be others.*

Lokor went on: "There were many on the *Kreltek* who sided with General Talak. They wish to avenge themselves for the general's death at the captain's hands."

Indignantly, Toq said, "Martok himself declared the captain's actions to be honorable."

"Fine, Commander." Lokor turned a pitiless gaze on Toq, to the point that the young first officer had to avert his eyes from the security chief's. "When one of the troops aims his *d'k tahg* at your heart, you should be sure to tell him that, and I'm sure it will stay his blade."

Now Toq turned and looked right into Lokor's eyes. "If you wish to go on without a *d'k tahg* aimed at *your* heart, Lieutenant, you will never speak like that to me again, am I understood?"

This time it was Lokor who looked away. "You are, Commander."

"Good." Toq grabbed the last two serpent worms from his *gagh* bowl. "I will have to bring your concerns to the captain, but I will recommend he accept them."

Lokor nodded. "And all of you be on your guard, especially with anyone who transferred from the *Kreltek*. Also, be wary of Kurak."

At that, Leskit laughed, splurting his bloodwine. "Are you mad?"

"No," Lokor said, "are you?"

"Quite possibly, but I also know Kurak. The idea of her being involved in a conspiracy against the captain is idiotic."

22

"She is a malcontent," Lokor said, "and she has a particular loathing for Klag—and for me."

"No, she doesn't."

"Leskit—" Toq started, not wanting to see the pilot and the security chief get into a pointless fight over this. Any other time, he would welcome the diversion, but if Lokor was trying to make a strong show of force among the senior officers, having two of them start a duel would not aid in that cause.

However, the pilot insisted on speaking. "Trust me, Lokor, you do not need to waste your time worrying about Kurak. Our esteemed chief engineer will never, under any circumstance, participate in any kind of conspiracy against the captain."

"And you're sure of this because you share a bed?"

Toq wasn't surprised by Lokor's knowledge. Leskit and Kurak's liaisons were not secret, though some didn't believe it, despite the fact that, on one of the *Gorkon*'s first missions, Leskit and Kurak both reported nearly naked for duty during a battle.

Leskit didn't answer Lokor's question immediately. He took a long sip of bloodwine, then chewed on his *taknar* gizzards. Finally, he spoke. "I'm sure of this because I've come to know her very well—in part, yes, because we share a bed. And what I know is that her hatred isn't so simple as to be for the captain or for you or for me or for any one person. What she hates, my friends, is the Klingon Defense Force. She would not try to overthrow Klag because it doesn't do anything to help her. What she wants is to get out of the Defense Force."

"Which she cannot do until her nephew Gevnar is old enough to enroll," Lokor said.

Toq blinked. "She has a nephew?"

Rodek stared at Toq. "Is there a reason why she should not have one?"

Shrugging, Toq said, "I simply cannot imagine Kurak having a family. It is too—ordinary."

Baring his teeth, Leskit said, "There's nothing ordinary about that woman, believe me." The pilot then looked at the security chief. "Don't worry about Kurak, Lokor. She is quite incapable of caring enough to involve herself in a mutiny."

"Perhaps." Lokor leaned back. "But there are many who do."

"Lokor," Rodek said, "the troops from the *Kreltek*—they were used to fill holes in the squads, correct?"

"Yes."

"A pity—they are able to sow the seeds of their discontent in a variety of squads. It would have been better to put them together in squads of their own. That makes it easier to slice them out." Rodek smiled. "Something similar happened on the *Hegh'ta*. We took care of it very efficiently."

Toq regarded Rodek for a moment, then looked at Lokor. "Is there any reason why we cannot do that? Rearrange the squads?"

Leskit said, "Then they'll know you suspect them."

"I already told you," Lokor snapped, "I *want* them to know. It might provoke them into tipping their hand sooner if they are indeed plotting against the captain. Rushing their timetable will lead to their being sloppy."

"You hope," Leskit said.

"If this were an exact science, old man, there would be no such worries on *any* ship."

"Enough!" Toq said. "Lieutenant, talk with the *QaS DevwI'* about reorganizing the troops. Which of them do you trust most?"

"Vok," Lokor said, "but I'm hardly going to put these *toDSaHpu'* in First Company."

"What of the lesser companies, then?"

Lokor considered. "Grotek. We have served at several posts together. He commands Twelfth Company."

Nodding, Toq said, "Have the *Kreltek* transfers be placed there."

"Yes, sir." With that, pausing only to give Leskit an annoyed glance, Lokor rose and left the secondary bridge, heading straight for the mess hall's exit.

Leaning back in his chair, Leskit laughed heartily. "Oh, I *like* him."

Dryly, Rodek said, "The feeling would not appear to be mutual."

"That's why I like him. He shows excellent taste in enemies."

Just as Toq was wondering if he was ever going to understand Leskit—and hoping that someone would be kind enough to slit his throat if he ever went that insane—the intercom speakers sounded with the voice of Lieutenant K'Nir, the second-shift duty officer. "*Commander Toq to the bridge.*"

"Perhaps we've found something worthy of our attention," Leskit said.

Rodek shot the pilot a look. "Were you not the one

who said you were looking forward to tedium after San-Tarah?"

"That was six weeks ago." Leskit grinned. "When you get to be my age, it takes the blood a little while longer to boil—but it *does* still boil."

Rising from his chair, Toq said, "I don't intend to live to your age, Leskit. I will have died in battle long before I get to the point where it takes my blood *any* time to boil."

Holding up his bloodwine mug in salute, Leskit laughed again as Toq departed.

Perhaps it is another planet where we may plant the flag. It would be glorious indeed if we were to find another world to add to the empire so soon after San-Tarah.

Toq was joined at the turbolift by one of the *bekks* from First Squad. After a moment, Toq placed him as Beyr.

When the lift arrived, Beyr followed Toq inside, and did not indicate a deck to be taken to. Since Beyr was from the first, Toq assumed that he was now assigned to be the first officer's bodyguard. *As usual, Lokor wastes no time.*

Upon Toq's arrival on the bridge, Beyr moved to stand amid the aft consoles, while K'Nir, an unusually tall woman, got up from the first officer's chair, to the right of the captain's; only the commanding officer sat in the center seat. Toq had not given the second shift much thought until he became first officer. Since then, he'd come to appreciate her value in keeping the ship running during "off hours." Plus, since she reported to him, he grew to appreciate her beauty, from her luminous red hair to her muscular legs. *Pity that our duty shifts make it difficult to arrange an off-duty liaison.*

At K'Nir's serious expression, however, Toq put lustful thoughts in the back of his mind. "Report."

"We have arrived at the star system designated Kavrot *vaghmaH*. There are some indications of dilithium and diamonds on one of the moons, and we have set a course for it."

A snarl began in Toq's throat. "That is *not* why you summoned me here." He did not phrase it as a question.

As if appalled by the very notion, K'Nir said, "Of course not, sir. When we arrived in the system, we did a standard long-range scan. Ensign Kal has picked up a great deal of warp activity near Kavrot *wej'vatlh wa'maH vagh.*"

Toq thought through the reports from the other Chancellor-class ships that were also exploring the Kavrot sector. "That sector was mapped by the *Kravokh*, was it not?"

"Yes, sir. It is where they were setting course for when last they reported in."

"When was that?"

K'Nir fixed Toq with a hard look. "That is why I called you to the bridge, sir. It's been eight weeks. The last message from the *Kravokh* was a report—"

"Yes, I remember," Toq said, waving her off. He had still been second officer then, and he was the one at operations when the dispatch came in. The *Kravokh* had encountered an alien vessel that could detect them while cloaked and then fired on them. Captain Wirrk retaliated and destroyed the vessel, and his crew was able to translate some of the aliens' language. Their enemy was part of some kind of multiplanet nation.

Toq also remembered how the report ended: that the enemy's transmissions were directed to Kavrot *wej'vatlh wa'maH vagh*, and the *Kravokh* was traveling there to investigate.

The first thought that came to Toq's mind was of battle. He walked over to Kal at the operations console, K'Nir on his heels, to view the long-range sensor report. "Show me the scan," he told the ensign, who obeyed instantly.

All the *Gorkon*'s sensors could determine from this distance was the presence of warp activity, but just the fact that there was enough *to* detect meant there had to be a lot of ships.

"Where is the captain?" Toq asked.

Without hesitation, K'Nir said, "On the holodeck."

Toq smiled. *Protocol required she alert me first, but she made sure to locate the captain as well.* Once again, he admired the woman's efficiency.

"Ensign Koxx, plot a course for Kavrot *wej'vatlh wa'maH vagh*. Ensign Kal, prepare a report to be sent to General Goluk, but do not send it until you receive orders from myself or Captain Klag."

Both ensigns gave their affirmations. Goluk had been assigned to take over Talak's duties in the Kavrot Sector expansion. If any of the Chancellor-class ships found a planet worthy of being conquered, they would begin the process, and summon the general's fleet, which would complete it, leaving the Chancellor ship in question to continue its exploration. Besides San-

Tarah, two other planets, Brenlek and Nayyvrrra, had had the Klingon flag planted on their soil, the former by the *K'mpec* prior to the San-Tarah mission, the latter by the *Azetbur* two weeks ago.

K'Nir looked confused. "Will you not be summoning the captain to the bridge?"

Toq smiled. "The captain does not wish to be disturbed when he is on the holodeck. I will be in his office."

Without another word, Toq walked to the door located to the right of the captain's chair. As first officer, he was permitted to use the office when the captain wasn't on the bridge, and he needed privacy for what was to happen next.

Although his words to K'Nir were true, the captain's desire for privacy was not the real reason for his not having the captain summoned over the intercom. If Lokor was as efficient with the captain as he was with Toq—and that was a reasonable supposition, all things considered—then a second guard would await him at the holodeck exit. Toq had not discussed Lokor's plan with the captain yet, and did not think it would be good to surprise him with a second guard.

Beyr had taken up a position outside the door to the office. When the door rumbled to a close behind him, Toq was alone. As soon as that was the case, he touched a control on the captain's small, metal desk. "Toq to Lokor."

"*Lokor.*"

"Send the second guard you were going to assign to the captain to the holodeck."

"Bekk *K'Varia* is already there."

No surprise. "Have him escort the captain and Leader Morr to the bridge. Tell him the captain may confirm it with me."

"Of course, Commander. A wise course of action. Out."

Smiling, Toq turned the computer station around so that it faced him—he would use the captain's office, but he would not presume to sit in Klag's chair—and called up the long-range sensor readings once again.

The Kravokh *simply cannot be causing that on its own. It could be an entire fleet.*

Whoever these people were, their first encounter with the Klingon Empire was a defeat at the empire's hands. If they were massing a fleet, it could mean battle.

Toq smiled. *I'll get that glorious death sooner than you might think, Leskit. . . .*

For the fifth time this week, Tenth through Fifteenth Squads checked the weapons in the *Gorkon's* armory.

Leader Wol of the fifteenth finished the last of the hand disruptors in her row. "Finished," she said, turning to her counterpart on the fourteenth, Leader Ryjjan. "I am happy to report that these same ten disruptors are in exactly the same condition they were in a day ago."

Ryjjan laughed. "I'm sure that the enemies of the empire are quivering in their boots at that."

Mak, the leader of the thirteenth, hissed. "Be careful what you say, fools! If the *QaS DevwI'* hear you—"

"They will agree with you," said a jovial voice from behind Wol, which she recognized instantly as the *QaS*

DevwI' in charge of all six squads currently checking the armory.

Wol turned around to see Vok's portly form and smiling face, framed by stringy brown hair. Vok had been the one to promote her to leader upon her arrival on the *Gorkon* when she had expected only to be simply another of the many troops assigned to the vessel. Thus far, Wol had done all she could to justify the *QaS DevwI'*s faith in her.

Vok continued: "I do not mind, Leader Mak, if you decry the duty for being tedious. After all, it *is* tedious. That does not make it any less necessary." He laughed, resting his hands on his ample belly. "By all means, complain all you wish—" Then he moved to stand face-to-face with Mak. "—as long as you *perform* the duty in question."

Straightening, Mak said, "Yes, *QaS DevwI'* Vok!"

Grinning, Vok turned to Leader Hovoq of the tenth. "Report, Leader."

Hovoq stood up so straight that Wol feared his spine would disengage from his hips. "The inspection is complete, sir. No malfunctions have been reported, sir."

"Again," Ryjjan muttered only loud enough for Wol to hear. Wol managed to contain her reaction.

"Does this mean we can leave now?" came a voice from the narrow corridor behind Wol.

Wol turned and looked down the corridor. The walls on either side were lined with hand disruptors, and the four troops in her squad had finished checking them over. She noticed that only the newest recruit to the fifteenth, Kagak, stood at attention. Goran might have, but his great height forced him to stand stooped in the narrow corridor. Trant and G'joth, though, simply stood awaiting their orders, both looking like they wanted to be somewhere else.

G'joth had been the one to ask the plaintive question, which prompted Vok to walk over to Wol and ask, "Is there a problem in your squad, Leader?"

"Not at all, sir," Wol said without hesitation. "They are simply following your orders."

"How so?" Vok asked with a frown.

"You said for the troops to complain all they wish, sir," Wol deadpanned.

Vok stared at her for a moment; then a belly laugh exploded from his mouth. When that happened, Ryjjan and Wol laughed as well, as did two of the other leaders. Mak and Hovoq, though, remained at attention. Wol also heard some chuckles from her own squad behind her.

Eventually, Vok stopped laughing. "Certainly *Bekk* G'joth is best qualified to carry out that order, Leader. In fact, he is correct—you may leave now. Report to the holodeck at the beginning of the primary shift in the morning."

That got everyone's attention. Wol hoped that meant battle drills. The tedium of maintenance and inspections was wearing on them. Vok was the first among the twenty *QaS DevwI'* assigned to the *Gorkon*, the fifteen five-soldier squads under his command comprising the cream of the crop of the fifteen hundred troops on the Chancellor-class vessel. However, the curse of being among the elite is that they were rarely given mundane assignments such as cargo duty, or assisting in engineering, or waste extraction, or any of the other duties assigned to the troops when there was no combat.

Instead, we polish disruptors, Wol thought bitterly, though they had been given cargo duty shortly after leaving San-Tarah. Officers were permitted a small section of the cargo bay to store personal items, and the items belonging to the ones who transferred over from the *Kreltek* had to be placed there by troops who had not been given that privilege.

Were I still Eral, daughter of B'Etakk, of the House of Varnak, I too could be an officer now. That thought was even more bitter, but she dismissed it quickly. *Were I still Eral, I would never have joined the Defense Force. Were I still Eral, I would have been disgraced when my family chose to back Morjod when he tried his coup against Martok.*

And were I still Eral, I would have raised my son in luxury instead of killing him on the battlefield of San-Tarah.

Cursing to herself, she shoved those thoughts to the back of her mind. She focused instead on Vok, who was still talking. "Before we arrived at San-Tarah, Lieutenant Lokor and Commander Toq devised a holodeck program that would simulate conquering a world." The *QaS DevwI'* smiled. "It was not utilized, as the real thing arrived soon after that. However, the program is still there, and tomorrow we shall make use of it. *QaS DevwI'* Klaris and I will supervise a drill during which you will conquer a small, industrial city." He turned to Ryjjan. "Do you think the fourteenth will be ready for that, Leader Ryjjan?"

Ryjjan grinned. "Absolutely, sir."

"Excellent!" Vok looked at each leader in turn. "You're all dismissed."

Vok turned on his heel and departed. The other five leaders turned to look down the armory corridors that they stood at the forefront of and dismissed their squads.

Wol, however, did not.

The fifteenth had done well at San-Tarah, but since leaving that planet, Wol had not liked the direction the squad was taking. Her words to Vok notwithstanding, there *was* a problem in her squad. Both G'joth and Trant lost friends at San-Tarah, and they had become more withdrawn. Kagak was a transfer from the *Kreltek*, but he had kept to himself. When she first took over the fifteenth, it was as solid a unit as existed on the *Gorkon*. But first they lost Krevor and Davok, and then they were betrayed by Trant's friend Maris, who was subsequently killed. While Davok was a tiresome malcontent, he was as nothing compared to Trant, who would have to improve tremendously to be as inoffensive as "tiresome." As for G'joth, Davok's death had put the normally jovial old soldier in a permanent bad mood.

Not that I've been the happiest of my life, Wol thought. Once again, she shoved aside thoughts of her son and her long-since-destroyed honor.

Thinking back over the past six weeks, she found that what was missing was the useless conversation. G'joth and Davok were past masters at it, and they encouraged the others. But all Trant did was whine,

Goran was never much for conversation, G'joth had become withdrawn, and Kagak spoke less than Goran.

Time to change that. Thinking back on the cargo duty she'd had six weeks ago, she had an inkling of how to do so. It involved finally making use of a piece of intelligence she'd acquired while on that duty, one that simply awaited the right moment to be utilized.

Her nondismissal of the fifteenth had not gone unnoticed by the four who served under her.

"Is something wrong, Leader?" Goran asked, sounding confused.

"No," she lied, "but you are not dismissed. Instead, you are to adjourn"— she smiled—"to the mess hall. I will meet you there in five minutes. Move!"

The four troops exchanged confused glances, then they all moved out of the corridor and headed toward the nearest turbolift.

For her part, Wol ran in the other direction, toward the leader of the fourteenth.

"Ryjjan!" she cried when he was in earshot.

The tall, lanky warrior stopped and turned to face Wol. "Yes, Leader?"

"You are hiding four barrels of bloodwine in the cargo bay. I want one of them."

Ryjjan's mouth opened, then closed. "I—how did—I haven't—" He shook his head. "You speak madness, Leader. To do such a thing would be in violation of—"

Rolling her eyes, Wol said, "Spare me the attempt at outrage and innocence, Ryjjan. I saw the barrels in the areas designated for the ship's pilots."

The leader's hands clenched into fists. A snarl escaped his lips. "How did you find out?"

"I noticed that the bloodwine was from the Pelgren vintner."

"You know your bloodwine." Ryjjan seemed surprised that she would be able to distinguish vintners. "There are not many of our station who do."

I could hardly not be familiar with the vintner once owned by the House of Varnak, she thought. "Come now, Ryjjan, you should know by now that I'm not typical of those of our station."

At last, Ryjjan smiled. "That is certainly the case." The smile fell. "So once you recognized the vintner—"

"I questioned Ensign Koxx. I assumed it was his or Leskit's, and the ensign has expressed a fondness for me in the past." In fact, Koxx had been drooling over her from the moment she reported on board, but she'd managed to stave off his advances. That didn't stop her from taking advantage of his infatuation when it served her purpose.

Ryjjan shook his head. "And he told you about our deal."

"He said you sent a barrel of bloodwine to each of their homes on Qo'noS in exchange for their cargo space to put your four barrels." She smiled. "Did he lie?"

Angrily, Ryjjan said, "No. I have connections—they were selling the older vintages cheap, because they were produced by the old owners. They were supporters of Morjod's coup, so they were disgraced. The new owners don't want anything to do with the back stock, and my connection was trying to unload the older barrels. And now you want one of them in exchange for what?"

"My silence. I don't think Vok or Lieutenant Lokor would be terribly amused by your flouting of regulations."

Ryjjan spit. "If anything happens to me, it will also happen to Koxx and Leskit! They'll never—"

At that, Wol laughed. "Do you truly imagine Lokor will care about offending the officers of this ship?"

That brought Ryjjan up short. Anyone else might hesitate to anger his fellow officers, but not Lokor.

Letting out a long breath, Ryjjan said, "Fine, you can have the *khest'n* barrel. But I suggest you finish it soon, before Lokor finds out and asks you where you got it."

"Thank you. I'm in your debt."

That got Ryjjan's attention. Had she simply taken the deal, that would have been all, but she knew that Ryjjan was truly doing her a favor by giving her access to the wine. *Especially since my threat was an empty one—Lokor knows all about the barrels, because he told me after I reported it to him. He couldn't care less who uses the cargo space, as long as the ship is secure.*

Ryjjan's eyes traveled up and down Wol's body. "You can expect me to call in that debt *very* soon."

Wol sighed. She had expected something like that. Ryjjan had been more subtle than Koxx—he could hardly not be more subtle than the ensign—but she had noticed his interest in her. Wol preferred her bedmates shorter and with more body mass, but she supposed she could live with sharing a bunk with him for one night. *Perhaps he'll surprise me.*

"I'll have one of my *bekk*s take care of it," Ryjjan said. "Where should I have it sent?"

"The mess hall. My squad is waiting there."

Ryjjan nodded. He was about to activate his communicator when Wol said, "Ryjjan, a question."

"What?"

"Why have you been hoarding those barrels, anyhow?"

He smirked. "I've been waiting for a special occasion."

Wol frowned. "Our victory at San-Tarah didn't qualify?"

Sneering, Ryjjan said, "Hardly. Oh, our battle there was necessary, and honor was on our side, but we were fighting our fellow Klingons in a battle to save a species who will only be *jeghpu'wI'*. That is *not* what I would call special."

"I suppose." Wol didn't agree, but she could see Ryjjan's point. "I look forward to the bloodwine."

Grinning, Ryjjan said, "And I look forward to the payment."

Gripping the *bat'leth* tightly in his hands, Klag moved through the underbrush, his boots sinking slightly into the loose dirt.

The scents were muddled in this overgrown jungle. An ancient mining station was located nearby, and the fumes from its primitive workings interfered with any attempt at gaining an olfactory picture of one's surroundings. Klag found himself reduced to depending on sight and sound only.

Not that he wasn't up to the task of finding and defeating his foe. He was a Klingon warrior, a member of the Order of the *Bat'leth*, captain of one of the finest ships in the fleet.

A rustle in the bushes to his left caught his attention. *But no*, he thought after a moment, *that movement is too minimal to belong to a being the size of my enemy. It is probably a small animal.*

Besides, his foe was too canny to be that obvious.

The *bat'leth* Klag held in his hands was an ordinary one that he had replicated. Good weight, good size for his hands; it was completely adequate as a weapon. It certainly was sufficient for the task he engaged in today: to win the battle, and to do so while wielding a *bat'leth*.

Once, that would have been no challenge at all. Klag was as skilled with the *bat'leth* as any warrior, and more than most. Then came the Dominion War and the Battle of Marcan V. It was there that Commander Klag lost many things—his beloved ship, his hated captain, and his good right arm—but gained a label: hero. He slew several Jem'Hadar and one Vorta on the plains of Marcan V after he had lost his limb, and paved the way for victory in the Allicar Sector.

His reward had been the captaincy of the *Gorkon*.

Slowly, he moved out from the underbrush and took up a position behind a thick tree. Still, he heard and saw nothing. The only smell was that of the smoke that belched from the mines.

Then the clouds cleared away, bathing the area in bright sunlight. Klag saw a glint of metal in the bushes to his right, and then he knew he had his foe. Though he saw no other evidence, nor heard anything, the glint was unmistakably the sunlight reflecting off the metal of a blade.

After the war, Klag came to realize that he was less of a warrior with only one arm, and so had the arm of his recently deceased father grafted onto his body. But, although Dr. B'Oraq had successfully attached the limb, she could not make it function. That would come only with hard work.

At first, Klag had been unwilling to do the work, assuming his prior proficiency to be enough to carry him through. He made a fool of himself during his drills with his bodyguard, Leader Morr, his own position as captain preventing Morr from telling him what he needed to hear: He was not improving. Not that it mattered, as B'Oraq *did* tell him that, but he did not listen.

No, it took a humiliating loss to the leader of the Children of San-Tarah to disabuse Klag of that notion, and he'd spent the weeks since departing San-Tarah pushing himself to achieve the same level of skill he'd once had with the *bat'leth*.

Coming out from behind the tree, he crouched down and started moving swiftly in a direction parallel to where he had seen the glint. *I will not reveal that I have seen my enemy until the last second.*

As soon as he passed the location of the glint, he unholstered his *d'k tahg* and threw it to his right in one fluid motion, hoping to wound his foe.

Then he was attacked from the left.

His foe was a Klingon, one armed with a *bat'leth* also. Klag knew that there was only one foe, and that he was cannier than the captain had expected.

No, it is not canniness to spring a trap that is older than Kahless's great-grandmother. I am simply the fool who has fallen for it, Klag thought as he rolled with the attack, he and his foe turning over and over again on the grassy ground. His foe had left a weapon in the bushes in order to fool Klag into thinking he was there. *Addled and with only one arm, I had more sense against a dozen Jem'Hadar on Marcan V, yet this one Klingon plays me for a* toDSaH.

They ended with his enemy on top of him, swinging his *bat'leth* down toward Klag's head. Klag—using his right arm—brought his own *bat'leth* up in front of his face in order to block the blow. The sound of metal clanging against metal echoed off the flora. Klag twisted his weapon and locked the inner blades of his *bat'leth* with that of his foe, then he thrust it down and to his left, using his right hand for most of the power of the thrust.

His enemy's weapon fell to the ground.

"Computer, freeze program, erase opponent."

The voice belonged to B'Oraq, who, along with Morr, was supervising Klag's drills.

As the foe disappeared in a puff of photons, Klag clambered to his feet. The auburn-haired doctor stood before him, clutching the end of the braid that extended past her right shoulder. Morr stood next to her, towering over her, yet looking much more staid than B'Oraq, who carried a fierce mien even when she was relaxed.

Walking up behind them was a third person, a *bekk* whom Klag recognized as being a member of Morr's squad. "What is the meaning of this?" he asked.

"My apologies," the *bekk* said, and Klag finally remembered that this was K'Varia, "but Dr. B'Oraq terminated the program at my request. Commander Toq has requested that I escort you and Leader Morr to the bridge immediately. You may verify this with the commander if you wish."

Klag frowned. This was unusual—Toq could have just called him. "Klag to Toq."

"*Toq. Has Bekk K'Varia come to escort you, sir?*"

"Yes, he has. What is the meaning of this, Commander?"

"*I will explain when you arrive, sir.*"

Letting out a long breath, Klag said, "Very well. Out. Computer, end program."

The holodeck reverted to the simple grid pattern that indicated no simulations were running.

"It seems it is my lot in life to be irritated by my first officers."

B'Oraq laughed. "I believe, Captain, that that is the primary duty of a first officer."

"I'm not in a position to judge. I spent my unnecessarily lengthy time as a first officer being irritated by my captain." Klag spoke with a certain bitterness. Captain Kargan was an incompetent *petaQ* whose family connections provided him with a lofty position and also made it impossible to remove him from it. Instead, he let Klag, his first officer, do all his leading for him, a state of affairs that remained for almost a decade before Marcan V finally freed Klag from his position under Kargan's boot.

However, while Klag stayed first officer of the *Pagh* for nine years, he was now on his fourth first officer in only nine months on the *Gorkon*. Klag had gotten rid of Drex as fast as he could, and both Tereth and Kornan had died in battle. The captain had faith in Toq based on his stellar performance since the shakedown cruise, but that faith was leavened by the commander's relative youth. "I wonder now if I promoted Toq too quickly."

Smiling, B'Oraq said, "Give him a chance, Captain. I'm sure he has a good reason for his peculiar behavior."

Morr and K'Varia exchanged a glance, but of course said nothing. Klag had a suspicion that the two soldiers knew something their captain didn't.

Klag stared at K'Varia. "Speak."

The *bekk* gave Morr a quick look, then said, "I would not presume to speak for the commander, sir. He'll explain it all." He hesitated, then added, "But I do believe his reasons are sound, sir. Things on this ship are not what they were."

Throwing his head back and laughing, Klag said, "Things are *never* what they were on this ship, *Bekk*. Change has been the hallmark of the *Gorkon* since its shakedown. It would be unwise of us to expect otherwise." He moved toward the exit.

B'Oraq walked alongside him. "You did well, Captain. That thrust led with your right—I think the new limb is becoming as strong as the old. You're also minimizing use of it, not straining it constantly." She smiled. "If you had realized this a few months ago, things might have gone differently on San-Tarah."

Klag shook his head. B'Oraq studied medicine in the Federation, and from them she had learned the tiresome proclivity for wasting energy wondering what might have been. Done was done; only a fool speculated on what could not be changed.

Still, B'Oraq is no fool. Quite the opposite. She has been my best advisor since I took command of this vessel. So much so that I am willing to indulge her tiresome speculations.

"Perhaps," was all he said in reply. "We will continue our drills tomorrow." To Morr and K'Varia, he said, "Come, let us see what it is that Toq needs me to be aware of in so mysterious a manner."

CHAPTER TWO

Seven weeks ago . . .

Avrik had never been in the government sphere before. Generally, non-strata didn't go into the sphere unless they were menial workers—certainly never to see the first oligarch, as Avrik was doing today. He had seen the sphere—in truth, many spheres linked by tubes—several times, mostly on the news. It always looked impressive, situated in the middle of the Gorram Grasslands on top of a hill. The sun always rose behind it, causing the sphere to glow as if Doane himself favored the Elabrej.

Intellectually, of course, Avrik knew that the news usually just recycled the same image of the sun rising behind the sphere, but the effect was the same. When he saw the sphere, he was proud to be a hegemon.

Seeing the place on the news, particularly with the sun behind it, had not adequately prepared him for the real thing, which turned out to be a massive disappointment. By standing close to it, as he did upon disembarking from the conveyance that brought him and Yer Maskrol, his supervisor, to this meeting, the place lost most of its grandeur. Up close, he realized to his chagrin, it simply looked like just another sphere.

He had, of course, expected to go through several levels of security. One didn't go anywhere in the Elabrej Hegemony without going through several levels of security. It was the price they paid for living in an orderly society, and to keep them safe from the separatists. Just this morning, the news reported that the separatists had destroyed a military moon shuttle as it was departing the First World. Not only were two dozen soldiers killed, but so were several civilian workers at the dock. Nobody knew for sure if it was the separatists—at least one aviation expert said it might have been mechanical failure—but the oligarchs seemed to think that the separatists were responsible, and Avrik believed them.

But if what I saw today is what it appears to be, the separatists will be the least of our problems.

As the security scanners looked him over to make sure he was carrying nothing dangerous into the heart of the hegemony's government, Avrik looked over at his supervisor. Only the presence of a stratad individual like Yer Maskrol allowed Avrik to even consider coming here. Indeed, Avrik would have been happy to stay at the office, but Maskrol insisted that Avrik come along, since he was the one who made the discovery.

It took the better part of an *atgret* to go through security, as they checked both Avrik's person and his pouch, in which he carried the recordings he'd made.

The process was far longer than the usual, even at Avrik's own workplace. The space center was a prime target for the separatists, since it coordinated most of the spacefaring activity, as well as for religious fanatics who believed that the extrasolar-vessel program was an affront to the Demiurges. Avrik had thought that the space center's security procedures were endless, but they were as nothing compared to what he went through here. Then again, as a worker at the space center, his process would be shorter by virtue of his having the proper identifiers. As a visitor here, he was not so fortunate.

Plus, this *was* the government sphere.

When they were finally cleared, they were led by two people, who carried weapons in each of their midlegs, to the inner sphere.

Avrik was surprised to see that the halls of government looked just like any other office sphere. Simple workstations, occupied by normal people. For some reason, Avrik expected something more—spectacular?

It doesn't matter. The important thing is to let the oligarchs know what has happened.

The armed guards led them to a waiting sphere, complete with hammocks for both of them. "Wait here," one of the guards said. He then left the sphere; his companion remained.

Avrik asked Maskrol, "What's happening?"

Maskrol, having already climbed into the hammock, waved her hindlegs. "Don't worry, Avrik. The first oligarch is very busy. He'll see us when he can."

"Will we even get to see him? I'm surprised they

didn't just send us to one of the other oligarchs." Avrik got into the hammock as he spoke. His legs had been aching for *sogrets*, and standing in security for so long was just aggravating them, so he was grateful for the chance to sit.

This time, Maskrol waved her forelegs. "I've already spoken to the fifth and second oligarchs. They were the ones who told us to come here and speak to the first oligarch."

That explains a lot, Avrik thought. He didn't think that a mere Yer could command an audience with the first oligarch just like that. The fifth oligarch, however, made sense; she probably was the one who brought it to the second oligarch's attention.

Speaking of whom, the second oligarch entered the sphere. At his presence, Avrik climbed out of the hammock, as did Maskrol.

"Yer Maskrol, it's good to see you again."

"Same here, Vor Brannik. This is Avrik—it was his department that verified Vor Ellis's transmission, and also the one that detected the—"

"Let's go inside," Second Oligarch Vor Brannik said quickly, before Maskrol could say the words *alien conveyance* out loud.

Avrik didn't blame the second oligarch for being discreet. This knowledge was very dangerous.

Unlike the rest of the government sphere, the first oligarch's office sphere was lavish, decorated with the finest sculpture and a most elaborate mural on the wall. The mural portrayed Doane and Gidding creating the solar system, a perfect re-creation of the mural that also decorated the inner wall of every holy sphere in the hegemony. Avrik spent only a moment noticing this, because his attention was quickly taken by the other people in the room. As expected, First Oligarch Vor Jorg was present, standing inside his rather elaborate workstation, which was made of tree bark rather than the usual metal. Also present were the third and fifth oligarchs, joined now by the second when he escorted Avrik and Maskrol in.

What surprised and concerned Avrik was the presence of First Cleric Vor Hennak, as well as First Defensor Vor Ralla. *If nothing else*, he thought, *they must be taking what I found seriously, if both the head of our spirituality and our military are here.*

Avrik was now especially grateful for the presence of Maskrol and the fifth oligarch, who were both of the Yer strata. Being in a room with so many Vors would likely have sent Avrik into a panic. As it was, all six legs were now aching, and it wasn't the usual aches and pains he lived with every day.

History is being made here and, Doane help me, I'm part of it.

Brannik said, "First Oligarch, this is Yer Maskrol, the head of the space center. She's the one who brought this to our attention."

Vor Jorg waved his right midleg in greeting. "I'm pleased to meet you, Yer Maskrol. The space center is doing excellent work."

"That is one opinion," the first cleric said.

"We're not here to discuss religious dogma," Brannik snapped. "There is a crisis—"

"That's enough, Brannik!" The first oligarch then waved his forelegs and midlegs with respect. "My apologies, First Cleric, the second oligarch is simply letting his emotions get the better of him. Yer Maskrol, if you please, tell us what it is that you found."

Maskrol waved one midleg toward Avrik. "With your permission, First Oligarch, I would like my subordinate, Avrik, to make the report. He is the one truly responsible for this discovery, and can provide the most detailed account. I realize," she added at the distressed armwaves her request provoked, "that it is unseemly for a non-strata to give such a report, but given the direness of what has been discovered, I believe that the protocols should be relaxed in this instance. Clarity is what's of greatest import here, not proper forms."

Third Oligarch Vor Anset waved her midlegs with irritation. "The proper forms are what make the hegemony great, Yer Maskrol. I hardly think—"

Brannik interrupted his fellow oligarch. "If this discovery means what we think it means, we're going to have to get used to a lot of changes in how we do things."

The first cleric let out a puff of annoyance through his windpipe. "Ridiculous," he muttered.

"I hate to say it, but Vor Brannik is right," the first oligarch said. "*This once*, I'm willing to allow it. Avrik, I give you leave to speak to me. Tell us all what you saw."

To Avrik's surprise, the aches in his legs lessened. *This is it*, he thought.

"Yesterday, we received the latest transmission from

Shipmaster Vor Ellis's exploration conveyance. Instead of a straightforward report on the *digret*'s activities, this was a continuous feed." He reached into his pouch and took out the recorder onto which he had copied Ellis's transmission. Avrik held the recorder in his right mid-leg while touching a control with his right foreleg. A low-resolution holographic image of the flight sphere of Ellis's conveyance appeared over his hand.

Avrik had watched this recording dozens of times, so he focused his attention instead on the reactions of the others in the room.

The first cleric looked horrified, and then dismissive. All of the oligarchs looked concerned, as did Maskrol. First Oligarch Jorg was inscrutable—but Avrik supposed that was part and parcel of his position.

What surprised Avrik was the reaction of the first defensor. Ralla looked as if he knew what was coming.

There were gaps in the transmission, but one thing that came through clearly was the aftermath of Ellis firing her conveyance's batteries.

"This is not possible," First Cleric Vor Hennak whispered. "Shipmaster Ellis has obviously faked this transmission—"

For the first time, First Defensor Vor Ralla spoke. "*Vor* Ellis is one of the finest shipmasters alive. She would never falsify records in this manner. I find your accusation offensive."

Avrik tried to keep his legs from waving. One did not challenge a cleric so brazenly, least of all the first cleric.

"And I find this entire proceeding offensive!" Hennak said. "Those images are heresy!"

Maskrol said, "These images are reality, First Cleric. And they are only the beginning."

Pointing at the holographic image, which Avrik had paused pending his being given permission to continue his report, Hennak said, "That image cannot be real! Nothing natural looks like that!"

"I'm afraid it gets worse." Maskrol waved his foreleg at Avrik. "Continue."

Avrik started the recording again, but said nothing. The images spoke for themselves. Everyone in the first oligarch's office watched as the alien conveyance fired a weapon of its own, an energy beam as devastating as the batteries were, which tore through the *litrarin* hull like it was parchment. They watched as Ellis's crew were blown into the vacuum of space. They watched as the conveyance died.

They watched until the transmission ceased, its source destroyed.

Hennak muttered a prayer to Doane for the preservation of the souls under the shipmaster's command.

"Thank you, Avrik," the first oligarch finally said after a long silence. "It would seem—"

"Excuse me, First Oligarch." Brannik's interruption surprised Avrik, but if anyone could do so without fear of reproach, it was the second oligarch. "I'm afraid that is only the *first* of the reports from Yer Maskrol's employee."

First Oligarch Jorg's forelegs waved with agitation. "There's more?"

It was Ralla who answered. "Yes, sir, there is."

Avrik's legs started aching again. *What does the military know about this?*

Touching another control on his recorder, Avrik said, "This morning, shortly after we were able to clean up Shipmaster Vor Ellis's transmission to the quality of the images you saw, our outer telescope detected an object headed directly for hegemony space." The images of the telescope's scans shone over Avrik's hand. Each scan brought into greater focus the object in question. It matched the odd, angled shape of the very same alien that had destroyed Ellis's conveyance. "If they continue at the speed we have been detecting, they will reach the Ninth Outer Station in three *digrets.*"

Maskrol waved a foreleg at Avrik, indicating that he no longer was required to speak. Avrik was both grateful and disappointed. He had done well, and found that he enjoyed providing this briefing for the most powerful people in the hegemony—but these *were* the most powerful people in the hegemony, and he didn't want to push his luck.

Then Maskrol said, "Our theory is that the aliens were able to trace Vor Ellis's transmission. We believe that they wish to continue their aggression against us."

"I still think—" Hennak started.

Ralla cut him off. "There's more, First Cleric—First Oligarch," he added in a conciliatory tone. "One of our rim patrollers detected the same thing that the space center's telescope saw. The configuration is such that it cannot be a hegemony vessel."

"What is your opinion, First Defensor?" the first oligarch asked.

"Despite what the clerics would have us believe, there *are* other people elsewhere in the universe, and one of them is about to break down our sphere and try to destroy us."

Brannik said, "We don't have any proof that they're hostile to us."

Waving her midlegs in amusement, Fifth Oligarch Yer Blos said, "What, destroying Vor Ellis's conveyance wasn't enough?"

"Vor Ellis fired first."

"Yes," First Oligarch Jorg said, "with our most powerful weapon—and they just shrugged it off."

"Not quite, First Oligarch," Ralla said. "It was our *second*-most-powerful weapon. The plasma weapons are ready to go, and can be installed in all our military vessels."

Waving his hindlegs in irritation, First Oligarch Jorg said, "I was told that the plasma weapons were still in the testing phase."

"We had been taking a cautious approach with the testing," Ralla said, "since we were in no hurry to implement them. Now we have a reason to be quick— those aliens will be here in three *digrets*, and we need to be ready for them. The batteries aren't going to be sufficient."

The first oligarch then did what Avrik had been waiting for: he spoke to the first cleric. "Vor Hennak, what do you think?"

It was half an *engret* before the first cleric finally spoke. "I think that this is madness. But I also cannot deny the evidence. No Elabrej could possibly have made that monstrous *thing* that is flying toward our skies. And no Elabrej would so wantonly destroy one of our conveyances. Whatever those things are, they are an affront to the Demiurges and they must be stopped."

Waving one foreleg in affirmation, Jorg said, "I agree. First Defensor, begin implementation of the plasma weapons and prepare a battle plan. I want to be ready for those aliens when they arrive." To Maskrol, he said, "Thank you, Yer Maskrol, you have done a great service to the hegemony today. I want you to return to the space center immediately and continue scans. Direct all our telescopes to the effort, and send all your intelligence to Vor Ralla."

"Of course, First Oligarch. It is an honor to be here."

With that, Maskrol turned and moved toward the exit. Avrik placed the recorder in his pouch and then followed Maskrol.

The entire meeting had taken place using the Common tongue, which Avrik had expected. He had heard stories that the oligarchs all conducted their meetings in Vlrinto, but he had no idea if that was true or not. That language was the exclusive province of the Vor, so Avrik would not have been surprised to find that it was true.

Then First Oligarch Jorg spoke to Second Oligarch Vor Brannik.

The Vlrinto tongue was a carefully guarded secret. It was illegal for any non-strata to know the language, and stratas who were not Vor were not encouraged to learn it either—for a non-Vor to speak it was considered a huge breach of etiquette.

For that reason, Avrik had kept his own knowledge of Vlrinto to himself.

No doubt, First Oligarch Vor Jorg felt confident that neither Maskrol nor Avrik could understand him when he said to Brannik in Vlrinto, "It looks like this may be it, Brannik. These aliens are the way to finally put down the separatists once and for all. The people will—"

Whatever else the first oligarch said was lost when the entryway to the sphere closed behind Avrik.

His legs ached even more as he and Maskrol headed back to the space center.

One way or another, it seemed, the hegemony was about to go to war.

Wirrk practically ran onto the bridge from his office when the alert came from Commander Komor that they had entered the Elabrej star system.

For a long time, Wirrk had never really appreciated the use of universal translator technology, the work of many Klingon linguists and programmers, with aid provided by their counterparts in the Federation. Wirrk had never seen the need to make it easier to communicate with non-Klingons, nor had he seen any need to understand the gutter tongues of aliens. *Let them learn a real language if they wish to be understood,* he had often thought.

It was Komor who had pointed out to him the intelligence value of being able to translate the languages of other species, and that benefit was proving itself several times over now.

When Komor had summoned him, he was reading the translation of the transmissions of the alien vessel they destroyed. They came from a governmental body that called itself the Elabrej Hegemony, and they were exploring beyond their home solar system.

The *Kravokh* was their first encounter with an alien species. Wirrk glowed with pride at the fact that he was responsible for making it one that would be remembered in song.

As he entered the bridge, he said, "Report!"

Komor was standing at the operations console with B'Etloj. "We are approaching the Elabrej home system. Sensors are detecting seven ships of similar configuration to the one we defeated."

"Do they have the same armament?"

Komor and B'Etloj exchanged a glance. Then Komor said, "It is impossible to be sure. These vessels use the same power source as the other one."

"What of the cloaking device?"

"Engineering still has been unable to effect repairs," Komor said.

Wirrk snarled as he sat in his command chair. He had given the chief engineer, a coward named Sak, one day to fix the cloaking device. When Sak failed to do so, Wirrk had personally sunk his *d'k tahg* in the *petaQ*'s chest. Sadly, his staff had been unable to make any progress in the two days since Sak's death.

Not that it matters all that much—these Elabrej detected us while cloaked before, so that advantage is not what it could be.

"Shields?" Wirrk then asked.

At that, Komor smiled. "Engineering *has* been able to adjust the shield frequencies to better defend us against the Elabrej weapon."

Laughing, Wirrk thought that Sak's staff were not quite the worthless animals their late commanding officer was.

"Alert status," Wirrk said. "Raise shields, arm all weapons."

As Komor moved to sit next to Wirrk, B'Etloj said, "Sir, we're receiving a transmission from the enemy vessels. It is in several languages—including the one we've translated."

Komor said, "What does it say?"

" 'Alien conveyance, you are not welcome in Elabrej skies. Surrender immediately, or we will destroy you.' "

Wirrk laughed. "Excellent. I prefer a foe that faces us with their eyes open."

"Disruptors and torpedoes armed and ready, sir," the gunner said. Even as he spoke, four warriors took up position at the secondary gunner positions. Those positions controlled the twelve rotating disruptor cannons placed at various points around the ship.

The pilot added, "We are now entering the star system."

"Slow to impulse," Komor said.

"When will we be in weapons range?" Wirrk asked.

"Two minutes," said the pilot.

Turning to his first officer, Wirrk said, "Let us not waste our torpedoes on these creatures *just* yet, Commander."

Komor nodded. "Train all fore disruptors on the ship that sent the transmission."

Wirrk approved of his first officer's course of action. That was probably the lead ship, and might well have contained the leader of this battle for the Elabrej.

"Sir," the gunner said, "that vessel is protected by the others—it is the innermost."

A *wise strategy*, Wirrk thought. *These foes are not unworthy. Good.*

"In range," the gunner said.

"Fire!" Komor cried.

Wirrk watched the screen, feeling the blood burn in his veins. Though these people had one devastating weapon, they were ready for it now. From the readings they'd taken of the debris, besides that one energy weapon they also had an impressive armament of explosive missiles, which would be dangerous if the *Kravokh*'s shields were to fail. *As long as our shields hold out, though, the missiles will be as useless as a dull* d'k tahg *against a* trigak.

Disruptor fire leapt from the emplacements throughout the *Kravokh* and struck the Elabrej ships. The closest ship's foremost sphere splintered and exploded, the effects cascading across the entire vessel until it was destroyed. Another of the Elabrej ships was damaged. Wirrk had been hoping for more devastation than that. *Whatever their hull is constructed of, it's strong.*

Then he realized what needed to be done. "The tubes." Turning around to the gunner, he said, "Aim for the tubes, not the spheres!"

"Yes, sir!" The gunner reprogrammed the firing pattern.

"Sir, there is an energy buildup," B'Etloj said.

"Where?" Komor asked.

B'Etloj looked up from her console. "In all the remaining ships, sir."

"Their energy weapon," Komor said dismissively.

"No, sir, these readings are not consistent with what we encountered before—it's an order of magnitude *more* powerful."

Wirrk turned around and stared at his operations officer, as did Komor. "Say that again, Ensign."

"The energy buildup is an order of magnitude more powerful than the weapon we encountered three days ago. I do not believe that our shields will hold against it."

As B'Etloj spoke, the *Kravokh*'s disruptor fire destroyed another of the Elabrej ships by striking at the tubes that interlinked the vessel's spheres, and it exploded in a fiery conflagration that gave Wirrk some comfort to ameliorate B'Etloj's words. Now only five vessels remained.

Wirrk turned back to the screen to see those five ships start to glow. "Gunner, prepare quantum torpedoes, full spread on all the enemy vessels and fire immediately!"

"Yes, sir."

Even as the gunner acknowledged the order, the glow on each of the Elabrej ships focused. Instead of surrounding the entire set of spheres, each reduced to one spot at the center of the largest sphere on each ship.

"Pilot, evasive maneuvers!"

"Yes, sir."

The gunner said, "Firing torpedoes."

In response, the *Kravokh* spit out half a dozen quantum torpedoes, one at each of the ships, with the sixth also going for the one at the center—the vessel that sent the message, its immediate protection now destroyed.

Even as the torpedoes made their way through space, the five glows then shot forward like *ghIntaq* spears in a thin stream of concentrated energy.

Wirrk frowned as he realized that the streams of energy were heading not for the *Kravokh,* but instead to a point several *qell'qams* in front of the ship's nose.

Most of the *Kravokh*'s torpedoes hit their targets, and many of them caused damage, though not as much as Wirrk would have hoped.

Not that that was his primary concern at the moment. There was much that was to be commended about the Chancellor-class vessels. They had the latest and best in sensor and tactical technology, they had a dozen disruptor emplacements, as well as one large disruptor cannon, a massive complement of both photon and quantum torpedoes, they could carry fifteen hundred ground troops, and they could travel between warp eight and warp nine with no strain on the engines.

What they could not do was maneuver well at impulse speeds.

The energy streams converged—no, *merged* into a single massive beam, at least three times the diameter of the five original beams—and headed straight for the *Kravokh*'s position.

To his credit, the pilot did the best he could to move the *Kravokh* out of the path of the beam, but the ship was simply too large. A quarter of a *qell'qam* long, a fifth of a *qell'qam* wide, the *Kravokh* presented too big a target for their foes to miss.

Wirrk's hopes that the shields would hold against this weapon were dashed instantly, as the beam's impact was felt throughout the bridge. Wirrk found himself starting to float out of his chair even as he heard the sounds of consoles exploding all around him. The stench of burned conduits assaulted his nostrils and smoke blinded him.

Alarms blared throughout the bridge, but B'Etloj made herself heard over it. "Shields are down! Communications offline! Warp engines offline! Artificial gravity offline! Hull breaches on decks—hull breaches on almost *every* deck! Impulse power down to—"

The helm console exploded, sending the pilot across the bridge in front of Wirrk. His corpse spun in the air in front of him. The captain gripped the armrests of his chair.

B'Etloj amended her report. "Impulse engines down. Engineering reports that a warp-core breach is imminent."

Komor managed to say the words "Eject the—" before the sound of wrenching metal blotted out his words.

Wirrk's ears popped as suddenly he felt himself pulled violently toward the ceiling. One of the hull breaches was on the bridge, and the air screamed as it was drawn toward the vacuum of space. Wirrk looked up to see that the hole was barely wide enough for a person to fit through.

Before he could think on that further, Komor

grabbed him by the shoulders and pushed him down. It did little against the pressure of the explosive decompression, but it was enough to make Komor strike the ceiling and go out into space first.

The commander straightened his body, raising his arms over his head even as he slid through the hole—

—partway. The bridge quieted as Komor's body sealed the hull breach.

For now. You have done well, Commander—your place in Sto-Vo-Kor is assured.

Wirrk fully expected to join him soon.

I underestimated these Elabrej. Even a baby targ can kill a trigak if its teeth are sharp enough and it bites on a vulnerable part of the body.

With gravity out, Wirrk was still floating in the air of his bridge. Around him, his crew did the same. B'Etloj, to her credit, had managed to spear one of the bridge support struts with her *d'k tahg* and used it to lever herself back down toward her console.

"The warp core has been ejected. Main power is fluctuating. Sir, we—"

Then Wirrk saw nothing. The lights went out, and emergency illumination did not replace them.

An explosion briefly lit the bridge as the aft gunnery consoles were destroyed. The heat burned Wirrk's face, and he was barely able to duck the limbs of the *bekks* who staffed those positions as they flew past him.

He once again thought back to Ty'Gokor and his wager with Klag. The last he had heard, the *Gorkon* had not yet engaged in battle, but Wirrk had faith that the son of M'Raq would find combat soon enough, thus enabling him to win their wager.

I regret that I shall not be able to watch you drink your bloodwine, Captain.

"I really don't appreciate being awakened like this."

Yellek expunged a great deal of air out of her windpipes at Mal Donal's tenth repetition of that particular phrase. He'd said it continuously since she came to his home sphere, explaining that she was under orders to escort Donal to the government sphere. They had taken a sky conveyance, Donal grumbling the entire time about how little he appreciated being awakened like this.

Somehow, Yellek managed not to ask what way he *would* have appreciated being awakened.

"And you don't have any idea what this is about, soldier?"

It was only the fourth time he had asked that. Yellek replied, "No, sir, I simply was ordered to escort you here." In fact, she knew precisely what it was about, but besides escorting Donal, she was also ordered not to say anything about the aliens.

Aliens. Yellek still had trouble wrapping her legs around the notion. She had believed what the clerics told her all her life: that the Elabrej were the only sentient life in the universe, that the Demiurges made them unique, and that Doane and Gidding watched over them and kept them safe.

Except we're not safe, are we? Three military space conveyances had been destroyed when the alien ship was captured, not to mention the explorer conveyance. Hundreds of lives had been lost. It was the highest body count in a hundred *ungrets*.

I wonder what the seps will make of this, Yellek wondered as she parked the sky conveyance in the hangar sphere. While she approached, the conveyance was scanned thoroughly by security. If they had any reason to doubt that she was anyone other than Soldier Yellek or that her passenger was anyone other than Mal Donal, the sky conveyance would have been destroyed.

Yellek opened the sky conveyance's doors. "Please come with me, Mal Donal."

"I really don't appreciate being awakened like this."

"So you've said, sir." Yellek couldn't bring the words back from her mouth, though she regretted them the instant they came out.

"What did you say, soldier?" Donal's forelegs and right midleg all waved in great annoyance.

"Sir, I—"

"I am a *Mal*, you non-strata buffoon, and I won't have you—"

"Harassing the troops again, Donal?"

Yellek turned at the new voice, and was so stunned at who it was that it took her an extra half-*engret* to stand at attention, as was required when in the presence of the second oligarch.

Donal waved his left hindleg toward the new arrival. "Brannik? What in Doane's name is going *on*?"

"Follow me," the second oligarch said. He started moving down a corridor that Yellek would not have been able to traverse were she not in the presence of a

Vor strata or someone of the rank of protector or higher. She did not question their going this way, though—she assumed that the aliens would be kept in this area, and she also had orders not to let Donal out of her sight. Although Vor Brannik had the authority to override those orders, he had not done so.

"Brannik, you still haven't answered my question." Donal was now whining.

"It's a very long story, and one you're not going to believe even though you're going to see it for yourself."

Waving his midlegs, Donal said, "What are you going on about? Look, I don't appreciate being awakened by—"

"Donal, last night, seven military conveyances engaged a conveyance of unknown origin. Three of those conveyances were destroyed, but the alien conveyance was defeated, and we captured ten specimens. They're being held in one of our facilities here." Second Oligarch Vor Brannik placed one midleg on Donal's torso. "You're the best doctor we've got."

Yellek knew that Brannik was lying. Donal was an adequate doctor, but he also had high-level clearance. *The oligarchs have to be real careful who they trust with this. Especially if the clerics start waving their legs around.*

The doctor was laughing. "Brannik, is this some kind of joke? Really, I understand that you government types like to—"

"Mal Donal, this is *not* a joke. Four hundred Elabrej have died at the hands of these aliens over the past few *digrets*. I need you to examine them, and I need you to do it right now. If you can't, I'll put you in prison for treason and find another doctor. Am I making myself clear?"

Donal's midlegs were waving so fast Yellek feared they would come off. "Are you mad? There's no such *thing* as aliens! The very idea—"

They turned a corner while Donal was ranting. They arrived at a small sphere with a large window. Donal's words cut off at the sight of what was on the other side of the window.

Yellek was glad nobody was really paying any attention to her, because her own reaction was very unmilitary. *Protector Yer Terris would have my legs for standing a post in this state.*

But she couldn't help it. Standing in that sphere were ten of the most peculiar beings Yellek had ever seen.

They had four legs rather than the usual six: hindlegs and midlegs only, and they seemed to use the hindlegs only for ambulation. They had no windpipe, no nasal slits, elongated torsos, an odd protuberance on top of those torsos, and only half the expected number of fingers at the end of each leg. They also had ridges all over their persons.

The protuberance was especially peculiar. It had one of those ridges, some odd openings, only one of which Yellek recognized as a mouth—and that only because it had teeth—the others of which were a mystery to her. The protuberances also had some kind of stringy substance atop it. Their bodies were, in fact, covered in the string, though the bulk of it was on the protuberance.

Not all of them had the same body type. Yellek assumed that they were the differences between male and female, though she admitted she was making a very big assumption there.

"Doane's limbs." That was Donal, whose own mouth hung open stupidly, making Yellek feel better about her own reaction. "What *are* those?"

Brannik again put a midleg on Donal's torso. "That's what we need you to find out. There could be more of these—these *things* out there, and they're obviously hostile and out to kill us all. The oligarchs need you to find out what they are, what they can do, and how we can destroy them all. Can you do that?"

Another burst of air came from Donal's windpipe. "Do I have a choice?"

"Not really. Get to work. Soldier Yellek has been assigned to you—if you need anything, ask her."

Just what I've always wanted, to be at the beck and call of an arrogant fool.

She dismissed her own thought as unworthy of her position. *I'm a soldier, I do what I'm told. Besides, would I rather have been assigned to one of those conveyances that these alien monstrosities destroyed?*

Yellek found she couldn't even look at the creatures. *I swear by Doane's limbs, I will do whatever needs to be done to keep you despicable things from murdering any more Elabrej.*

Second Oligarch Vor Brannik had taken to simply ignoring Fourth Oligarch Vor Mitol. He found that things moved more smoothly that way. They each sat in their respective hammocks in the meeting sphere. Normally such meetings of the oligarchs happened at the beginning of each day. Now, however, an emergency session had been called in the dead of night. While they waited for Mal Donal to finish his preliminary examinations of the aliens, the oligarchs would discuss what their options were.

"All right, what's next?" he asked.

Before any of the other oligarchs could move on to the next order of business, however, Mitol felt the need to keep talking. "This just isn't possible. Aliens from beyond our skies attacking us—it's like we're characters in a piece of fiction. A piece of very *bad* fiction."

"Mitol—" Brannik started, but the fourth oligarch refused to lower his legs.

"This is just a ploy by the military—you know that, don't you? They wanted to equip their conveyances with those horrendous weapons of theirs before they were done testing so they could use them on the seps. So they created this ridiculous—"

"Mitol, it's not a hoax."

His hindlegs waving back and forth, Mitol's voice seemed to be coming as much out of his windpipe as his mouth. "Of *course* it's a hoax, Brannik! This is the military's dream come true! Instead of constantly being stalled on appropriations, now they have a tailor-made mandate to spend as much money as they want on defense, and never mind where the money's supposed to come from."

Brannik let air out of his windpipe. *This is going worse than I expected.* "Mitol, I know it isn't a hoax—you know how I know that?"

"How?"

"I've seen the aliens. We've got them. Mal Donal is examining them right now."

"That's insane."

"If you want, I'll take you to see them."

First Oligarch Vor Jorg finally spoke. "No, you won't, because Mitol is finished wasting our time." Before Mitol could reply to this, Jorg continued. "You're right, Mitol, this *is* a dream come true, but not in the way you think. The seps have been constantly crying that we tax them mercilessly, that we line our own money pouches while letting the people of the hegemony go to rot. Well, I don't know about you, but I've heard as much of that as I can stand from people who think nothing of committing seditious acts, and of stealing from their betters, and of releasing legitimately held prisoners. Now that these aliens have come, we can show them exactly whose welfare we're concerned with."

"First Oligarch, this—" Mitol started, but this time Brannik interrupted him, which gave the second oligarch a certain pleasure.

"Mitol, it was the space center that first saw this, not the military. *They're* the ones who came to us with the report that Vor Ellis's conveyance was destroyed by these aliens, complete with images from Vor Ellis herself." Brannik placed his hindlegs down on the floor as a show of resolve. "These aliens are *real*, Mitol. And the sooner you wrap your legs around that, the sooner we can move on and *deal* with it."

Before Mitol could reply, the door parted to reveal

one of the soldiers. Brannik could never keep track of their names. "Oligarchs, Mal Donal has finished his preliminary report. May he enter?"

"Absolutely," First Oligarch Jorg said. "Escort him inside."

Waving her left foreleg in acknowledgment, the soldier disappeared for a moment, then came back with Donal.

The doctor's legs all hung limply at his side. *I guess he was able to wrap his legs around the problem eventually.*

"Amazing," he was muttering.

"Mal Donal," Brannik said, "what have you learned?"

"Truly amazing."

"Mal Donal!"

"What?" The doctor's legs started to perk up. "I'm sorry, I just—yes, I—I have a report to give." He removed a recorder from his pouch with his left midleg. "The first thing I'd like to explain is how they are like us."

"They're not like us at all." Brannik was revolted by the very notion. They were disgusting, malformed creatures, and Brannik couldn't believe they had anything in common with the Elabrej.

"Actually, they are in a few ways. For one thing, they respirate similarly to us—they inhale oxygen and exhale carbon dioxide. They have a skeletal structure augmented by muscles and flesh, just like us, even if it's arranged differently. They seem to be divided into male and female, like us, and their genitalia seems to be arranged in roughly the same manner—although the females have odd growths on their torsos whose purpose

71

I've yet to determine. Still, in very general terms, they are carbon-based life, like us."

Jorg waved his left midleg. "Get to the part where they're not like us."

"Well, First Oligarch, there's the obvious way in which their bodies are shaped. They are stunted, having only two useful legs. Their midlegs are too weak to support their weight, and they have no forelegs at all. My guess is that their midlegs have atrophied from lack of use. Honestly, First Oligarch, I have no idea how these creatures could possibly have evolved. They violate every known tenet of survival."

"In what way?" Jorg asked.

Brannik let out air through his windpipe. "How is this relevant?"

Jorg folded his midlegs together. "I believe what Mal Donal is about to tell us is how they are weak."

Then Brannik understood. *We have to know our enemy's strengths—but their weaknesses are important, too.*

Peering at his recorder, Donal said, "The most interesting thing is that odd growth atop their torsos where their forelegs should be. Not only does this growth contain their mouths, but I did a variety of scans only to discover that they keep their craniums there, as well as their primary olfactory passages."

"How odd," one of the oligarchs said.

"Indeed it is." Donal was speaking now with the enthusiasm of a scientist, which suited Brannik as long as he stayed on topic. "It's very impractical—their brains are located on the top of their bodies instead of being centrally located. True, they have a bony ridge that protects them, but it still leaves them appallingly vulnerable, especially given how hampered their movements are with only two usable legs. Plus they have limited dexterity, with only five fingers per leg instead of the usual ten. Honestly, I don't see how they could have built anything, with their bodies designed like that. In point of fact, I don't see how they survived long enough to attain sentience. Any decent predator would have done them in centuries ago."

"I'm more interested in what can do them in *now*, Mal Donal," Jorg said gently.

"Of course, First Oligarch." Donal pressed a control on his reader. "You said you were looking for weaknesses—well, I have one that will stun you. This, more than anything, leads me to believe that these aliens are weak creatures that will be easy for us to swat like insects: they have no vision worth mentioning."

Third Oligarch Vor Anset waved her hindlegs. "You mean they can't see?"

"Well, I suppose, if you stretch the definition, they can. It took me quite some time to figure it out. I could find no evidence of optic nerves anywhere in their bodies except on two of the holes in the brain pouch."

Jorg puffed briefly through his windpipe. "Brain pouch?"

"Sorry, First Oligarch, that is the name I have given to the torsal growth."

"Of course, Mal Donal. Please, go on."

Donal consulted his reader for a moment. "The holes seemed unusually sensitive to light. Eventually, through trial and error, I was able to determine that the holes in their brain pouches were their only method of sight. First Oligarch, Oligarchs—these creatures can only see whatever's directly before those two holes."

Brannik waved his forelegs. "That's insane."

"It's true."

"How can they possibly function while only seeing—what, five percent of what's around them?"

Donal checked his reader. "My readings indicate that it's more like twenty percent, but that's still eighty percent of their environment that they are unable to visualize. One thing I will credit them with—their other senses do compensate to some degree. Their olfactory and aural senses are much greater than ours."

"What about language?" Anset asked.

"Grunts and growls." Donal waved a hindleg. "I suppose it makes sense to them, since they seem to be conversing. Oh, one other thing—they were wearing some kind of armor. We removed it, of course. One of the military people examined them, and they told the soldier escorting me that each of them carried several items that have been identified as weapons."

Naturally, Brannik thought.

Jorg asked, "What does that tell you, Mal Donal?"

"They are a violent people, First Oligarch."

"That, we already knew," Brannik said. "We saw what they did to Vor Ellis's conveyance, not to mention three military ones."

Donal said, "Still, they show very few signs of intelligence. I suspect that they are only dull-witted animals. During my testing, they committed several violent acts against their prison. There's been no direct interaction with any Elabrej, and I would suggest that remain the case. These savages would probably cause a great deal of damage if left unchecked."

Brannik started to wonder if bringing the doctor in was such a good idea. "Mal Donal, these aren't animals. They built spacefaring conveyances."

"Do you have any proof of that?" Donal asked archly. "All we know is that they *operated* spacefaring conveyances. My theory is that another species keeps them as slaves of some kind, gives them basic instruction on how to operate machinery and tools, and then sends them out as cannon fodder. It's the only explanation that makes sense—there's simply no way beings like this could possibly have survived and evolved without outside help from a superior species like the Elabrej. Their evolutionary weaknesses are legion. I believe that they can be easily defeated simply by using complex strategies against them. I doubt they have the cunning for that."

Jorg folded his forelegs over his midlegs. "These are just preliminary tests, you said?"

"Yes, First Oligarch, and I will conduct more, of course, but I do believe that my basic premise is right. These aliens are weak, they are vulnerable, they are stupid, and they will be easily defeated should any more darken our skies."

Brannik took in some air before expunging some.

Jorg waved his forelegs. "Thank you for your report, Mal Donal. Soldier Yellek will escort you back to the holding sphere so you can continue your tests."

That's her name, Brannik thought.

Waving his forelegs back in acknowledgment, Donal said, "Thank you, Oligarchs."

Donal and Yellek both departed.

Jorg leaned forward in his hammock, his hindlegs solidly on the floor. "Thoughts?"

"I'm not sure I believe Mal Donal's assessment," Brannik said. "I don't think we're going to succeed by underestimating these creatures. Just because they're different doesn't make them inferior."

Mitol said, "Oh, and you're a scientist now, are you?"

"Look, Mitol, I respect Donal, but—"

"I respect him too, Brannik, and I respect his credentials. I wouldn't expect him to make a sensible judgment about how to run a government, so frankly, I'm not going to believe you over him when it comes to what makes a viable intelligent species. If he thinks they're dumb animals, I'm inclined to believe him—especially given how physically inferior they are."

"Maybe, maybe not, but that doesn't really matter," Fifth Oligarch Yer Blos said. "The point is, these beings, whatever they are, are out there. Whether they did it themselves or had help doesn't matter—the point is, they are flying through the skies in conveyances that have broken the light barrier, just like we did. They were first encountered flying through an uncharted star system, just like we were. And they fought with energy weapons, just like we did."

"What's your point, Blos?" Jorg asked.

"My point, First Oligarch, is that it's reasonable to assume that if they have done so much that we have also done, they also have the ability to communicate over interstellar distances."

Brannik saw where Blos was going with this. "You think that they were able to let their fellow aliens know about what happened to them?"

"Vor Ellis was able to warn us."

Jorg waved his forelegs. "In which case, we have to assume they did the same to their people."

Seventh Oligarch Yer Gosnot said, "We have to mobilize."

"Definitely," Sixth Oligarch Vor Markus said with a wave of her forelegs.

Anset added, "We have to finish re-arming all our conveyances, and then we have to mount a defense. It will take several *sogrets* for the buildup to reach full strength, even if we start immediately, but I believe we must do so."

"I think that's premature," Mitol said.

Brannik expelled a huge amount of air. "Mitol—"

"I'm still not convinced that this isn't all an elaborate ploy by the military, Brannik."

"It isn't." The first oligarch spoke with authority and finality. "Fellow oligarchs, this is an unprecedented opportunity. We've been plagued by separatist attacks on our government and on our people. This ends now. It was one thing when the seps were our only concern, but now we have a bigger problem, one that affects *all* Elabrej, not just the government, not just the people, not just the seps—*all* of us. Gosnot, Markus, and Anset are correct—we have to defend ourselves. Are we agreed?"

All the oligarchs save for Mitol raised their hindlegs in agreement.

"Vor Mitol," Jorg said, "I understand your reservations, but—"

Mitol raised his hindlegs. "I agree, also, First Oligarch—with those reservations, but I do agree. I ask only that we be careful."

Brannik said, "We can't afford to be careful. These things are coming. We can't let them destroy us."

CHAPTER THREE

"**A**nd then—and *then*—the *petaQ* fell on top of my *tik'leth!*"

The Imperial Intelligence agent who went under the name of *Bekk* Trant gulped his bloodwine while he listened to Leader Wol's story, secure in the knowledge that his anti-inebriation implant would keep him from feeling any ill effects.

"It was absurd—he had me on the ground, poised to make the killing blow—and he *passed out!*"

Laughter echoed throughout the mess hall, mainly because, aside from the five soldiers of the fifteenth and the Pheben steward cleaning the tables on the far side of the hall, the room was empty. Wol had ordered them here, only to show up accompanied by *Bekk* Tolark from the fourteenth and a barrel of bloodwine.

"The only problem was, he fell on my *tik'leth*—and my sword arm."

Goran asked, "Why was—why was—why was that

79

a—that a problem?" Though he was twice the size of the average Klingon, the big man, as he was called, could not hold his liquor.

Wol poured a large amount of bloodwine toward her face. Most of it entered her mouth; she swallowed that quantity before answering Goran's question. "He weighed a *ton*. I couldn't move my arm!"

More laughter. Trant joined in it, making sure to bray as loudly as possible. *After all, I should be as drunk as the rest of them.*

G'joth kept rocking back and forth on his feet. Kagak sat at a table constantly swatting a nonexistent insect near his head. And Wol was gripping the back of one of the mess-hall chairs for dear life, as if letting go of it would be fatal.

However, their drunken state wasn't what was important—rather it was that they were relaxed. Trant's observations since arriving on the *Gorkon* had been that troop morale on the ship depended a lot more on the squad leaders than the *QaS DevwI'*. One of Trant's assignments from I.I. was to report on this phenomenon, which Trant attributed to the greater number of troops on a Chancellor-class ships. Smaller units would rely more on the *QaS DevwI'*, but the sheer number of troops present made the squad leaders' role that much more crucial.

Wol's unit was of particular interest. Wol was a highborn Klingon woman who had successfully reinvented herself after being cast out of her House. Trant had targeted her as a possible I.I. recruit, going so far as to get himself (as well as the late *Bekk* Maris) demoted from the seventh to the fifteenth to keep a closer eye on her. Her squad was a standout on San-Tarah, and the morale difficulties since leaving that planet were surprising to Trant.

This night of debauchery, however, seemed to be accomplishing what Wol wanted.

Wol's was the latest in a series of stories. G'joth had told the story of his unexpected trip to Narendra III, during which a Federation ambassador shot Davok. This led to several other stories of G'joth and Davok's exploits. Goran told a story from when he was a prison guard at Rura Penthe. Trant even made up a tale on the spot, claiming it was from early in his career. Wol then shared some of her war stories, of which this duel with a drunken soldier was the latest.

"Kagak," she said suddenly to the fifteenth's newest recruit, "you've been pretty quiet."

"I haven't had anything to say." Kagak swatted at his invisible insect again.

"Pfaugh," G'joth said. "You haven't had anything to say for six weeks. I was starting to think that a *targ* had eaten your tongue."

"I—I knew someone whose—whose tongue was eaten by a—by a *targ* once." Goran let out a long, loud belch—Trant swore the bulkheads rattled from the sound of it—before proceeding. "It was on—on Rura Penthe right after—after I became a guard there on Rura Penthe when I was—I was a guard."

Swatting his insect some more, Kagak said, "Well, nobody took my tongue, s'just—I just—I don't feel so good."

G'joth laughed. "Not used to the good stuff, eh?"

Playing along, Trant also laughed.

"Well, you haven't done your share," Wol said. "All of us—even Trant—have told a story. Except you. Tell us about yourself."

"Yes," G'joth said. "Tell us why you're worthy."

"Excuse me?" Kagak sounded befuddled.

"This is the fifteenth!" G'joth bellowed, holding his mug up toward the ceiling. "We held the road against the San-Tarah! We defended the prize! We won the day at the Prime Village and then took back the village of Val-Goral from General Talak's troops! Krevor—Davok—even that *toDSaH* Maris—they all died with honor!"

"Yes!" Trant cried, even though he knew that Maris's death had nothing to do with honor. Thanks to a lapse that still shamed Trant—and for which he fully expected to be put to death when the *Gorkon* returned to Qo'noS and he was fully debriefed—Maris had found some of Trant's I.I. gear and used it to feed intelligence to General Talak's troops. Trant had put the traitor to death, and the rest of the fifteenth believed that he died in an unfortunate accident during battle. *Even that false report is not truly dying with honor, but G'joth is trying to prove a point here. . . .*

G'joth walked on unsteady legs to stand in front of Kagak. "So tell me, why are you worthy to follow in their noble footsteps?"

"I have always served the empire with honor, and I have always done my duty to the High Council."

Before Kagak even finished, G'joth was laughing so

hard he fell onto the deck. Trant, who joined in the laugh, moved to pick him up, as did Wol. Between them, they were able to drop G'joth's weight onto one of the mess-hall chairs—certainly not with any help from G'joth himself, who apparently was saving all his strength for mocking Kagak.

The young *bekk* himself seemed outraged. "What is so amusing about serving the empire?"

"You sound like a recruitment enticement, infant," G'joth said. "That's the kind of answer I'd expect from the button-pushers on the bridge. But you're no officer, you're a working warrior just like the rest of us. So tell me again—why are you worthy?"

Now G'joth was fixing Kagak with a sharp gaze. Trant noticed that Wol had retaken her seat, and was content to watch this play out. But despite the amount she had drunk, Trant knew that she was as aware of what was happening as he. *She's gauging Kagak's reaction, and how it will affect the squad.*

Kagak didn't seem to be able to make his mouth move.

When Trant reported to the fifteenth, he had shown his support for Captain Klag's call to arms against General Talak—who had called for the captain to go against the word he had given to the Children of San-Tarah—by playing the malcontent and questioning Klag's actions. Those who supported Klag spoke out in his defense, helping to persuade those who might not be sure on whose side their loyalties lay.

Now, though, I think the time for playing malcontent is past. He stood next to G'joth. "Why don't you answer?"

he asked belligerently, as befit the amount of bloodwine he'd drunk. "You've been assigned to the finest squad on this vessel!"

As expected, G'joth looked at Trant with shock. "What did you say?"

"Leader Wol is the noblest of the soldiers on this ship—she has led the fifteenth to honor and to glory!"

Wol smiled. "What led you to this new conclusion, Trant?"

Trant turned to Wol. "I know I questioned you—and the captain—in the past, Leader. But Chancellor Martok himself approved of Klag's actions, and I do not disobey my chancellor."

G'joth snorted, sending spittle flying across one of the tables. "That's it? Chancellor One-Eye says all is well and you're no longer a whining little Ferengi?"

"I may be slow to see honor, G'joth, but I do see it eventually. I am proud to be a member of the fifteenth." He turned to Kagak, who still looked mildly stunned. "And so should you be. But what we want to know—what Leader Wol and G'joth and Goran and I want to know—"

Trant was interrupted by a very loud snore. He looked over to see that Goran had passed out.

All of them laughed at that sight, especially since Goran's mouth was hanging open and drool was pouring down his beard like the *nagh* waterfall.

"Very well, then," Trant said. "What Leader Wol and G'joth and I want to know is—why are you worthy to be among us?" Pointing at Kagak with his bloodwine mug, he added, "And be warned! It would be better for you if we *liked* your answer!"

Kagak took a long gulp of bloodwine. Then he got up and stumbled unsteadily toward the barrel—which had very little left at this point. He scooped up as much as he could, then drank it all down.

Then, finally, he turned to face the rest of the fifteenth, dropping the mug in the process. It clattered across the deck, the noise echoing.

"Well?" G'joth asked.

"In truth—I'm not sure I am. I was a good soldier on the *Kreltek*. I thought that Captain Triak was the greatest captain in the fleet. We had seen many campaigns together, and always we were victorious! Especially during the war . . ."

After Kagak was silent for a moment, Wol said, "Go on, *Bekk*."

Shaking his head, as if to revive himself, Kagak then said, "Then Captain Vekma—well, she was Commander Vekma, then—Commander Vekma killed the captain, saying he had chosen the path of dishonor. That the Order of the *Bat'leth* had been summoned to glory and Captain Triak had ignored it—in fact that he belittled the order. I was stunned. I could not believe that the great warrior I served under would do such a thing. Then when we found out that Vekma was taking us into battle against our fellow Klingons—worse, that we were going into battle against General Talak—and there were many of us who thought—who thought—who thought that this was wrong!"

Kagak moved his hand to his mouth as if to drink

more bloodwine, only to realize that his mug was gone. Without a word, Trant handed Kagak his own mug. The *bekk* grabbed the mug and drank down its contents eagerly.

"This," Kagak said, "is a *good* vintage."

"Yes, it is," Wol said. "Continue. What was 'wrong'?"

Trant noted that Wol now sounded completely sober.

"One of our *QaS DevwI'*, an old warrior named Krox, said that the captain who summoned the order was Klag, son of M'Raq. We knew him as the Hero of Marcan, but *QaS DevwI'* Krox portrayed him as an animal who mutilated his body and was not a true warrior."

G'joth moved forward, his *d'k tahg* out. Trant didn't think the old razorbeast was fast enough to unholster his blade while sober, much less drunk, but at the insult to the captain, he managed it. Wol intercepted him, and in response to her actions, Trant did likewise.

"Let him finish, G'joth," Wol said.

Struggling against both Wol and Trant's grip, G'joth asked, "Why? I will not let Captain Klag be spoken of that way!" Trant thought he would pass out from G'joth's breath, which combined the worst elements of bloodwine and *gagh*.

Kagak's bloodshot eyes had gone wide. "You were the ones who called the officers 'button-pushers'!"

At that, G'joth laughed. "They are! But the captain is still the captain, and no one insults him and lives."

"I *said* let him finish, G'joth." Wol's voice was deep and dangerous. "When he is done, if he has not explained his slander—we will *all* kill him where he stands."

Wol let go of G'joth, Trant doing likewise a moment later. Snarling, G'joth paced back to another table and sat angrily in a chair. He kept his *d'k tahg* unsheathed, though he closed the secondary blades.

"It was Krox who slandered Captain Klag, *not me!* But I knew only that Captain Triak was in *Sto-Vo-Kor* and that his killer was leading us into dishonorable combat. So we planned a mutiny."

"*Did* you?" G'joth bared his teeth and, with a telltale click, again unfurled the *d'k tahg*'s secondary blades.

"What came of your mutiny?" Wol asked.

"Nothing! The battle ended before Krox could implement his plan, and then the *Sword of Kahless* showed up, Talak was disgraced, Martok gave Klag his blessing—and Krox committed *Mauk-to'Vor.*"

"Coward." G'joth snorted as he made the accusation.

"Perhaps he was. But I know that I was wrong. And when I was reassigned to this ship, I hoped that I would be able to regain the path of honor that we all lost on the *Kreltek*. But—"

Wol stepped forward, now standing nose-to-nose with Kagak. "But what?"

"I know that we were wrong to plan that mutiny, that to have done so would have dishonored us all. But—"

Again Kagak cut himself off at that word. Trant said, "Speak your words, boy, because we will not restrain G'joth a second time."

Kagak looked at Wol, then at Trant, then at G'joth,

then even at Goran's slumbering form. "There are those who served on the *Kreltek* who still believe Krox's words."

Normally, Trant's training would have required him to control his reaction to this, but shock and anger would have been expected from a *bekk*, so he allowed himself to express outrage at this. "What are you saying, boy?"

Kagak drank down the rest of Wol's bloodwine before answering. "I'm saying that you should all watch your backs. My former shipmates may not be happy with the command structure on this ship. And I've— I've heard things."

"What kind of things?" Wol asked.

"That they may have some officers on their side as well."

G'joth spit. "I wouldn't count on that."

In truth, Trant didn't think it likely either. Klag had not chosen most of his command staff; if any of them had any problems with Klag's leadership, it would have come out months ago. Certainly, it would have at San-Tarah. If these theoretical mutineers had the support of any officers, they weren't high-ranking ones.

However, in the interests of maintaining his cover, Trant said, "How do we know? Kagak could be right, there could be officers involved."

"*If* officers are involved," Wol said, "it's their problem. All we need do is watch our own backs—and watch Kagak's former crewmates." She turned to Kagak. "And him as well."

"Me?" Kagak's voice broke when he bellowed the word. "I've confided in you! Why won't you trust me?"

Wol barked a laugh. "You've been with this squad six weeks, and this is the first we've heard of *any* of this. We've seen no battle together, so we do not even know if you are a worthy warrior. We *do* know that you will sell out your former crewmates."

"Only those who choose the path of dishonor!" Kagak's eyes were now darting back and forth among the three of them. "I would never betray honorable warriors! And I had to be sure."

"Sure of what?" Trant asked, though he knew the answer.

"That you were the same creatures of honor that I now know our captain to be."

"We are." Wol put a hand on Kagak's shoulder. "If you're very very lucky, Kagak—you'll live long enough to find out for sure."

"And if *we're* very lucky," G'joth added, "you won't."

Trant sighed. G'joth had said the same thing to Trant and Maris during the San-Tarah campaign. *For someone who once fancied himself a writer, G'joth, you have very little by way of original material.*

"We shall see in due course." Wol walked over to the barrel, noticed it was all but empty, then looked at her squad. "And we shall do so together. But more than anything else, G'joth—Trant—Kagak—" She smiled. "And Goran, if he were awake—as long as I am here, I will *always* lead you to victory."

"Of that, Leader, I have no doubt," Trant said.

"You know," G'joth said, finally holstering his *d'k*

tahg, "*you've* been with this squad *seven* weeks, and this is the first we've heard of any of this, either, Trant."

Trant grinned. "It would seem I'm a slow learner."

Wol returned the grin. "Learn faster next time. You and this infant have very large boots to fill." She checked the chronometer on the wall. "It's late. We have a drill in the morning. C'mon, G'joth, let's get the big man up."

As Wol and G'joth moved to rouse Goran, Trant walked over to Kagak. "You were wise to confide in us, boy."

"I know I was. And I will be on your side."

That's truer than you know, Trant thought. Right now, his primary duty as one of the I.I. agents on this ship was to make sure this potential mutiny never happened. Klag was one of the most important captains in the fleet right now. Ever since the end of the war, and the unsuccessful coup by Morjod, Martok had been attempting to bring the empire back to the honorable path, to the true way of honor as codified by Kahless. By his actions—in general, since he took command of the *Gorkon* nine months earlier, and in particular at San-Tarah—Klag had proven himself to be an important piece on Martok's game board.

Trant would make sure that nothing happened to jeopardize that.

Klag spoke as soon as the door to his office rumbled shut behind him. "Has Dr. B'Oraq given you reason to think that I have weakened in any way, Commander?"

Toq had been standing on the guest side of the desk,

studying something on the viewer. At Klag's entrance, he stood up straight. "Of course not, sir," he said quickly, sounding appalled at the very idea.

As well he should be. "Then explain why there is a need for me to be guarded by three warriors. Did I not slay a dozen Jem'Hadar on Marcan V? Did I not defeat General Talak within the circle on San-Tarah?"

"Yes, sir, you did, but—you are not guarded by three warriors. The guard who stood outside this door when you entered was mine."

Klag had played enough games. He sat down in the chair behind his desk. "Explain."

Succinctly, the young first officer told Klag of a report he'd gotten from Lieutenant Lokor regarding possible disaffection among the transfers from the *Kreltek*.

Klag considered Toq's words. In truth, he'd had few dealings with such issues. He had been fortunate early in his career to serve with honorable captains. Then he came aboard the *Pagh*. While there were many thoughts of mutiny under Captain Kargan, none dared put those thoughts to action for fear of reprisal. Kargan was kinsman to Councillor K'Tal and General Talak both, and no one dared challenge a scion of the House of K'Tal unless they wished to number the hours remaining in their own lives on the fingers of a single hand.

Since his own elevation to the captaincy, he had received no inkling of any consideration of removing him from the command chair. That meant either that no one wished to do so, or that Lokor had done his job well in containing such wishes.

"Very well," Klag finally said. "Keep me apprised. Is Lokor not concerned that he is tipping his hand?"

"He says he has done so on purpose, that he wishes any possible conspirators to be fully aware that he is on to them."

"You believe this to be a wise strategy?"

Toq replied without hesitation. "Yes, sir, I do. At worst, it drives the conspirators further into hiding, which keeps them from acting on their desires. At best, it drives them to act quickly—perhaps too quickly."

Klag nodded. In fact, he agreed with Lokor's decision, for the very reasons Toq gave, but he wished to make sure that Toq himself understood Lokor's thinking.

"Plus," the first officer added, "Lokor has earned a reputation. Knowing that he is aware of them may frighten the conspirators."

Chuckling, Klag said, "Indeed. I assume you did not cut my *bat'leth* drill short to inform me of this."

"No, sir, that could have waited until you were finished." Toq turned the viewer back around so that Klag could see the screen. "Lieutenant K'Nir reported that a long-range scan detected heavy warp activity near Kavrot *wej'vatlh wa'maH vagh*. That system is also the last known destination of the *Kravokh*—eight weeks ago."

Klag frowned. "There's been no report from Captain Wirrk since they destroyed that ship?"

"No, sir."

Shaking his head, Klag cast his mind back to Ty'-Gokor and his and Wirrk's wager. *I've won it now, my friend—I only hope that you are still alive to revel in my victory.*

Klag stood up quickly. "How far are we from *wej'vatlh wa'maH vagh*, Commander?"

Again, Toq spoke without hesitating. "Five days at warp eight-point-five."

"Good." He walked around to the other side of the desk to face Toq directly. "Is General Goluk still at Nayyvrrra?"

"According to the most recent reports, yes, sir, though they should be leaving within a day or so. A governor has already—"

Uninterested in the minutiae of the conquering of Nayyvrrra, Klag held up a hand and interrupted. "We must speak with the general immediately."

"I've had Ensign Kal prepare a report—"

"No." Klag shook his head. "Not a report—we must speak directly to him. Have Kal open a channel to the general's flagship."

Toq nodded and headed for the exit. "Yes, sir."

Klag considered the report. Wirrk was not one to go silent for so long without reason. True, warriors need not check with their superiors at every step of a battle like children learning *klin zha* for the first time, but eight weeks was more than enough time. If the *Kravokh* was in a battle that had taken that long, they were in need of assistance, warrior's pride be damned—and if they had lost a battle, then they needed to be avenged.

Moving to sit back at his desk, he called up the last report from the *Kravokh* two months earlier. He remembered when Toq's predecessor Commander Kornan brought it to him: *"The Kravokh defeated an alien ship that appears to be part of a small confederation. They're investigating further to see if they are worthy of being conquered."*

According to the report Wirrk's operations officer filed, the vessel they encountered penetrated the *Kravokh*'s cloak and then took out the cloaking device—as well as several other systems—with one shot. *Which was*, he noted, *the same number of shots Wirrk needed to destroy them entirely.*

At the time of the transmission, they had translated enough of the enemy's communications to know that they called themselves the Elabrej Hegemony.

Then he called up the readings that Ensign Kal was taking even now on long-range sensors.

Toq's voice sounded over the room's speakers. *"Captain, I have General Goluk."*

Klag switched the viewer to the gray-maned visage of Goluk, son of Ruuv. Goluk was a respected general, winner of several battles against foes ranging from the Cardassians to the Romulans to the Federation—during the year that the empire withdrew from the Khitomer Accords—to the Jem'Hadar and the Breen. Not only had he always been victorious, but he was never in any danger of being defeated. His battle plans were legendary. For many years, he had been prevented from advancing because he did not approve of Gowron when the latter served as chancellor, and Gowron had little tolerance for those who did not approve of him. It was not until Martok ascended to the chancellorship that the gruff old veteran was given his long-overdue promotion to general.

In addition, Goluk was, like Klag, a member of the Order of the *Bat'leth*. Perhaps the greatest statement of approval of Klag's actions at San-Tarah that Martok could have made was replacing Talak with a member of the order.

"General."

"*Captain. Speak.*" Goluk also was not one for wasting words.

Klag reported what his people had found. "In addition, sir, our own long-range sensor readings have been refined over the past twenty minutes or so. The energy output of the warp activity is similar to that of the ship the *Kravokh* destroyed." He smiled. "Of course, it's also similar to Breen, Vulcan, Ferengi, and Andorian propulsion systems."

"*What is your opinion, Captain?*"

The smile remained on Klag's face. Goluk's question was as much a test for Klag as the captain's earlier question to Toq was a test for the first officer. "I believe that the *Kravokh* traveled to this Elabrej Hegemony and found far more than one vessel. I believe that they may well have been destroyed, which is why we have not heard from them in eight weeks. And I believe that this warp activity is an aggressive buildup of forces to defend against more Klingon ships coming to their space."

"*I concur.*" The general paused a moment. "*Chancellor Martok is on his way to Bajor—they're joining the Federation, apparently, and he's an invited guest.*"

Klag frowned. "I thought Bajor joined the Federation during the war."

"*Apparently not. In any event, I will need to contact him, but the distance will delay matters. However, Captain, as you are closest to the Elabrej, I want you to set course there immediately. What is your travel time?*"

"Five days at top speed."

"*Very well. Proceed to this Elabrej Hegemony, Captain. I will be alerting the other Chancellor ships to stand by until I can speak to Martok.*"

"What will your recommendation to the chancellor be, General?"

Goluk seemed surprised at Klag's impertinence, but Klag did not regret it. He wished to know his commanding officer's mind, and this was the only way to do it.

"*I will suggest that all ten remaining ships in the Kavrot Sector be diverted to Elabrej. Unfortunately, thanks to the events at San-Tarah, those are the only ships that will be able to respond to this initial aggression. Further reinforcements will take weeks to arrive.*"

Klag ignored the rebuke. He had no regrets about their actions at San-Tarah, and the fact that it left the Defense Force comparatively weak in this sector for the time being was something he could ill afford to be concerned with when a matter of honor was at stake.

"*After I have spoken to Martok, I will contact you again. Screen off.*"

Goluk's face faded from the screen. Klag activated the intercom. "Commander Toq, report to the captain."

Seconds later, Toq entered the office. "Yes, sir?"

As soon as the door closed behind him, Klag asked,

"Can I assume that a course for Kavrot *wej'vatlh wa'maH vagh* has already been set?"

Toq smiled. "You may indeed, sir."

"Excellent. Proceed out of the system at full impulse on that course, and execute at warp eight-point-five when we've cleared the system."

"Immediately, sir. What are our orders?"

"Just that for now—but expect those orders to be amended fairly quickly. Have operations on both shifts continue intensive scans of that system. I want to know everything there is to know about the home of this new foe of ours."

"Yes, sir." With that, Toq left at a quick pace, eager to carry out the captain's orders.

Klag rose from his chair with ease. Although it would soon be time for him to sleep, the captain found that he was more energized than he had been since they left San-Tarah. *I may as well take advantage.*

He activated his intercom. "Klag to B'Oraq."

"B'Oraq." The doctor's voice sounded sleepy.

"Report to the holodeck immediately, Doctor. We have a drill to finish."

Now sounding wide awake, B'Oraq said, *"Right away, sir."*

Trant climbed gingerly into his bunk, pain shooting through his lower back.

The *Gorkon's* centralmost deck was a maze of corridors, lined with sets of five bunks inset into the bulkheads, stacked from deck to ceiling. Generally, the leader slept in the lowest of the bunks, which were two meters in length, one meter in width, and half a meter in height. However, Goran's girth made it necessary for him to take the bottommost bunk, as it was reinforced by the deck, leaving Wol to take the second one. Trant had been placed in the middle bunk, beneath G'joth and Kagak.

At first, Trant had been grateful for the placement, as it put him one bunk removed from Maris, who had what was now Kagak's bunk. Maris tended to mutter in his sleep. Unfortunately, G'joth snored, loudly. G'joth had denied this when confronted with it the first morning after Trant's assignment to the fifteenth, and he had continued denying it for seven weeks (and counting).

G'joth was already asleep and snoring by the time Trant got to his bunk, since Trant and Kagak had been given big-man duty. All attempts at rousing Goran had proven futile, so, as the newest recruits to the squad, Trant and Kagak had the unenviable task of hauling Goran's massive form out of the mess hall and to the turbolift, and thence to the bunks. It took the better part of an hour, partly because Kagak kept almost passing out himself, partly because of the difficulty in getting the big man into the turbolift without any parts protruding. By the time they finally crammed Goran in, Trant was quite ready to simply cut off any parts that didn't fit.

The work was sped up considerably when they decided not to bother trying to lift him, but rather dragged him by his feet. Eventually, they were able to roll him into his bunk, with only one arm hanging out of the confines of Goran's two meters.

All Klingon soldiers were expected to keep their entire lives in the two-meter space of the bunks. In Trant's case, he kept everything in a satchel that had a hidden compartment. Until recently, he never bothered with the compartment, as none of the specialized equipment was generally recognizable to the average soldier, and few would go through a warrior's personal items in any case.

Maris, however, proved to be both smarter and more dishonorable than expected. He had gone through Trant's things, recognized the I.I. transmitter for what it was, and used it to betray the *Gorkon*. Since then, Trant made a point of using the compartment, and also of checking its contents every chance he got.

After settling into his bunk, he reached through the various innocuous personal items and touched the bottom of the satchel. It recognized his DNA; a flap opened to allow him ingress.

To his surprise, one of the items in the compartment was flashing.

Taking a quick glance outside to make sure no one was around—he saw nothing, and heard only G'joth's snoring—he removed the item.

This is not good. The item in question was a receiver to be used only by I.I. agents in case of a dire emergency. Field agents were all equipped with subcutaneous transmitters that could send a tight-beam subspace transmission to receivers like this one. The transmissions were directed, but the agent was unable to control that direction, so—particularly in an area as far from the boundaries of the empire as the Kavrot Sector—there was no guarantee that the transmission would be received.

Trant removed a small earpiece from the receiver and placed it in his right ear. Then he touched the flashing light, which stopped blinking.

Naturally, the message was in code. The first words were a number, indicating which code it would be.

The agent's report that followed chilled Trant. Worse, after the report, a computerized voice indicated that this was the fortieth attempt by the agent to send the report, but the first to be received by an I.I. agent.

This is not good at all. I need to see Klag immediately.

It was, however, not that simple. As a mere *bekk*, proper procedure was for him to go to his squad leader, then to his *QaS DevwI'*, then the chief of security, then the first officer, then, at last, the captain.

Trant could not afford to waste time with so many steps.

Leader Morr's *bat'leth* came careening toward Klag's head from his left. In order to parry the blow, he would need to bring his own *bat'leth* up from his right side to block it—which meant all the power from the parry had to come from his right arm.

That power had not always been there. Many times in the past six weeks, Morr had sparred with Klag, and every time the captain had to parry from his right, it was weak and ineffectual.

Tonight, however, Klag was, for whatever reason, feeling good. Perhaps it was the call to battle, however vague it was at present. Perhaps it was the good feeling he had about Toq. His first second-in-command was Drex, the son of Martok, and whose own honor was a shadow of his father's; Klag had him transferred as quickly as he was able. After that was Tereth, an excellent officer who was killed saving the life of a worthless *toDSaH* named Vralk at Narendra III; she deserved so much more. Finally, Kornan, neither as talented as Tereth nor as worthless as Drex, died saving the ship in the San-Tarah campaign.

Through all that, Toq had served with distinction as second officer, and, despite his youth, Klag felt it was finally time for him to take on the mantle of first officer. So far, Klag was happy with what he saw.

And when he successfully parried Morr's strike with a resounding clash of metal against metal, he was happy with that, as well.

"Well done, sir," Morr said.

B'Oraq approached the pair. "Indeed. The arm is gaining strength, and you're growing more accustomed to it."

Klag was about to point out that the doctor, like many of her kind, was stating the blindingly obvious, but before he could, the intercom sounded with Lokor's voice. *"Lokor to Klag."*

The captain blinked. *Lokor wouldn't contact me unless it was important.* "Klag."

"I need to speak with you immediately, Captain."

"Be in my office in five minutes."

"Bekk Trant and I will be there, sir."

Klag had no idea who that was. *What is a lowly* bekk *doing having a meeting with the captain and the security chief in the middle of the second shift? Does it have to do with the potential mutiny?* He sighed. *I will find out soon enough.*

"Computer, end program and exit." The holodeck reverted to its grid form and the doors parted, revealing K'Varia standing guard outside. To B'Oraq, Klag said, "It would seem, Doctor, that it is our lot to be cut short tonight."

"Such is the way of things, Captain. I'm just heartened to see the progress you're making. It provides me with a weapon to use."

Frowning as he made his way to the exit, Morr and B'Oraq both following, Klag asked, "Weapon?"

"A doctor named Kowag published a monograph some time ago excoriating me, calling the procedure I did on you barbaric, and predicting that, within four months, your new right arm will have atrophied and will need to be removed or else risk you dying of an infection."

"When was this article published?"

B'Oraq smiled and tugged on her braid. That nervous habit of hers had abated, mostly owing to Klag pointing it out to her, which made her self-conscious about it, but she still occasionally indulged in it, her fingers wrapped around the clasp with the emblem of her House that held the braid together. "Four months ago."

Throwing his head back, Klag laughed to the ceiling. "Excellent! I'm glad I'm able to provide you with a *d'k tahg* to sink into this Dr. Kowag's chest."

Grinning, B'Oraq said, "Oh, I intend to use something much larger than a *d'k tahg*. He's one of the physicians on duty at the Great Hall, mainly due to belonging to the House of Ch'vak. His surgical methods are horrendous, and he's been the cause of more than one death due to internal bleeding. Admiral McCoy took his work to task when he and I toured the Great Hall medical ward after his talk to the High Council—I'm sure that's what led him to write that monograph in the first place."

"I wish you success in your battle, Doctor," Klag said as they approached the turbolift. The doors parted, and Klag entered with the two guards. Since the medical bay was on the same deck, B'Oraq did not join them.

As they rode toward the bridge, Klag asked, "Who is Trant?"

"He's a member of the fifteenth, sir," Morr said. "He was with the seventh, then was moved to the fifteenth after the contests on San-Tarah."

It was unusual for troops to move downward through the ranks like that, but Klag did not pursue the question. The intricacies of the troop arrangements were best left to Lokor and the *QaS DevwI'*. Klag had enough to deal with without adding that to his burden.

As the turbolift slowed, Klag said, "Morr, I want you with me in the office when Lokor and Trant report. K'-Varia, you remain outside."

"Yes, sir." Both spoke in unison.

K'Nir stood when Klag entered the bridge. "Lieutenant Lokor is waiting for you in your office, sir."

Klag nodded to her, and went straight toward the door to his office.

It parted to reveal Lokor's powerful form as well as a *bekk* who was fairly nondescript. His crest was ordinary, his beard trimmed in a popular style, his height and build average for a warrior his age.

Looking at Morr, the *bekk* said, "The leader cannot be in here."

Angrily, Morr stepped forward. "Who are you to speak to me that way, Trant? I can have you—"

"Stand down, Leader." Lokor's voice, Klag noted, was tinged with a barely suppressed fury. The security chief was more controlled than that, out of necessity for the work he did, so his betrayal of this much anger told Klag much about what the tenor of the upcoming conversation would be.

Morr turned to Klag with a questioning look.

Lokor added, "Captain, Trant is correct—what is spoken of in this room cannot be said in front of a mere soldier."

Pointing at Trant, Morr said, "*That* animal is a 'mere soldier'!"

Klag considered for a moment. "Does this have to do with why I've had my guard doubled?"

"No, sir."

Not the mutiny, then. "Wait outside, Morr."

Keeping an angry gaze on Trant, Morr said, "Yes, sir." Even as he moved to the door, he did not take his eyes off the *bekk* until the door rumbled shut in front of him.

"*Bekk*," Klag said to Trant as he walked around his desk and took his seat behind it, "I would strongly advise you stay out of Morr's way."

"That is not a concern, Captain."

"Sir," Lokor said, "Trant is not a mere *bekk*. He is an I.I. agent."

Suddenly, Klag's stomachs felt as if they were trying to meld into one. "What?"

"I am an I.I. agent," Trant said slowly, "and I must invoke imperial privilege and take command of this vessel on behalf of I.I."

Before saying anything else, Klag turned to Lokor. There was a procedure for this sort of thing, after all.

His arms folded in front of his massive chest, Lokor said, "I have verified his credentials, sir. He provided a DNA sample, which I ran through the computer; he then provided the code word that unlocked his I.I. file and matched it to that DNA sample. He is who he says he is. And I verified it in—other ways as well."

At that, Trant looked over at Lokor. "What other ways would those be?"

Without looking at Trant, Lokor simply said, "I can imagine no circumstances under which I would reveal my sources, my methods, or my secrets to you, Trant— or whatever your true name is."

"Don't be so sure of that, Lieutenant."

Klag stared at Trant. *No wonder he is so nondescript.* I.I. agents often had their crests surgically altered to something that was not identifiable with a particular family, and he was sure that Trant's unimpressive affect served him well as a field agent.

Still not looking at Trant, Lokor said, "I have done what duty requires me to do. I have verified your status and brought you to see the captain. There is nothing more I will do for you, unless the captain orders me to do so."

"As of this moment," Trant said, "*I* am the captain of this vessel."

"No, Trant, you are not." Klag got up from his chair. "I am under no obligation to turn this vessel over to you unless you have dispensation from the High Council."

"And if I said I did?"

"I would ask you to produce it—not that it matters, since you would have produced it by now if you had it. I am not a fool, Trant, and you would be wise not to treat me as one."

Trant said nothing.

"Absent such dispensation, in order for me to relinquish control of my ship, you must prove to me that such an action is required by circumstance and that it supersedes any and all existing missions. Right now, this vessel is operating under orders directly from General Goluk to proceed to Kavrot *wej'vatlh wa'maH vagh*."

Trant smiled, an expression his face was ill suited for. "In that case, Captain, proving my case to you will be easier than either of us might have imagined, because my first instruction upon taking command will be for this vessel to proceed at maximum warp to that very star system."

Klag returned the smile which, to the captain's glee, caused that of the I.I. agent to drop. "If anything, that provides me with less reason to turn over my ship to you."

"May I assume," Trant asked, "that we are going to that star system—which is the home of the Elabrej Hegemony—to investigate the disappearance of the *I.K.S. Kravokh?*"

"May I assume that you have some method of tapping into the *Gorkon*'s computer?" Klag asked in a tight voice.

"Actually, I don't." Trant looked again at Lokor. "The computer is quite secure."

That got Lokor to smile, though he still would not favor the I.I. agent by meeting his eyes.

Trant continued: "No, Captain, I got that information from a fellow agent who served on the *Kravokh* as her operations officer—and is one of only eight survivors of an Elabrej attack on that ship."

Klag's stomachs went back to grinding together. "What happened to the ship?"

"Damaged beyond repair. The battered remains of the hulk were taken to their capital planet."

"Where are the survivors?"

"Also on the capital planet—as prisoners of the Elabrej, including Captain Wirrk."

Now Lokor looked at Trant. "They were taken *prisoner?*" Lokor sounded as disgusted by the notion as Klag felt.

"From what the agent said, they were not given any other option."

Involuntarily, Klag's left hand went to the wrist of his right arm—the one that once belonged to his father. M'Raq had been captured by Romulans and not permitted to die. Those pointed-eared *petaQpu'* kept him prisoner for years before he finally escaped, giving them no intelligence. He then went back to Qo'noS and waited for death. It took over a decade, but he finally died in his sleep like an old woman, honorless; Klag had taken it upon himself to win back his father's honor by using his good right arm in battle.

I will not allow Wirrk and his crew to suffer the same fate.

Trant continued. "Also there *were* ten survivors of the battle, but two have died during their imprisonment. One when attempting to escape, the other while the Elabrej—experimented on them."

"Experimented?" Klag had mistakenly thought his outrage was complete at Wirrk's crew being taken prisoner. This revelation proved him wrong.

"Apparently, the Elabrej have spent much of the last two months attempting to learn everything they can about us. According to B'Etloj—that is the agent on site—they have made attempts to translate our language, though the prisoners have done all they can to stymie those efforts. The Elabrej have also conducted biological tests, which she believes are geared toward forcing the prisoners to provide intelligence."

"Truth drugs?" Lokor asked.

"That is B'Etloj's theory, yes." Trant fixed Klag with an intense gaze. "Captain, we cannot allow this to continue. B'Etloj has a translator implant, and she has overheard several conversations that indicate that the Elabrej is massing a fleet to take up arms against us."

Klag tapped a finger on his desk. That certainly matched the warp activity.

When Klag had not spoken for several seconds, Trant apparently felt the need to continue. "I believe, Captain, that I have demonstrated ample reason why—"

"All you have done is prove that our assumptions

regarding the long-range scan of the Elabrej combined with the disappearance of the *Kravokh* were correct. Your petition is denied."

"Captain—"

Klag snapped. "That is *enough*, Trant! Speak further without prompting, and you will be executed on the spot."

Trant wisely said nothing.

"You will provide Lieutenant Lokor with a full transcription of the message you received. You will then report back to the fifteenth and maintain your cover."

Trant opened his mouth, then closed it. "Permission to speak, Captain."

Grinning, Klag said, "Denied. I have no interest in hearing your words, Trant. You could easily be charged with mutiny for your actions. I do not take kindly to those who wish to take my command away from me. Remember that for the future—should you live that long. You may both leave."

"Yes, sir." Lokor then turned to Trant. "Come with me."

Klag watched the pair leave his office, Lokor with a smile on his face, Trant looking rather like a child whose pet *targ* had been killed. Had Trant simply come to Klag with his intelligence, Klag might not have treated the I.I. agent so harshly; he might have even considered the possibility of giving the agent command of the specific mission to attempt to rescue the eight prisoners. The one thing he would never do without explicit instructions directly from the High Council was give over command of his ship to I.I.

While he waited for Trant's transcript and for General Goluk to contact them again, Klag went to the bridge to get a status report, which told him nothing new. By the time he returned to his office, Lokor had sent him the full transmission—or at least what Trant claimed was the full transmission. The transcript matched what Trant had reported verbally.

Then, finally, Ensign Kal's voice came over the intercom. *"Bridge to Captain Klag."*

"Klag."

"I have General Goluk for you, sir."

Activating his viewer, Klag said, "Put him through."

In addition to Goluk's grizzled face, the viewer also had an inset image of Chancellor Martok. "Chancellor!" Klag said in surprise.

"Greetings, son of M'Raq. It seems that once again you are at the heart of trouble in the Kavrot Sector."

"Not quite the heart, sir," Klag said with a smile.

"Perhaps not. Still, General Goluk informs me that there is trouble."

When he first encountered Martok, shortly before the *Gorkon*'s inaugural mission, he didn't think much of the chancellor, but time had shown Klag that the one-eyed former general was an honorable man, far more so than most who'd led the High Council. In particular, his support of Klag's actions at San-Tarah meant a great deal to the captain.

In response to Martok's statement, Klag said, "There is, Chancellor, and I have learned more since last the general and I spoke." He quickly filled in both the general and the chancellor on what Trant had told him.

Goluk's face twisted into a snarl. "*Spies. I do not trust them.*"

"*Nor do I.*" Martok then chuckled. "*But then, if we did trust them, they would be very poor spies. You believe this Trant's intelligence?*"

"Yes, sir, I do."

"*Very well. General, I will be following your recommendation, with one amendment. Who is the seniormost commander of the remaining Chancellor-class ships?*"

"Vikagh. He commands the Ditagh."

"*I assume the K'mpec is not yet ready for battle?*"

Klag winced. The *K'mpec* was commanded by Klag's estranged brother Dorrek, who had sided with General Talak against Klag at San-Tarah. His ship was badly damaged, but Dorrek survived, only to have Klag cast him out of the House of M'Raq for disobeying his elder brother.

"No, sir," Goluk said. "*It won't be for another month.*"

For that, Klag was grateful. He was not prepared to deal with Dorrek again so soon after discommendating him.

"*Pity. Very well, have the nine remaining ships rendezvous somewhere appropriate. Captain Vikagh will be the fleet commander. In the meantime, Captain Klag, you are to continue under cloak at maximum speed to the Elabrej home system. Your task is to rescue the survivors and cause as much damage behind the lines as you can. General, how soon can the fleet assemble?*"

Goluk was checking something on his workstation, then he looked up. "The *Ditagh, Kaarg, Azetbur, Kesh, and Gowron* can all be at *Kavrot* wejmaH *within three*

111

days. The other four will not be able to join them for another five to six days."

"That system," Klag added, "will put them only three days from the Elabrej. Right now, we're five days away."

"I do not wish to wait that long," Martok said.

"Nor do I. Vikagh should lead the fleet he has in three days' time—the others can join the battle when they arrive." Goluk paused. *"Chancellor, my own fleet can join the Azetbur. I can leave behind three birds-of-prey on Nayyvr-rra."*

Martok did not hesitate. *"Very well. In that case, General, you shall be fleet commander."* The chancellor then regarded Klag with his one good eye. *"Captain, you are to reduce your velocity to add a day to your travel time—I would prefer that your attacks be simultaneous with the fleet's engaging of the Elabrej forces."*

Klag nodded. His instinct was to go into battle sooner rather than later, but it was a wise strategy. He also could not help but be amused at the fact that his last campaign in the Kavrot Sector had a general take his fleet from a newly conquered world into battle, leaving behind three birds-of-prey, and escorted by a Chancellor-class ship. Then it was Talak leaving Brenlek with the *K'mpec* to engage Klag and the forces he'd amassed at San-Tarah. May this battle be more decisive.

Goluk added, *"This I.I. agent of yours should attempt to gain more intelligence from his source. Anything he learns is to be shared with the fleet."*

"Naturally." Klag hesitated. "Chancellor, am I to give command of this mission to Imperial Intelligence?"

"I see no need for that." Again, Martok chuckled. *"I*

suspect that decision will lead to my being subjected to a lengthy harangue by the head of I.I. Rest assured, my friend, you shall retain control of your ship and your mission. I.I.'s job is to gather intelligence for the empire, and they may continue to do so without interfering with the command structure of the Gorkon."

"Thank you very much, Chancellor." Klag fully intended to show Trant a recording of that statement—either before or after he broke the agent's legs.

"You have your orders. General, I want an update by the time the Sword of Kahless arrives on Bajor."

"Yes, sir," Goluk said.

"Qapla', all of you." Martok closed his right fist over his chest.

Both general and captain returned the salutation, and then the communication ended.

Klag rose smoothly from his chair and came out from behind his desk. Pressing the communicator on his wrist, he said, "Commander Toq, Ensign Kallo, to the bridge immediately."

He then proceeded to the bridge. K'Nir rose at his entrance, but the captain motioned for her to remain at the first officer's position. Klag meanwhile strode across the bridge, heading not to his own command chair but to the helm.

"Pilot, at what speed would we need to travel in order to arrive at the Elabrej home system in six days rather than five?"

Ensign Koxx quickly entered some commands into his console. "Warp seven-point-nine, sir."

"Reduce speed to warp seven-point-nine." He

turned to the second-shift gunner, Zaloq. "Ensign, engage cloak. Inform engineering that we will be maintaining cloak for the next six days at least. When the inevitable complaints come from Commander Kurak, direct her to me."

Looking puzzled, Zaloq said, "Yes, sir."

Klag recalled that Zaloq was one of the many transfers from the *Kreltek*, replacing the second-shift gunner and backup gunner, who both died at San-Tarah. "You have not encountered our chief engineer, have you, Zaloq?"

"No, sir."

"Be grateful, then, that the she-beast has not seen fit to sink her verbal fangs into your hide. Perhaps you will retain that distinction, but I doubt you will be so fortunate."

Several of the bridge officers chuckled in response. Only when that happened did Zaloq do so as well.

The turbolift doors opened to reveal Toq, Kallo, and Beyr. Klag walked over to the operations console, and the two officers correctly assumed that was where the captain wished to meet with them, along with Ensign Kal, who currently staffed the station. "Toq, we now have six days before we reach the Elabrej. By the time we arrive, I want to know everything there is to know about them. You and our two ensigns here are to study everything in the *Kravokh*'s report, as well as everything the *Gorkon*'s long-range sensors tell us. From what Captain Wirrk reported, the Elabrej were able to detect them even while cloaked. If there is a way to counteract that, I want you three to find it."

With his usual eagerness, Toq said, "Yes, sir. We will begin immediately."

"No," Klag said. "There is no need for haste. Ensign Kal may begin tonight, but I want the pair of you rested for the morning shift. Only a fool rushes into battle, and our battle is not for six more days." He smiled and quoted Kahless. " 'Hasty warriors are soon dead warriors.' "

"Understood, Captain," Toq said.

Kallo simply nodded.

Toq looked at Kal. "I want a full report of all long-range sensor readings by the time the first shift begins tomorrow."

"Yes, *sir*," Kal said.

"But first," Klag said, "address intraship."

Nodding, Kal did so. Klag strode to the front of the bridge and stood between the viewscreen and his chair, facing the officers and *bekk*s who had second-shift bridge duty, as well as Toq, Kallo, and the guards.

"Warriors of the *Gorkon*—we have been called into battle. Our brother ship, the *Kravokh*, has encountered a new enemy for us to fight, a discovery for which that mighty vessel was destroyed. Captain Wirrk, along with seven members of his crew, have been taken prisoner by this new foe, who call themselves the Elabrej Hegemony. One of their ships fired upon the *Kravokh* with no provocation; Captain Wirrk destroyed them, then was attacked in turn when he investigated. Our other brother ships are being dispatched along with General Goluk's fleet to do battle with this new enemy—but we will not be joining them. Instead, we are to take the battle behind the lines, to attempt to defeat the enemy from within—and also to rescue our fellow Klingons from their wretched fate. We will arrive in six days, and by then I want all of you to be prepared to claim victory."

Klag moved forward, his fists clenched. "We go now to battle! We go now to victory! We go now to *glory!*"

Cheers rang out from those on the bridge. Over the com system, he heard several groups of warriors break into song. After a moment, Toq started leading the bridge crew in a rousing rendition of "Don't Speak."

Lending his deep voice to the song, Klag took his seat, ready to face the coming battle.

CHAPTER FOUR

Imparter Mal Sanchit attempted to be enthusiastic as she read her day's lecture. She looked out over the young Vor children in her care, sitting in their hammocks and following along on their readers, and decided that they weren't convinced by her attempt at enthusiasm. *Then again, they don't seem to be putting any effort into seeming enthusiastic about what I'm saying, either, so perhaps we are even.* Still, she had to make the effort. After all, her job was to provide them with knowledge to prepare them for life as the best of the hegemony.

What a pathetic sham.

For *ungrets,* Sanchit had fought to expand the mandate of the schools to include all Elabrej, but all she had been able to do was convince the oligarchs that it wouldn't be too damaging to allow other stratas to mix in with the Vor and take classes together. Sanchit suspected that the recent appointing of two Yers to the oligarchy had a lot to do with that, and she had to admit that it was progress. A generation ago, the idea of mixing stratas in classes was unheard of—as was anyone other than a Vor serving as an oligarch.

First Oligarch Vor Jorg tried to cast himself as a reformer, but the truth was that it was politically expedient to allow two Yers to replace the oligarchs who had died three and five *ungrets* earlier. That one very public gesture, which had comparatively little bearing on the daily lives of the average hegemon, made it easy for the oligarchs to quietly block reform on virtually every other level.

Now, of course, there was a military buildup, with concomitant budget increases, all of which were taken away from social programs, infrastructure maintenance, and so many other vital functions—all so the military could find more ways to blow up sep redoubts.

She paused in her lecture notes. Her thoughts had turned to all the friends, all the colleagues, who had died when the military destroyed the cave system on Magna For. That had been a major sep hideout, and they had lost dozens of people. It had been a devastating blow.

Sanchit forced herself not to think about it. Especially now when she was supposed to be doing her job as an imparter. *If they even suspect I'm connected to the seps, I'll be arrested by Enforcement, interrogated—probably tortured—and then, when they're finished, a public show trial.*

Forcing those thoughts to the back of her mind, she ended her lecture, and then opened the room for questions. This was the part of the class that Sanchit both enjoyed and dreaded the most. On the one hand, the free exchange of ideas was much more conducive to the learning process than dry lectures; indeed, Sanchit was one of the few imparters who encouraged this kind of conversation with the students. On the other hand, the extemporaneous nature of such discussions increased the risk that she would expose her separatist leanings to the students, none of whom would hesitate to report her to Enforcement.

As usual, Vor Tammik was the first to ask something. "I don't understand why the oligarchy decided to separate the clergy from the oligarchy, as if government and religion weren't integrally connected to each other. Hasn't making the first oligarch and the first cleric two separate posts simply made the rule of government that much more complicated?"

Sanchit waved her midlegs with amusement. *Every term, someone asks that question.* It wasn't an unreasonable one, either—to the average hegemon, the separation of church and state seemed only to add to the bureaucracy.

"That's a good question, Tammik," Sanchit lied, "but the mistake many people make is to think that it was done in order to keep religion and government from interfering with each other. While there are some who believe that, it had little to do with the oligarchy's decision. Note the time frame of that decision: it was only a few *ungrets* after the Fourth World was added to the hegemony. With each new world, the amount of work needed to govern it increases exponentially—if not logarithmically. It simply was no longer practical for only seven oligarchs to maintain the civic and spiritual well-being of the hegemony. They could have expanded the oligarchy, or they could have separated the two—and, while there is considerable overlap between them, the two functions *are* separate—and they wisely chose the latter option."

Vor Larrab then posed a query. "But what about when the clergy and the oligarchy disagree? Like with the exploration program. The first cleric objected to the space center's initiative to explore skies beyond the home system."

Sanchit's instinct was to say that she agreed with the first cleric, but that was more overtly political than she was comfortable being in her class. Still, she had always found the space center's idiotic mandate to be an appalling waste of time and money that could be better dedicated to—well, almost anything. So many in the hegemony were poor or hungry, so many were struggling to survive, that the notion of sending expensive conveyances on long-term missions to far-off skies for no discernible practical purpose sickened Sanchit. It was one of several examples of the financial mismanagement that was leading the hegemony to ruin.

However, she could say none of this aloud to her students. "The first cleric's interpretation of holy writ meant that he had to object. The oligarchy's interpretation differed. That will always be the case. Laws are subject to interpretation as much as holy writ—sometimes more so." Several students laughed at that. "The oligarchs do not always agree on those points of order, either. What makes us Elabrej, what separates us from the animals and plants, is that when we disagree, we discuss it, we compromise, we argue, and eventually we figure out a way to live with or alter our disagreements. That doesn't change with the clergy separated from the oligarchy."

Before any other student could talk, the viewer built into one section of the learning sphere lit suddenly to life with the image of someone Sanchit didn't recognize.

"Hegemons, attention, please. We must interrupt your lives in order for the first oligarch to speak to all of you."

This surprised Sanchit. Jorg hadn't given an address that wasn't preplanned since he was elevated to first oligarch.

The image switched to that of Vor Jorg, seated in the hammock in his office sphere. *"Greetings, hegemons. I apologize for intruding on you like this, but it is necessary. Many of you are aware of the fact that there has been a military buildup over the past few sogrets. Rumors have been spreading, and many of the newsgivers have speculated as to the reasons for this unprecedented military activity."*

Sanchit expelled quite a bit of air in reaction to that, an outward show of negative emotion that she quickly regretted. It wasn't just the newsgivers who were speculating, though they certainly were—everything from massing an attack on the seps to a hastily covered up mining disaster on Timnor For—but also the seps themselves. At the last meeting, several had put forth a variety of theories. Of all the ludicrous notions presented, Sanchit's favorite was the most nonsensical: an attack by aliens. Gansett had insisted that his sources were reliable, but Sanchit knew the idea was absurd. It was as the clerics said: Doane and Gidding made the Elabrej unique in all the universe. The idea of alien life-forms was patently absurd. It was why she shared the first cleric's objection to the exploration program.

Jorg continued. *"Before I continue, I must warn you that the images you are about to see are quite graphic and violent—but it is necessary that you understand the extraordinary circumstances in which we find ourselves. As many of you know, the space center has sent several conveyances to explore beyond our skies. These images are from the flight recording of one of those conveyances, led by Shipmaster Vor Ellis, who made sure to warn us of this impending threat before she and her valiant crew were murdered so very far from their home skies."*

A commotion ran through the class at the thought of a Vor being killed. Sanchit was less concerned, in part because she didn't share the arrogant notion that the Vor were almost divinely superior, but mostly because of her own feeling, shared by most of the seps, that the best Vor was a dead Vor. Sanchit was far more interested in why anything involving that idiotic program of the space center's was of such concern that it necessitated interrupting what was turning into a particularly lively discussion.

The image on the learning sphere wall changed to that of some kind of full sphere. Oddly, it had workstations all over the interior. After a moment of watching the various people tethered to those workstations, Sanchit realized that they were in a gravity-free environment. *Of course*, she realized, *there is no gravity in the skies*. Yet another reason why this project was an abomination. *Elabrej should be able to place all their limbs on the ground*.

She recognized the one sitting in the elaborate cushioned seat at the center of the sphere: Vor Ellis, who had appeared with many of the newsgivers before her conveyance left hegemony skies, being treated as if she were engaged in the most noble endeavor imaginable, rather than the boondoggle it truly was.

After a moment, the image changed to that of a section of the sphere that showed an outside view. Sanchit saw only the stars and blackness, and wondered what the significance was of this. Then one of those electronic weapons shot out from the sphere and hit—something.

Sanchit had no idea what it was the weapon could have hit, but half an *engret* after it struck, something became visible.

Never in her life had Sanchit ever seen anything like what appeared on the screen then. She hoped never to see anything like it again. Her windpipes dried up, and her limbs fell limp.

It looked like some kind of giant predatory bird suddenly appearing in the sky in order to swoop down and destroy everything.

A moment later, the bird spit fire.

The image switched back, then, to the rest of the sphere. As Sanchit watched, horrified, a piece of the sphere ripped apart, drawing the people within toward it. Sanchit did not see all of them die as the sphere came apart, but she did see several of them lose their lives, though Vor Ellis was still alive when the image stopped transmitting.

Children would always talk, or at least whisper, so Sanchit did not concern herself with the fact that there was a low murmur while the first oligarch was speaking. Now, however, the sight of that—that *thing* wiping out an entire conveyance full of people left the room utterly quiet. Larrab dropped his stylus onto the floor, and it echoed throughout the room as if someone had fired a weapon. But Larrab, whose limbs were limp with the shock, didn't even move to pick it up.

Jorg's face came back on. "*I apologize for showing you those images, but you needed to see the gravity of the threat we face. For many ungrets, we have believed ourselves to be alone in the universe. We now know that to be false— but I assure you, I do not seek to belie holy writ. The clerics tell us that Doane and Gidding made us unique in the universe, and they are not at all wrong—for these creatures who appeared out of nowhere and murdered our people with no provocation are nothing like us. They were not created with the divine touch of Doane, but rather belched forth from some foul nether region. I have spoken at great length with First Cleric Vor Hennak, and he has assured me that these beings were sent by Doane to test us, and that it is our duty to eliminate them from the galaxy.*"

The first oligarch continued to drone on, but Sanchit paid little attention, because there was one thing in the image that played back that struck her even more than the presence of any kind of alien life.

We fired first. They didn't murder our people without

provocation—the provocation was right there. *We fired a weapon at them, and they fired one right back at us.* If Doane did send them as a test, Sanchit had a very bad feeling that the Elabrej had already failed it.

"*Furthermore,*" Jorg said, "*we now know for sure that these foul creatures will be returning in force to destroy us as they destroyed Shipmaster Vor Ellis. Their sacrifice will not be in vain, I assure you. We are massing our fleets into a fighting force that is to be reckoned with.*" Jorg paused and folded his midlegs. "*I know that there is unrest among some of you. I know that there are a select few who believe that times are difficult, even though the hegemony is more economically stable than at any time in its history.*"

This time Sanchit managed to hold back her disgusted expelling of air, but it was difficult. The hegemony was only "economically stable" if you were a Vor or a Yer.

"*Those few have had the flame of discontent fanned by arrogant, unpatriotic separatists who believe that everything should be handed out indiscriminately—*"

Sanchit managed to keep her limbs under control. *As opposed to now, when things are handed out discriminately.*

"*—rather than earned by their own labors, and who believe that sedition and disloyalty is the only way to get what they want. But now is not the time for divisiveness. Now is a time when we must all come together to face a common foe. Because no matter what you may think of me and my fellow oligarchs, whatever you may think of the Elabrej Hegemony, I can tell you this for sure: The aliens do not care about our differences. They only want to see us dead.*"

And the only way they will fail is if we stand together. I am calling for all able-bodied hegemons to enlist with the military to aid in our efforts to expel these demonic invaders. Our military conveyances have received upgraded weaponry guaranteed to blow these foul aliens out of our skies permanently."

Yet again, Sanchit had to hide her dismay, as she wondered what service vital to the needs of the average hegemon would be reduced or eliminated to pay for these new recruits and for this new weaponry. She also wondered what the basis of the first oligarch's guarantee was.

"The digret that Vor Ellis and her conveyance were destroyed was a dark one indeed, but the digrets and sogrets ahead will be the greatest we have ever seen. Doane will wrap his limbs around us and we will be strong."

Jorg continued on with some tiresome patriotic speech or other, but it didn't matter. Sanchit's main concern was what would happen next.

We have to have a meeting. We need to have a meeting now, and we need to figure out what to do.

Imparter Mal Sanchit was sure of one thing: First Oligarch Vor Jorg had it completely wrong. The *digrets* and *sogrets* ahead were likely to be the *worst* they had ever seen.

When Sanchit went back to her private office sphere, she found a message waiting for her inviting her to a surprise gathering for a friend's natal day. It was the common code used by the seps—an emergency meeting. *Good*, she thought.

The class had ended after Jorg's speech, and the students were unusually quiet. What little they did say as they climbed out of their hammocks and left the learning sphere was determination to do everything they could to help defeat the wicked aliens.

When Sanchit and the other separatists gathered at Jammit's home sphere for the alleged surprise gathering, Gansett wasted no time in starting the meeting. All six of his legs quivering as he sat in one of the guest hammocks, he said, "I *warned* you, didn't I? My sources at the government spheres have *always* been reliable, and they *assured* me that aliens were involved."

"That doesn't mean—" Altran started, but Gansett interrupted.

"It *does* mean, Altran, because I was talking to one of my sources *today*, and he told me something. You know how Vor Jorg said that the new weapons were 'guaranteed' to destroy the aliens?"

Sanchit said, "That was just his usual posturing. What I'm—"

Gansett interrupted her this time. "It *wasn't* posturing, it was truth. Those aliens who destroyed Vor Ellis's conveyance? They headed *straight* here, and were engaged by a military fleet, where they used that new weapon they've been testing." His forelegs waved agitatedly. "The fleet *destroyed* the alien conveyance, and brought *ten* of them back here. They're being held in one of the government spheres."

Several people spoke at once.

"There are aliens *on the planet?*"

"They came here?"

"But if we destroyed them, the threat's over, right?"

"Don't be stupid."

"Where are they being held?"

Gansett answered that last question: "I don't know. I'm trying to find out, though."

"This is terrible." Altran's forelegs were waving. "What're we going to do?"

"We don't have to do anything," Viralas said. "Look, whatever else we think of the oligarchy, this has to be more important. These aliens want to destroy us."

"No, they don't," Sanchit said. "At least, we don't know that for sure."

"What're you talking about?" Altran said. "They blew Vor Ellis's conveyance to pieces."

Waving her left midleg, Sanchit said, "Yes—*after* Vor Ellis fired on them. They were simply defending themselves. And then they came here. How do we know what their intention was? For all we know they were coming here to apologize for their actions."

"That's a long leap of logic, Imparter." Bantrak, an old-fashioned sort, always referred to people by their titles. "First Oligarch Vor Jorg did say—"

"What we wanted to hear—what he needed to say in order to whip all hegemons into a frenzy. But since when have we ever believed what the oligarchs tell us? In the very same speech where he told us about these aliens, he also told us that we were stronger economically than we've ever been—which, I'm sure, is a surprise to the people living in poverty in the cities of each of the Four Worlds."

"What's your point, Sanchit?" Altran asked.

"My point is, we don't know anything about these aliens, except what the oligarchs are telling us, and the oligarchs have no reason to tell the truth. That moon shuttle that exploded was due entirely to their own incompetence and poor maintenance, yet the first thing they did was blame us for it, even though we've never committed violent acts on anywhere near that level. If they were willing to do that, then why wouldn't they use this new discovery to turn public opinion against us? It gives the hegemons a common foe to face, someone who can serve as a patriotic rallying cry that will simultaneously discredit us."

Bantrak let out a puff of air. "You speak like an historian, Imparter, but you are denying the possibility that what we think has happened has happened. That we are about to face a foe that wants to destroy us."

"Based on what evidence? We only know that they engaged our forces because Gansett found out. Vor Jorg did not mention that in his speech, did he? And, again, you assume he's telling the truth, and I say, why would he start now? The oligarchy has always lied to us and claimed it was for the greater good when in fact it was for their own good only. The foe we face is one that may not even *be* a true foe, but people simply defending themselves against an unprovoked attack. Bantrak, you say I talk like an historian, but that's because I *am* one, and one thing I've learned from history is that the time when the government is most likely to lie to its people is in times of conflict."

There was silence for almost a full *engret* before Altran spoke. "Let's say you're right, Sanchit—what difference does it make? We're *still* going to war, and the oligarchs *are* going to use this opportunity to turn public opinion against us. Why doesn't really matter so much as how we're going to react."

"Assuming this is all real."

Sanchit blew out a puff of air. She was amazed it had taken Yannak this long to provide his own absurd theory.

"Yannak . . ." Altran started.

"Hear me out," Yannak said, waving his forelegs. "How do we know that any of this is real? What if these aliens are all a hoax to accomplish precisely what Altran just said—a propaganda tool to be used against us. What if it's just an excuse to use those new weapons, not on some ridiculous aliens, but on *us*? Those images Vor Jorg showed weren't beyond the realm of fictional effects. Look at some of the fictions that Entertainment provide. They could easily re-create something like that."

"No, they couldn't have." Bantrak spoke quietly. "I've been alive more than any of you, and never—not in any fiction, not in any speculation, not anywhere have I ever seen or imagined anything as awful as that alien conveyance."

Once again, Sanchit felt her mouth and windpipes dry up as she remembered that terrible creature that materialized in front of Vor Ellis's conveyance. She feared she would see the image in her mind's eye for many *ungrets* to come, and that those images would deny her sleep.

"Besides," Altran added, "the clergy would never go along with that kind of hoax, even if it was possible.

Vor Hennak was probably completely shrivel-limbed when he saw the footage and gave his blessing to this whole enterprise."

"Unless," Yannak said, "they have fooled the first cleric as well."

"No," Bantrak said authoritatively. "Whatever we may think of Vor Jorg, even he would never stoop to deceiving the first cleric."

Everyone muttered affirmative noises at that—except, Sanchit noticed, Yannak.

Altran blew out a puff of air. "Which brings us back to the question of what our next step is."

Gansett spoke quickly. "I think we *have* to go further underground, at least for the time being."

Waving his midlegs in agreement, Bantrak said, "I agree. It is the prudent course of action."

Several others gave their consent.

Part of Sanchit was tempted to go along with everyone. Altran was right, they were going to have a harder time of it now. Supplies for their guerrilla attacks would be harder to obtain, their methods of releasing underground publications would be curtailed if not taken away outright, and even gatherings like this would become suspect and bring them to Enforcement's attention. Communications between the sep leaders here and their people on the Tenth Moon would be almost impossible, as most verbal traffic would be given over to military use. That last was probably the biggest reason to scale back; so much of the sep success had come from the ability of their people on the Tenth Moon to make physical attacks while keeping their redoubt on that moon a secret from Enforcement.

But a much larger part of her felt differently.

That part is what enabled her to speak. "I say that prudence is the worst course of action. What we need to do now is make a bold gesture, one that will show the oligarchs that we are not so easily cowed. And I think we need to let the hegemons know the truth about what is happening here."

"How do you propose we do *that*, Imparter?" Bantrak sounded incredulous, and understandably so.

Waving her midlegs a bit, she said, "I think we should free the aliens from their prison."

CHAPTER FIVE

Kurak was drunk.

This was not an unusual state of affairs for her of late. Being drunk was, she found, the only way to keep her life tolerable. Who she blamed for this state of affairs varied from moment to moment.

Sometimes she blamed Kornan, the damnably attractive former first officer of the *Gorkon*, who managed to ruin wind-boat riding for her on San-Tarah before getting himself killed saving the ship. She liked blaming him because he was dead and unable to defend himself.

Sometimes she blamed the Dominion. After all, it was only when war with them broke out that her father insisted that she join the Defense Force. All her life, Kurak had believed the Defense Force to be made up of incompetents and fools, and the three years she'd spent as a commander in it only served to reinforce that opinion. But—and the words were like a mantra to her and everyone in her family—the House of Palkar must always serve the empire. By the end of the war, all the qualified people in her House who could serve were dead, except her. So she remained obligated to stay in the Defense Force until her nephew, young Gevnar, came of age and enrolled.

Sometimes she blamed her father, who insisted on enrolling her when the war started.

Sometimes she blamed Palkar, the long-dead warrior for whom her House was still named, whose service defending Emperor Sompek led to that tiresome insistence on his House always defending the empire.

Sometimes she blamed Moloj, the House *ghIntaq,* if for no other reason than she had spent most of her life blaming that tiresome old *ghISnar* cat for whatever might irritate her.

Sometimes she blamed Lokor, who threatened harm to Gevnar if Kurak did not perform her duties to his and Captain Klag's satisfaction. Never mind the fact that true engineers should not have to do their jobs under fire without proper testing facilities. . . .

Sometimes she blamed Kahless, simply because the existence of the empire was, for all intents and purposes, his fault.

Sometimes she blamed Leskit, because she shared her bed with him and he therefore provided a much readier target for her wrath than any of the others.

She didn't understand Leskit. He made her laugh, made her feel more like a Klingon than she had since her father dragged her away from the Science Institute and her work for the great shipbuilder Makros. But

Leskit was also a Defense Force officer, and one who believed in what he did. He stood for everything she despised. Yet she kept inviting him back. It confused her, which led her to drink more.

If her drinking interfered with her duty, she wasn't aware of it. That was primarily because she didn't care all that much. The worst, absolute worst they could do to her was demote her—which would change nothing, as she would continue drinking—or kill her—which would put her out of her misery.

She sat on the comforting cold metal of her bunk, a mug of *warnog* in her hand, with no idea of how long she'd been sitting there. Her thoughts kept running away from her—like the horizon whenever she sailed down the mighty *tlq* river on Qu'vat, always a certain distance away no matter how far she sailed.

The door chime to her cabin rang. A noise came from her lips, which was apparently enough to convince the computer that she wanted the door to open, for it rumbled aside to reveal Leskit.

"What're you doing here?" she asked.

Leskit sighed. "I wanted to make sure you were ready for duty. I'm glad I did—don't you know what time it is?"

"No."

The pilot pointed at the display unit on her desk. "It says so right there."

"I know. I looked at it before."

"And?"

"There were some numbers on it, but they could mean anything."

Then Leskit laughed. "Well, in this case, the numbers mean that first shift starts in twenty minutes."

"So?"

"You're out of uniform."

Kurak looked down. For the first time, she realized that she was wearing only a nightshirt. "So I am."

"You should perhaps get *into* uniform. I already took the liberty of stopping by the medical bay for an anti-inebriant."

Kurak snorted, phlegm flying out of her mouth. "Don't want one of those."

"Why?"

"Because I'm drunk."

Slowly, Leskit said, "That's the idea, Kurak—taking the pill will make you not drunk."

"I want to *be* drunk."

"If you're drunk on duty—"

Kurak stood up from the bunk, stumbling slightly, but regaining her footing in half a second. "If I'm drunk on duty I'll still be four times the engineer than *anyone else* in that group of incompetents the Defense Force has saddled me with, if you can even *call* them engineers, given that none of them can . . ." Kurak trailed off, and tried to pull her thoughts together, but they remained on the horizon, ever out of reach. "What was I talking about?"

"You were talking about putting on your uniform, taking the anti-inebriant, and reporting to engineering."

The thoughts congealed, at least a little, and she found herself able to remember things. "No, that's what *you* were talking about. That's what you're always talking about. What I'm talking about is staying here and not reporting for duty, because it means I won't have to listen to that idiot child Kallo and watch her drool all over Toq while she tells him how to alter our cloaking shields."

"And why do you object to that?" Leskit asked.

"Because you don't alter the functioning of as sensitive a piece of equipment as the cloak based on vague theories, secondhand sensor readings, and no proper testing equipment. We don't even have a proper laboratory." She looked up at Leskit. Her thoughts were becoming clearer with every second, which simply meant that she needed to drink more. Unfortunately, her *warnog* mug was empty, and she didn't have the wherewithal to refill it. "And I have to ask something."

"What?"

"Why?"

Leskit grinned. "Why what?"

"Why do you keep coming here? Why do you take me to your bed?"

"I don't—you take me to *your* bed. Mainly, I suppose, because your cabin is bigger than mine."

Kurak waved her hands in front of her face—which caused a dizzy spell, and she stumbled forward. Leskit caught her in his strong arms, and she suddenly felt the urge to rip his uniform off and take him right there.

"Come, Kurak, let's get you ready."

She grinned. "I'm ready for you now, Leskit."

"I meant for duty."

"I didn't." She started to take her nightshirt off.

He stopped her. "I know you didn't. But I *did* mean it." Grabbing her by the shoulders, he straightened her up and gazed into her eyes, the Cardassian neckbones he wore rattling. "I like you, Kurak—Kahless knows why. You're unpleasant in every possible way, but I find myself drawn to you like a *glob* fly to the swamp pits. Unlike that insect, however, I will not let you drown me. You will get dressed and sober up and we will *both* report to duty. Then, tonight, after dinner, I will come back here, you'll be on your fourth or fifth *warnog*, and we will have excellent sex, then you will yell at me, blame me for your plight, and throw me out while pouring your fifth or sixth *warnog*, and then I'll come back here and get you to engineering on time and sober despite your best efforts. Just as we have every day since we left San-Tarah."

Leskit then walked over to the corner of the cabin where Kurak had casually discarded her uniform when she came off duty the previous night. She found she couldn't bear to wear the metal and leather uniform any longer than was absolutely required, and indeed she was often naked when Leskit arrived, as it saved time.

He picked up her uniform.

"This," Kurak said as she removed her nightshirt, albeit not for the purpose she had originally intended, "is all your fault, Leskit."

Smiling while holding up the uniform, Leskit said, "Of that, I have no doubt."

Klag sat at the head of the wardroom table. Kurak sat perpendicular to him on the right, staring off into space blankly. Rodek sat to Kurak's right. Toq and Kallo stood in front of the viewer, which showed a sensor schematic of some kind.

Kallo had spent the last several minutes explaining the adjustments that needed to be made to the cloak in order to keep the Elabrej from detecting it. Every time Toq tried to make a comment, Kallo interrupted with a clarification of some kind. Toq looked like he was ready to swallow his own face, and Klag had to admit to being highly amused by it.

Finally, before the young woman could go off on another explanation of how she extrapolated the sensor readings the *Kravokh* took, Klag said, "Enough! I am convinced that you believe this will work, Ensign. Commander—do you agree with the ensign's theories?"

The Toq who had once served confidently as Klag's operations officer—and who had never let his captain down—came back to the fore. "I would not have wasted your time with this meeting if I did not, sir."

Klag turned to his gunner. "Rodek?"

"The response time for decloaking is reduced by several seconds. That could prove fatal in combat."

"Not nearly as fatal," Toq said, "as being detected while cloaked, as the *Kravokh* discovered."

"True." *Now comes the part I dread*, Klag thought. "Kurak?"

The engineer turned and looked blankly at Klag. "Hm?"

"What are your thoughts, Commander?"

"Oh. That this is a waste of time, of course. Ensign Kallo's theories are supposition."

"*All* theories are supposition." Kallo's words sounded defensive to Klag's ears.

"No, infant," Kurak snapped, "all *hypotheses* are supposition. Theories are actually based on facts. You have no facts here, only guesses based on interpretations of another ship's sensor data. What you have, in fact, is nothing."

"It is much more than that," Toq said, "and you would know that if you had paid attention to any of this briefing."

"Have you even tested this adjustment? No, you have not, because we don't know what the parameters of the test are, and even if we did, we have no way of creating the conditions."

A thought occurred to Klag. "Yes, we do."

Everyone looked at him.

"We have a holodeck. The Federation often uses their holodecks for scientific testing."

Kurak did not sound placated. "It will not be a wholly accurate test."

"I thought you were a scientist," Kallo said. "I remember reading your monographs, viewing the specs of the *Negh'Var* and all the other ships you designed—and I remember thinking it was an honor to serve with you when I was assigned to the *Gorkon*. But now I see that your reputation is a sham." The ensign leaned forward, her fists resting on the wardroom table. "No test can possibly be wholly accurate. I believe that you are simply too cowardly to implement these changes and are making excuses."

Rising from her chair, Kurak said, "Believe what you will."

Klag also rose. "You have not been dismissed, Kurak."

The chief engineer stayed standing, though she seemed to wobble a bit on her feet. "Of course not, *sir*."

After glaring at his chief engineer for several seconds, pity mixing with disgust, Klag turned to Toq. "Commander, program the holodeck with the parameters of the new cloak and the specifications of the Elabrej ships, and conduct your tests immediately."

"Sir, the *QaS DevwI'* are conducting training exercises in the holodeck until second shift."

Klag hesitated. The holodeck was the best cure for indolence among the troops, who often went for months without activity, or performing menial tasks, before being pressed into combat duty.

"Compose the program. Work with Commander Kurak on it," he added, ignoring the look of irritation the chief engineer gave him. "Begin the testing when the *QaS DevwI'* have completed their drills."

"Yes, sir."

"You are dismissed—" Toq, Kallo, Kurak, and Rodek moved toward the door. "—except for you, Kurak. Remain."

Kurak stopped, turned, and sat—fell, really—back into her chair.

When the other three were gone, Klag said, "I grow weary of you, Kurak. Kallo was correct about you—your reputation for brilliance has not been in evidence on this ship, and you have proven yourself a coward."

"I am *not*—"

Klag slammed a hand down on the wardroom table. "You were directly challenged! And you disregarded it!"

Laughing bitterly, Kurak said, "Must I pay attention to the mewlings of infants now?"

Leaning over the engineer, Klag could smell the *warnog* on her breath. In truth, he could have smelled it if he were on the bridge and she in the aft portion of the port wing. "The only thing you *must* do, Kurak, is follow my orders. You have, to date, done a poor job of it."

"Then it is your duty, *Captain*, to kill me and replace me with someone who will do the job better." Then she widened her eyes in mock surprise. "But, wait! There *is* no one who will do the job better! This is, after all, a ship of fools and imbeciles, led by the captain of *petaQpu'* himself, who—"

Whatever else Kurak was going to say was cut off by Klag's fist striking her face, which sent her sprawling to the floor.

Klag stood over her prone form. "My duty, Kurak, is to run this ship as best I see fit. Right now, I feel the best way to do that is to remind the chief engineer that death is an honor. To die in service of the empire is the hope of any warrior. Therefore, I would not waste any energy providing you with a death that might, for some reason, lead you to *Sto-Vo-Kor*. The Black Fleet does not deserve the likes of you. And neither does this ship. The crew of this vessel has fought and bled and died for honor and for the empire. Many of them have suffered. But you? All you have done is lose a wind-boat competition and whine about being ordered to do your job."

Kurak spit on the deck. "You think I have not suffered? To be forced to work with my inferiors, to—"

This time Klag interrupted Kurak by slamming his boot down on her left leg. Based on the cracks that echoed throughout the wardroom, he broke her leg in at least three places.

To her credit, she did not scream, though she did bite down on her lower lip sufficiently hard to draw blood.

Then Klag knelt down next to her. "You may call what you have endured suffering, but it is nothing compared to what will come. I have been patient with you, Commander, because of your reputation and indeed because of the lack of viable alternatives. But my patience has run out." He stood upright and activated his communicator. "Klag to B'Oraq. Report to the wardroom. Commander Kurak is injured."

Klag heard the slightest whimper of pain as he left the wardroom without looking back.

"Your leg will be stiff for a few days, but it should heal just fine."

Kurak barely heard Dr. B'Oraq's words. Instead she stared at the ceiling of the medical bay and hoped that she would be released soon so she could go drink some more. At least this injury meant she would not have to participate in the captain's idiotic exercise on the holodeck.

How much more of this must I endure? she asked herself, even though she'd known the answer since the end of the war: until Gevnar came of age.

So typical, she thought as she looked down at her leg,

which B'Oraq had healed with a bone-knitter. *Only the Defense Force would use such tactics for discipline. Much better to kill the offending officer and be done with it.*

With a start, Kurak realized that she was wishing for her own death. *It would certainly be preferable to this. Perhaps that is why I have continued drinking—in the hopes that Klag would kill me.* It was truly her only alternative; suicide would send her straight to *Gre'thor*, and there was no one on this ship with whom she could entrust *Mauk-to'Vor*.

"This is interesting."

Kurak looked over at the doctor, who was studying a readout on the display over the engineer's biobed, but said nothing.

B'Oraq stared down at her and smiled. "Don't you want to know what's interesting?"

"I don't care all that much." Kurak looked away as she spoke, going back to staring at the ceiling and thinking about *warnog*.

"You have something I've never diagnosed in a Klingon before. Plenty of humans, Betazoids, Tellarites, and Vulcans, but never a Klingon."

This confused Kurak at first; then she recalled that B'Oraq had studied medicine in the Federation, and therefore probably treated several of their species for whatever illnesses their weakened bodies contracted. Kurak had visited the Federation once, and despised it. She was falsely accused of killing a Ferengi scientist in secret, which offended Kurak—when she killed someone, she did it face-to-face. Besides, this Ferengi was actually a skilled scientist whose work on metaphasic shields was groundbreaking; she would as soon kill her mentor, Makros. She didn't see how B'Oraq could have tolerated being among these weaklings for longer than the fortnight Kurak had spent, much less the eight years required to learn how they practice medicine.

The doctor continued: "You, Kurak, have alcohol poisoning."

That got Kurak's attention, and she looked back at the doctor. "How can alcohol poison one?"

Chuckling, B'Oraq said, "Alcohol *is* a poison, Kurak, but it's one for which the Klingon system has a very high tolerance. But drink enough *warnog,* and even those tolerances can be exceeded."

"I don't know what you're talking about," Kurak said defiantly.

"Don't be stupid, Kurak. I did a full examination while I was setting your leg—you've got more *warnog* than blood in your veins right now." B'Oraq tugged at the braid that hung down on her right shoulder. Kurak felt a sudden urge to tear the braid from her scalp. "Looks like you've been off the wagon for two months. Sorry, a human expression," she added with a chuckle, though Kurak hadn't really been paying close enough attention to care. "In any case, if you keep up this pace, you'll be dead in two days." She looked over at the nurse, who was sitting in a corner with a reader. "Gaj, prepare a hypo of Broxmin-C."

The nurse seemed irritated at the instruction, but got up from her reading and prepared the hypo. *If one of my engineers acted like that,* Kurak thought, *she'd already be dead.*

Looking back down at Kurak, B'Oraq said, "It will help break down the alcohol in your system, and ease you out of the addiction. You'll be nauseous for a few days, and if you touch anything with alcohol in it, you could die instantly."

Gaj walked over with the hypo, but Kurak grabbed the nurse's wrist to prevent her from handing it to B'Oraq. "No. I will not take this drug."

"It'll make the withdrawal much easier, Kurak," B'Oraq said.

"I do not intend to withdraw from anything."

"If you keep drinking, you will *die*, Kurak. It's as good as committing suicide."

"That is not your concern." Kurak did not believe the doctor's words. Alcohol was *not* a poison, unless you were one of those weak Federation species like humans or Betazoids. They made Kurak sick to even be near them. She started to rise from her bunk. "I will no longer—"

B'Oraq touched a control next to the biobed, and suddenly Kurak felt as if she had slammed into a duranium wall just above the biobed. She slumped back down onto the metal bed. "What have you done?" she asked with a snarl.

"It's a restraining field. I won't force the medicine on you, but I *can* keep you confined to the medical bay until further notice."

Kurak decided that after she ripped the braid from B'Oraq's scalp, she would strangle her with it. "You have no authority to do that! Only the captain does!"

At that, B'Oraq laughed. "Have a good relationship

with the captain, do you? Klag considers me to be a valued advisor, Kurak. You, he considers an irritant at best—and, I might add, he shares that opinion with everyone on this ship, with the possible exception of Leskit. Which of us do you think he will believe?"

Seething, Kurak said nothing.

"However, since you wish him to make the decision, I'll be happy to bring him down here."

B'Oraq then left the medical bay, leaving Kurak alone.

No, not alone—the nurse was there, also. She put the hypo away, but did not go back to her corner. Instead, she leaned over Kurak.

"I can help you."

That earned the nurse a sneer. "How can *you* help me?"

"You do not believe that the son of M'Raq is a good captain."

Kurak said nothing.

Gaj continued. "You are not the only one who feels that way. Many of us wish to see Klag removed from power on this ship. He leads us to dishonor, and consorts with the *bolmaq*."

"The what?" Kurak asked, confused.

"That creature who just left. I call her the *bolmaq* because she reminds me—"

Getting the joke, Kurak actually smiled. A *bolmaq* was an annoying little marsupial native to Boreth that made a bleating sound and tended to run around in circles. "The name fits. Go on."

"We are organizing. Lieutenant K'Nir is on our side, as are Ensign Zaloq and most of the second-shift bridge crew. So are Lieutenant Rovar, Lieutenant Yaklan, and Ensign B'Mar. So are many of the troops."

This conversation was starting to bore Kurak. "How many of the troops?"

"Many," Gaj said unconvincingly. "All those who came from the *Kreltek,* for certain."

"Any of the *QaS DevwI'*?"

"Latkos and Karin."

Kurak snorted. Those two commanded Nineteenth and Twentieth Companies—the lowest of the low. "Any of the command crew? Toq? Rodek? Lokor?"

"No—they are among those who must be purged if this ship is to return to glory!"

Shaking her head, Kurak said, "You are all fools. A few transfers, some unimportant officers, and the *QaS DevwI'* of the poorest soldiers on the ship are your revolutionary force?"

Sounding almost petulant, Gaj said, "Our numbers are growing."

"I'm happy for you." Kurak felt her thoughts clearing and her anger rising, and she desperately wished for a mug of *warnog.* "You asked if I thought Klag was a good captain. The phrase 'good captain' is an oxymoron. I will not participate in a mutiny that will simply exchange one *petaQ* for another. All of you are fools, and I only wish to be left alone until I can be rid of you." A question occurred. "What made you think I would be intersted in this insanity?"

"Yaklan suggested it. He and Ensign Zaloq both thought you'd jump at the chance."

Now Kurak laughed, though she had no idea who

Zaloq was. "Yaklan—that *toDSaH* has yet to come up with a thought that was worth voicing, much less acting on." Yaklan had been her assistant chief engineer for eight months, ever since Vall was left behind on taD to act as a figurehead planetary governor. Vall was irritating and Kurak had to restrain herself from killing him several times, but at least he was a skilled engineer. Had he been her assistant at the Science Institute, and had he not had such ludicrous notions as treating engineering conundrums as battles to be won rather than problems to be solved, Kurak would have welcomed him. As it was, she was happy to see the back of him.

But while Yaklan was more tolerable than Vall, it was mainly because he was so undistinguished as to be irrelevant. If Kurak actually cared about what kind of engine room she ran, she would have gone to the trouble of finding a new assistant who was qualified for the job, but by her lights that was impossible in the Defense Force. All the candidates were imbeciles by dint of their *being* in the Defense Force. So she simply promoted the one with the most years of service.

And now he wishes to mutiny, along with the other fools. "Yaklan was mistaken. Don't feel bad," she added at Gaj's sour expression. "Yaklan is usually mistaken. It is a direct result of his being awake." She looked away from the nurse, going back to staring at the ceiling. "Go away from me now."

Gaj stared at Kurak for several seconds before returning to her corner to continue reading.

By Kahless's hand, I want a drink, Kurak thought plaintively.

*   *   *

"Leaders of Fifteenth through Thirtieth Squads, report to the wardroom."

The command woke Wol out of a sound sleep, her naked body intertwined with that of Leader Ryjjan. When they went off duty yesterday, Ryjjan had called in his debt in precisely the manner she had expected, in his bunk.

Years of service had made it easy for Wol to get into uniform quickly while confined to two meters, even if she was sharing it with someone else. Ryjjan continued to slumber, making Wol wonder if the rest of his squad covered for him when announcements didn't awaken him.

To Wol's disappointment, but not to her surprise, Ryjjan was a thoroughly unimaginative lover. His technique showed only a basic brutality. She barely even had any bruises, and not a single welt. *I may as well have slept with a human.*

Still, the experience was not actively unpleasant, and it fulfilled her debt to him. Certainly, it was worth enduring one tedious night of dull sex in order to get her squad back in working order. Ever since the night of debauchery in the mess hall six days earlier, G'joth was back to his old self, Kagak was fitting in better, and Wol herself felt more alive and in control of her life. Only Trant was a problem, insofar as he had been acting no different since the night in the mess hall, despite his encouraging words.

No, that's not true, she thought as she pulled her boots on and clambered out of Ryjjan's bunk, now fully dressed. *He is acting different—as if he's distracted by something.*

She resolved to deal with it later. Right now she was more concerned with why she was going to this meeting. Sixteenth through Thirtieth Squads comprised Second Company under *QaS DevwI'* Klaris's command—she was the only leader attending this meeting who was part of First Company.

Entering the wardroom, she found herself even more confused by the presence—besides twelve of the other fifteen leaders, plus Klaris, Lokor, and Commander Toq—of Trant.

What in Kahless's name is he doing in this meeting?

Trant stood in the corner of the wardroom, his arms folded before him. He looked different—not the malcontent he'd been when he joined the squad, nor the distracted soldier he'd been the past week. Now he carried an arrogant affect, as if he were better than anyone in the room. Since it was Wol's considered opinion that that notion was precisely reversed in reality, she wondered what brought it on.

Deciding to confront the issue head-on, she did not take her seat at the table as the other leaders had, but instead walked over to the *bekk*. "What are you doing here, Trant?"

"You'll find out soon enough." Wol had never heard Trant use such a dismissive tone, not even during his arguments with Maris or G'joth.

"Do not *dare* to speak to me that way, Trant! I—"

Lokor interrupted her. "Leader—take your seat."

Wol whirled on the lieutenant. The security chief's

151

eyes were blazing with fury—and after a moment, Wol realized that it was directed, not at Wol, but at Trant. That, however, did not stop him from giving that order. *What is going on here?*

She turned back to Trant. Confusing her even more, Trant's face seemed apologetic. "It will all be explained, Wol. Trust me."

"Leader, take your seat," Lokor said again.

"I do not trust a subordinate who addresses me familiarly without cause, *Bekk.*" Wol put extra emphasis on the rank before turning her back on Trant and taking her seat next to Leader Gozak of the twentieth.

"Maybe they'll be telling us why the pointless transfers," Gozak muttered.

Wol frowned and spoke at a low volume, as Gozak had. "What do you mean?"

"I lost two of my troops. Zabyk over there lost one, half the thirty-first moved . . ."

Not having heard any of this—but also not having concerned herself overmuch with troop assignments that didn't affect First Company generally and Fifteenth Squad in particular—Wol asked, "Moved where?"

"To Twelfth Company. And you know what they all have in common? They were all transfers from the *Kreltek*. Something's going on here, and I do not like it."

Shaking her head, Wol said, "It's probably just some foolishness from on high, as usual. I long ago learned not to try to decipher the motivations of officers."

Gozak conceded the point. "Perhaps. But I still do not like it."

The final three leaders came in then. One of them, Ch'drak of the sixteenth, took the empty seat to Wol's left. Ch'drak had made his disdain for Wol clear at San-Tarah, and now he gave Wol a sneer, as if to say that she did not belong in this meeting.

Wol was not entirely sure that Ch'drak would be wrong in that assessment.

With everyone present, Toq moved to the view-screen inset into the wall. When he activated it, Wol saw a schematic of a series of spherical structures. *Half-spherical, really,* she mused, *unless there is a portion of them underground that completes the circle.* At present, it looked as if someone had sunk several ball bearings halfway into the ground.

Toq said, "You will all be joining a battle group under my command to the Elabrej homeworld, which we are orbiting under cloak. So far, we have gone undetected by the Elabrej military forces, most of which are amassed outside the system, and are about to be engaged by a fleet of Defense Force vessels."

Klaris then said, "You are probably all wondering why we are not joining that battle."

Gozak muttered only loud enough for Wol to hear: "Because this ship only fights other Klingons."

Wol noted Gozak's words.

"It is because we have a mission that is of equal import," Klaris said. "Eight Klingons, crew of the *I.K.S. Kravokh,* have been captured and not allowed to die. We will rescue them from the ignominy of imprisonment. They are being held in this complex, which is located on the Elabrej homeworld. Unfortunately, we do not know where." Klaris said this last with an undertone of irritation and a look at Toq.

The first officer seemed unconcerned. "The structure is proof against our sensors. Since it appears to be the center of the Elabrej government, this is not surprising. However, we have another method of locating the prisoners." With those words, he looked at Trant.

Stepping forward, the *bekk* said, "I am not what I appear to be. I serve Imperial Intelligence, as does one of the prisoners on the planet."

Wol felt bile rise bitterly in her throat. "What?"

Klaris was apparently as shocked as everyone else—only Lokor and Toq seemed unsurprised by this revelation—as he cried, "*That* is why this *petaQ* is here?"

"Mind your tone, *QaS DevwI'*," Trant said.

Lokor, who had been standing leaning against the bulkhead with his arms folded, now unfolded his arms and stepped between Klaris and Trant. "Mind yours, *Bekk*. Your allegiance to I.I. notwithstanding, you are a *soldier* on this ship, and you will comport yourself appropriately or you will be put to death."

Trant bared his teeth. "That would be unwise, Lieutenant."

"I doubt that very much."

Wol's fists were clenched with rage. She wanted Lokor to make good on his threat, as she wanted very much for Trant to die a painful death—and she had no doubt that Lokor would suffer no negative consequences.

Toq snapped, "Both of you, stand down! There are *Klingons* being held prisoner on that planet, and we will do whatever is necessary to liberate them—I will *not* have the mission compromised! Am I clear?"

"Perfectly." Lokor again leaned against the bulkhead, his arms folded.

"Thank you for leashing your *targ*, Commander," Trant said with a sneer. "Now—"

Now it was Toq who put himself in front of Trant. "I was speaking about *both* of you, *Bekk*."

"I am *not* a *bekk*, boy, I am an agent—"

Toq raised his arm as if to strike, but held back. Wol thought that wise; I.I. agents were exempt from challenges.

"An agent of I.I. you may be," Toq said, "but until we are told otherwise by the High Council—who have already denied your petition to take command of this ship—you are still crew, as Lokor said. You will behave as such." He finally lowered his arm. "Speak to me with disrespect again, and your life *will* be forfeit."

Wol grinned at that. *Typical of I.I. to try to take command away from those who have actually earned it.*

Toq turned his back on Trant. "It was because of Trant that we even know that Klingons were taken prisoner, and it was he who confirmed the *Kravokh*'s destruction. It is unlikely that we will be able to take the building, as scans reveal dozens of security measures, as well as several platoons of armed guards."

Trant added, "I can lead a detail to the prisoners' location after we beam down."

Klaris spoke up. "Why not now?"

"Excuse me?" Trant asked.

"Why not tell us where they are now?"

"The homing beacon has a limited range. It is only effective at a *qell'qam* or so."

Wol then asked, "Why *can't* we take the government complex?"

Lokor said, "The losses we would suffer would be too great for the minimal gain. We do not even know that the governmental body is *in* this location. They might well have been removed to a safer locale."

"However," Toq said, "the eighteenth through thirtieth can keep the forces guarding the complex busy long enough for the fifteenth, sixteenth, and seventeenth to penetrate the complex and liberate the prisoners. When you have completed that task, you must return to the beam-down point so the *Gorkon* can transport you out. The complex is made of an unknown alloy—we cannot be sure that the transporter will penetrate it. We have, however, detected an area in between two of the spheres that make up the complex where a beam containing a dozen patterns can go without risk."

Trant added, "These creatures do not have transporter technology. Indeed, they barely have accomplished faster-than-light travel. They have powerful ship-based weapons, but no defensive measures worth mentioning."

"Aside," Klaris said snidely, "from this unknown alloy that we cannot transport through."

Ignoring the *QaS DevwI*'s words, Trant said, "They will be easy targets."

Wol didn't like the sound of this. "Sir, I assume that the fifteenth was included in this mission because Trant is part of the squad?"

Lokor nodded. "Among other reasons, Leader."

"Then I must ask—who will be leading the team who rescues the prisoners?"

Trant said, "I will" at the same time that Lokor said, "You, Leader Wol."

That angered Trant, who stepped to the wardroom table and slammed a fist onto it. "This is *my* mission, Lieutenant! I will not—"

Lokor unfolded his arms. He stared at Trant with his pitiless brown eyes. *Anyone else*, Wol mused, *would have unsheathed his* d'k tahg. Lokor, however, did not need to.

Trant said nothing.

Toq spent the next several minutes going over the specific battle plan, which Wol paid only partial attention to. The information was also being downloaded to padds that they would bring with them. Her attention was focused on Trant, who stood fuming, and Wol realized something. *I do not wish to go into battle with him.*

However, what Toq and Lokor had said to Trant applied to her as well: She was crew, and would do as she was told.

When Toq was through with the briefing, he had one last thing to say. "The truth of Trant's status must remain a secret. Only the people in this room and Captain Klag are aware of it, and it must remain that way."

"No." Wol was surprised at the sound of her own voice. *What are you doing?* she asked herself, but after a second she realized that this had to be the way.

In a deep, dangerous voice, Toq asked, "*What* did you say, Leader?"

"I said no, sir. I will not go into battle with a *wam*

serpent in my midst. The soldiers of the fifteenth, sixteenth, and seventeenth—" She looked quickly at Ch'drak to her left and then across the table at Zabyk, the leader of the seventeenth. "—cannot be asked to fight alongside an I.I. agent without their knowledge."

"The decision has been made, Leader," Toq said in a tone that made it clear that further discussion would result in her death.

Wol, however, did not care. She would rather die than lie to her people for this bloodworm's sake. "Good soldiers died to uphold Captain Klag's honor at San-Tarah. General Talak cast aside the captain's good word for the sake of expediency. Is the honor of the troops less worthy of defense? Are you now to become that which we all fought so hard against?"

The room grew silent. Wol felt all eyes on her, but her own gaze was locked with Toq's. His job as first officer was to stand for the crew, and if he did not do so now, then Wol would do everything in her power to make the crew aware of it before they killed her.

However, she did not expect that to happen. She had served on this vessel long enough to have taken the measure of its command crew.

"Leader Wol is correct," Toq finally said. "Those who must go into battle with Trant may be informed—but *only* them, and only after the mission has commenced. Is that clear, Leader?"

"Perfectly." Wol was not concerned. The moment she, Ch'drak, and Zabyk told their troops, word would get around the ship quickly enough.

And that was all that mattered. While everything

Wol said was true, the honor of the fifteenth and the rest of the troops on the *Gorkon* was only part of her motivation for pushing Toq the way she did—the biggest part, certainly, but still only part.

Trant betrayed her, and betrayed the fifteenth. Officers may have had to kowtow to the whims of creatures such as Trant, but the troops had no such compunction. Once word got out of Trant's true identity, Wol had every faith that, should the I.I. agent survive the mission to liberate the prisoners, he would still be dead within a day.

When the meeting adjourned, the leaders were instructed to gather their squads. As they departed the wardroom, Ch'drak walked alongside Wol. "Well argued, Leader. You have served us all well."

Before Wol had a chance to react to this unexpected praise, Ch'drak walked ahead. She allowed herself a smile. Ch'drak was the leader of the top-ranking squad in Second Company, and had the mission been limited to that company, he would have been leading the rescue instead of her. *Obviously, defending the troops' honor earned back some respect. Good. I would prefer to have more allies on this ship, especially given what Kagak told us.*

CHAPTER SIX

G'joth's reaction to the revelation that Trant was an I.I. agent was predictable: He unsheathed his *d'k tahg* and asked Wol, "Is there any good reason why I should not kill this lying *petaQ* right now?"

"Several, actually," Wol said. "We need him to complete our mission."

They stood in transporter room twenty-three. Fifteenth Squad was assembled there, awaiting orders from the bridge. Right now, they were in a holding pattern until the *Gorkon* could safely decloak for the three seconds needed to beam eighty-three warriors to the surface. Commander Toq, Ensign Kallo, *QaS DevwI'* Klaris, and Sixteenth through Thirtieth Squads were in fifteen of the other thirty-four six-person transporter rooms on the *Gorkon*. Wol revealed Trant's true colors here, since silence would be of critical import for their part of the mission.

"I'm not convinced that's a good enough reason."

"Captain Wirrk and the other prisoners must be free," Kagak said. "Even if it means working with this lying *toDSaH.*"

"Perhaps." G'joth put his blade away. "But there will be a reckoning, Trant."

"There is something I do not understand," Goran said.

Wol thought, perhaps unfairly, that that was true of many things. Goran was as good a warrior as anyone could ask for, but thinking was not his strong suit. "What is that, Goran?"

"I thought that Maris was the I.I. agent."

Blinking, Wol turned to Trant. She had forgotten that Maris died under suspicion of being with I.I.—in fact, he had used an I.I. transmitter to betray the *Gorkon* to General Talak's troops at San-Tarah.

Trant merely stood placidly. "Maris is not your concern."

"Maris died under my command," Wol snapped. "That makes his death my very specific concern, Trant." She stared at Trant. Unlike most people at her station, Wol knew something about how Imperial Intelligence worked, from her days as the highborn daughter of a noble House, before Eral, daughter of B'Etakk, was forced to become the Houseless commoner Wol. One of the things she knew was that undercover agents always worked alone. "Maris wasn't I.I., was he? I.I. would never be so clumsy—nor would they work against Captain Klag. The Order of the *Bat'leth*'s return to its original mandate came directly from Martok—I.I. would *support* that."

"You know much about how we work, Leader." Trant bared his teeth. "One would almost think you were the scion of a noble House—or, rather, a formerly noble House."

Wol felt her blood run cold. *He knows. Damn his crest, he knows who I am.*

"What are you talking about, Trant?" G'joth asked.

"Oh, nothing you need concern yourself with, G'joth." Trant sounded entirely too smug.

But Wol refused to show her true emotions. "You know what I think, Trant? I think Maris stole your I.I. transmitter and you killed him to cover it up." Now it was her turn to bare her teeth. "In truth, I was hoping that you would either die on this mission or, failing that, die on this ship, but now I don't think I want that to happen. Because nothing that could happen to you on this ship or on Elabrej can possibly compare to what will happen to you when I.I. finds out how badly you failed. And they will find out. I will make sure of it."

Now Trant laughed derisively. "You? Once, perhaps, you would have had the ability to do me harm, but now you are nothing—a commoner woman who has attained pitifully minor status on a ship of almost three thousand."

Wol said nothing. She didn't have to. Her own connections were gone, it was true, but Lokor's were just fine. Lokor was one of the few on the *Gorkon* who knew Wol's true bloodline, and he would therefore believe her deductions as to the real fate of *Bekk* Maris.

However, she forced her face to appear crestfallen. *Let him believe he has beaten me.*

"Leader," Kagak asked, "what is he talking about?"

"He is simply spinning more lies." Wol hoped she sounded at least a little convincing. "It is what his kind does."

And yet he does not lie. I shamed Toq into allowing me to tell the truth about Trant to my squad, yet I, too, keep secrets from them. I told Krevor on San-Tarah, but that was when I knew she was on her way to Sto-Vo-Kor. Truly, am I no better than Trant?

She resolved then and there that, should she survive this mission, she would tell the fifteenth all about Eral, daughter of B'Etakk, of the now-defunct House of Varnak, and what happened to her. They deserved to know.

Klaris's voice then sounded over the speakers. *"Prepare for insertion."*

Without another word, all five of them stepped onto the transporter pad and pulled out their hand disruptors, save for Trant, who removed a device from his belt that Wol presumed was a locator of some sort.

"Soldiers of the fifteenth," Wol said, *"Qapla'!"*

Goran, G'joth, and Kagak all said, *"Qapla'!"* in perfect unison.

Trant, predictably, said nothing.

The dark walls of the transporter room faded into a red haze, then coalesced into a brightly lit corridor with walls that curved upward. Based on Toq's briefing, they were beaming into a tube that linked two of the spherical structures. Apparently, Elabrej architecture had few corners.

When the red haze completely disappeared, Wol felt lighter; this world had a much lower gravity than

Qo'noS. Looking around, she saw that the rest of the fifteenth had materialized with her, along with Ch'drak, Zabyk, and their two squads. The tube they stood in was not very high. Goran's head was rubbing up against the tube's highest point, and the remaining eleven of them could have reached up and touched the top.

Wol turned to Trant with a questioning gaze.

The I.I. agent was staring at the display on his locator. Then he pointed toward one end of the corridor.

Turning to Ch'drak and Zabyk, Wol pointed at herself and held up one finger, then at Ch'drak, then two fingers, then Zabyk, then three fingers, and finally at Goran, followed by four fingers. Both leaders nodded in understanding—the fifteenth would take the lead, following where Trant's locator took them, with the sixteenth in the middle, followed by the seventeenth, but with Goran's massive form bringing up the rear.

Quickly arranging themselves as Wol ordered, they moved as one toward the door at the end of the corridor where Trant had pointed.

The door at the end did not open at their approach, nor did it have any visible handles. It did, however, have a panel. Since this *was* a government complex with no doubt heightened security, Wol suspected that simply blowing the panel to pieces would be unwise. For all they knew, their beaming in had triggered an alarm somewhere. But in case it hadn't, stealth was called for here.

Remembering the makeup of the sixteenth, she looked at Ch'drak, then at the panel. The leader nodded, and gave *Bekk* Yojagh a look. Yojagh holstered his disruptor and jogged forward, pulling out a toolkit that he kept where most warriors carried their *d'k tahg*s. Wol recalled a conversation in the mess hall shortly after the *Gorkon* entered the Kavrot Sector when one of the engineers asked Yojagh why someone with his considerable technical skills didn't transfer to engineering. Yojagh's response was: "But then I don't get to shoot things."

Prying the cover off the panel, Yojagh took only ten seconds to get the door open.

It slid aside to reveal some of the most revolting creatures Wol had ever seen.

They stood slightly shorter than the average Klingon, though only slightly. It seemed, at first, that they were even smaller than they actually were by virtue of the fact that they didn't have heads. The Elabrej apparently had one big torso, four arms, and two legs. That torso had several features on it that no doubt corresponded to sight, smell, sound, etc., but she would never have presumed to guess which was which. She also realized after a moment that all the creatures' limbs could be used in locomotion, as some traveled on four, and others on the top ones that she had initially identified as arms.

Six of them were in the room on the other side of the door, two in hammocks of some kind, three walking around, and one standing at a door on the opposite end. The room in question was spherical, as expected. The one at the opposite door had odd markings on his torso, and was holding a long tube that Wol suspected was a weapon.

That one was, therefore, the first person she fired on.

To the creature's credit, as soon as the door opened to reveal twelve Klingons, the guard—if that's what it was—immediately pointed the tube at them. Even as Wol's own disruptor fire sliced through the air, some kind of energy burst emitted from the tube.

Next to her, the beam struck Trant, burning a hole right through his shoulder—a hole large enough to cause his left arm to drop to the floor, followed quickly by Trant himself, who, to his credit, did not scream in pain even though his entire left shoulder was now gone.

After seeing that the guard had also been hit by Wol's disruptor fire, the leader bent down to grab the locator, hoping that it was not keyed to Trant's DNA signature or retinal patterns or some other thing that would make it useless to them. Meanwhile, the report of nine more disruptors echoed in Wol's ears. Only Trant, Wol herself, and Yojagh—who was still kneeling at the door panel—didn't fire.

Moments later, Wol was holding the locator and there were half a dozen dead Elabrej in the room. The locator had a small screen that indicated the distance and direction of the signal from B'Etloj. Wol stepped forward and the distance lessened. *Good.*

She turned back around and saw that Trant was now lying in a pool of his own blood, which had come pouring out of the gaping hole where his left shoulder and left arm used to be. He would be dead in moments.

After all the plans I had for your death, Trant, it's almost appropriate that you dash them and die in combat. For a moment, she considered performing the death ritual on him, then decided not to bother. *Leaving aside any other considerations, we need to stay as quiet as possible.*

She waved forward with the disruptor in her right hand, while keeping an eye on the locator she held in her left.

At the report of another disruptor blast behind her, she turned to see Goran and two members of the seventeenth firing into the corridor behind them. Goran was using the ancient disruptor his father had given him, which supposedly belonged to an ancestor of the big man's who served with *Dahar* Master Kor at Organia over a century ago.

The weapons fire stopped a moment later; one member of the seventeenth was cut down, but Wol couldn't see past Goran to see what they fought.

Since the need for silence was now pretty much past, she cried out, "Goran, report!"

"There were five aliens with funny marks on their bellies. They had weapons and they attacked us. We stopped them."

Zabyk added, "*Bekk* Tamlik and *Bekk* Gor are dead."

Wol let out a breath. "Yojagh, get that door closed and *keep* it closed, then open the one that leads out of here."

"Yes, Leader." The *bekk* touched one control on something from his toolkit, and the door they came in through closed. As soon as it slid all the way shut, the panel next to it sparked; Wol assumed the panel on the other side did the same.

As Yojagh worked on the other door, Wol heard a hissing sound.

"Gas!" Ch'drak cried out. He pulled out a hand scanner. "Nature of gas unknown."

Wol aimed her disruptor at the panel next to the door Yojagh was working on. "*Bekk*, move."

The moment Yojagh was clear, Wol fired. The panel blew to pieces and the door opened. At the same time, a blaring noise started sounding through the speakers, and a voice sounded over some kind of public address system. Luckily, among the material sent by B'Etloj to Trant was a translation matrix for the Elabrej language, which Trant had programmed into all the leaders' communicators, so Wol understood the words being spoken.

"*Code violet. Code violet. Intruders in the twelfth sphere. Intruders in the outer grounds. Fortieth through ninetieth defensors to the twelfth sphere. All other defensors to the outer grounds.*"

Given the ground, Wol assumed that meant fifty soldiers, not fifty squads—or worse, fifty companies. That would have been overkill.

Then again, they destroyed the Kravokh, *so perhaps these headless creatures believe in overkill.*

"Move out," Wol said. "Shoot *anyone* you see that isn't Klingon."

Wol took point. The door she had just opened led to another corridor, albeit a much shorter one, which in turn led into another, much larger sphere. Again, the troops advanced; again, Yojagh was tasked with getting the door open.

And again, they were greeted by Elabrej. Wol counted at least thirty as the door slid open. Only this time they all had the markings that Wol was starting to understand indicated a soldier. They were also all armed with those energy tubes, and were all firing those weapons at the Klingon troops.

"The cloak continues to function within expected parameters."

Klag clenched the fist that once belonged to his father in acknowledgment of Rodek's words from the gunner's position behind him and to his right. All things being equal, he would have preferred to go into battle, but right now the most important thing was to rescue Wirrk and his comrades.

And also gain intelligence. "Ensign Kal, report."

With Kallo on the planet, Kal was at the operations console next to Rodek's. "Sensors are scanning the entire planet, sir. We have also received a nondirected coded message from the *Ditagh*."

"Decode it." Klag smiled. Because the message was not directed to any one place, its receiver couldn't be easily tracked. It also meant there was a chance that the *Gorkon* wouldn't receive it, but that was a risk worth taking.

"It is from Captain Vikagh, sir, and he says that the fleet has engaged the enemy."

"Good. The Elabrej will soon learn who it is they are—"

"Sir!" Kal cried. "I'm reading six Elabrej vessels coming into range—bearing directly on our position!"

Again, Klag clenched his right fist. "Status of cloak?"

Rodek double-checked his console. "Unchanged."

Kal added, "They'll be in weapons range in three minutes."

It could be a coincidence—or they could have penetrated the cloak.

He turned to the pilot's position to his left. "Leskit, change our orbital path—bring us to a higher altitude."

The old pilot grinned. "With pleasure, sir."

Moments later, Kal spoke. "The ships have changed course toward our new position."

There it is, then. Klag rose from his chair. "Alert status! Rodek, decloak, raise shields, and arm all weapons. Leskit, bring us about to an attack posture." Klag then recalled something from one of Toq's briefings on the records from the *Kravokh*. "When we're in range, Rodek, have the gunners aim disruptors at the tubes that interconnect the spheres."

"Aye, sir."

Even as Rodek acknowledged the order, four warriors came onto the bridge and took up position at the secondary gunner positions.

Kal then said, "The Elabrej are arming their weapons, sir. They do *not* match the energy signature of the weapon used on the *Kravokh*."

"The first time, perhaps—these are probably the weapons used to destroy the *Kravokh* when they arrived here."

Rodek said, "In weapons range."

"Firing pattern *loS*, Rodek, and disruptor cannons as needed. Tactical scan on screen."

Now Klag sat back down in his chair and watched with glee. The Chancellor-class ships were the cream of the Defense Force, the largest, most advanced, most powerful ships in the fleet. Originally designed to be used against the Jem'Hadar in the Dominion War, the conflict ended before the vessels could be deployed. Klag now relished the opportunity to use them against worthy enemies of the empire. Until now his battles had been against Kreel or Kinshaya, or fellow Klingon ships, whether the mind-controlled warriors at Narendra III or the honorless followers of General Talak at San-Tarah.

Songs will be written of this day.

He watched as the Elabrej ships fired their own weapons even as the *Gorkon's* disruptors leapt outward like arachnids spinning a web. However, all the weapons were firing at the *Gorkon's* previous position in orbit. They had not compensated for Leskit's aggressive posture.

However, three of them still hit.

Rodek, speaking as calmly and unconcernedly as ever, said, "Shields down to ten percent."

Klag whirled around to face his second officer. Only three hits, yet it was enough to make their shields all but useless.

"Sir," Kal said. "Engineering reports that shields cannot be reconstituted."

Klag snarled. "Inform the medical bay that Commander Kurak is to be released immediately."

"Yes, sir."

He turned back to the tactical display. Just as he did so, three of the Elabrej ships exploded.

"Enemy vessels preparing to fire again," Rodek said.

The captain sat back down in his chair. "Leskit, evasive. Take us away from the planet, full impulse. Rodek, continuous fire on disruptors. Ensign Kal, inform Commander Toq that we are leaving orbit and to stand fast until they hear from us again."

They had several seconds to readjust their firing pattern the first time and didn't. If the *Gorkon* wasn't where it was when the weapons armed, there was less of a chance of being hit.

"Captain, this is B'Oraq. Kurak is in no condition to run engineering, sir. She is suffering from detoxification effects."

Klag didn't even know what that meant. "Is it fatal?"

"Not really, sir, but—"

"Doctor, if Kurak doesn't report to engineering now, it *will* be fatal—for all of us."

To her credit, B'Oraq did not argue. *"Understood. I'm releasing her. She'll be in engineering shortly."*

Leskit said, "We're on course for the moon in orbit of the sixth planet."

"We have destroyed two more enemy vessels," Rodek said, "and one other has lost structural integrity and will collapse momentarily."

Klag nodded his approval, remembering that that moon had a powerful magnetic field that would probably confuse scans to some degree. After what they endured from the subspace eddies around San-Tarah, Klag had every faith in the ability of his crew to deal with this comparatively minor problem. The lack of industrial construction or orbital bases of any kind around the moon, in comparison to the large amount of both on the other twelve moons in the system, led Klag to believe that the Elabrej were not so skilled.

"Enemy weapons firing on our previous position," Rodek said.

Kal added, "They're now changing course to pursue— and seven more ships are now coming in range. They're setting course for the same moon, sir."

Which takes us from two to nine foes. They have no defenses worth mentioning—if our own evasive maneuvering weren't making targeting difficult, we'd have destroyed all of them by now—but their offensive capabilities are staggering. Klag smiled. *Oh yes, many songs will be written.*

Until now, Klag wished to be parsimonious with their photon and quantum torpedoes. They had been able to restock some after San-Tarah, mostly from the wreck of the *Kreltek*, but were still not at full capacity, and they would not be able to restock for some time. However, given the fragility of the Elabrej vessels, he wanted to try.

"Rodek, two photon torpedoes on the closest ship. Fire when ready."

A moment later, Rodek said, "Firing."

Two torpedoes belched forth from the *Gorkon's* aft section and struck the Elabrej vessel most proximate to them.

It exploded upon impact of the first torpedo.

That was enough for Klag. "Load all torpedo bays. One photon per vessel. Fire when ready."

"This ought to be good," Leskit muttered, then said louder: "Approaching the moon, Captain."

"Firing," Rodek said calmly at the same time that Kal said rather more frantically, "Enemy vessels arming weapons!"

"Engineering to bridge."

Klag did not recognize the voice. "Who is this?"

"Lieutenant Yaklan, sir."

"Where is Commander Kurak?"

"Uh, throwing up on the deck, sir."

"Elabrej weapons bearing directly, sir." Kal was practically shrieking. Klag made a mental note to discipline the ensign later for showing such poor combat skills.

Rodek put in, "As are our torpedoes."

Klag turned to the tactical display. All nine enemy vessels were destroyed as the torpedoes each hit their marks.

So did the Elabrej weapons.

All at once, Klag's senses were assaulted. The sound of exploding consoles and blaring alarms slammed into his ears. The stench of melted conduits and burning components filled his nostrils. Smoke burned his eyes and coated his tongue.

Rodek was shouting over the din. "Shields down! Structural integrity field at thirty-five percent! Cloak offline! Main power failing!"

From the pilot's console, Leskit said, "I've lost helm control—we're heading into the atmosphere!"

Swallowing down the bitter taste of the smoke—and of defeat—Klag asked, "What is the status of communications systems?"

"Offline!" Kal's voice sounded peculiar, but Klag did not have time to determine why. He was more concerned with the fact that he had left Toq and his team behind on the Elabrej homeworld. *Without us to extract them, they will die on that world. My abysmal luck with first officers continues unabated. A pity—you were a fine warrior, Toq. May you die well.*

"Entering stratosphere," Leskit said.

Klag gritted his teeth. "On screen."

The *Gorkon*'s main viewer switched from the tactical overview to the grayish moon that they had been orbiting—and which now was getting closer by the second. The image was laden with static, which Klag attributed to the world's magnetic field combined with the damage the *Gorkon* had taken.

"All hands prepare for crash landing!"

Now Klag had to wonder who would actually write those songs. . . .

As energy blasts sizzled over his head, Toq thought, from his vantage point lying facedown on the grass, that the plan had seemed to be a good one back on the *Gorkon*.

The complex of spherical structures where the *Kravokh* crew was being held was located atop a hill surrounded by a park. Toq admired the thought that went into the construction: the position was very defensible. Had Toq's objective been to take the complex, it would have been very difficult, especially without the ability to transport directly into the structures.

But all they had to do was hold the line until Leader Wol and her team could liberate Captain Wirrk and the other prisoners.

Sadly, that was proving more difficult than they had imagined. During the initial attack, the Klingons had the upper hand, killing any Elabrej they saw—once they got past their revulsion. Toq had seen many different living things in his life, from the animal life on Carraya, where he grew up living among Klingons and Romulans coexisting in harmony, to the various species he met first as the scion of Lorgh, then as an officer in the Defense Force. But never had he seen any creatures like these Elabrej with their numerous legs and headless bodies.

But once the Elabrej realized that they were facing a superior foe, they retreated into the complex, depending on weapon emplacements built into the structures and the fact that the park had no real cover. *QaS Devwl'* Klaris had lost twenty-one of his sixty-five troops since the Elabrej retreated, and that number was only going to grow.

"*Gorkon to Toq. Sir, this is Ensign Kal—the* Gorkon *has been engaged by Elabrej forces and is leaving orbit. Your orders are to stand fast until you hear from us again.*"

Toq muttered a Romulan curse that he learned at Carraya.

He cried to Klaris, who was just to his right, also lying facedown—as they all were—taking shots at the emplacements. "The *Gorkon* has left orbit, and we don't know when they'll return. We need to change our tactics."

"You're not suggesting retreat, are you, Commander?" Klaris asked as he fired another shot. The *QaS Devwl'* made no effort to hide the disgust in his voice at that thought.

"No," Toq said, though he did not share Klaris's revulsion at the concept of retreat. Still, leaving aside any other considerations, there was nowhere to retreat *to.* There were only forty-seven of them, and the city surrounding them was huge. True, they could likely lose themselves in the metropolis, but to what end? *Then they will be able to pick us off one by one—or if we stay in one place, they'll face us on their terms, not ours.* "We may have to consider trying to take the complex."

Whatever Klaris was going to say in reply was lost to Toq, as he was occupied with rolling away from one of the blasts. When he righted himself, he saw that the grass where he had been lying was burned to ashes.

Luckily, the roll brought him closer to the *QaS DevwI',* who repeated his words. "I doubt we can take the place with so few of us."

"Remember, there are more of us inside." Toq grinned. "Besides, Klaris, think how well we will die!"

"I try not to think about things like that, sir. I prefer living to fight again."

Toq laughed and fired at the weapon that had almost killed him. "Perhaps, but—"

A wrenching sound interrupted Toq, squealing loud enough to hurt his ears. Instinctively, he puts his hands to them. *What is that—?*

Looking up, he saw that a dark metal casing was rising from the ground and surrounding the complex. After a moment, as it rose, curving as it got higher, Toq realized that it was a sphere that would surround the smaller spheres, in essence encasing them. He removed his hand scanner. It revealed no more than his scans of the complex had—only that it was some kind of alloy the scanner's database didn't recognize. However, the scan confirmed what Toq had already guessed: This material was even stronger than what the various structures were made of, and it completely surrounded the area.

Retreating to the city was starting to look like a viable option.

Then Toq felt as if someone had grabbed him by the waist and thrown him into the air. As he landed back on the ground with a bone-jarring thud, he deduced that someone had set off an explosion underground, which was confirmed by the sight of the ground several meters to his left exploding upward—knocking aside two of the troops.

The one advantage to the protective sphere that was being erected was that it seemed to be bereft of weapons emplacements, so Toq felt comfortable breaking cover—if one could call lying on the ground "cover"—to investigate the explosion. *It might be a way in, if nothing else.*

Several Elabrej climbed out of the hole left by the ground. The troops nearby took aim, but Toq cried, "Hold your fire!" These Elabrej were unarmed, and they did not have the same markings on their torsos as the ones who fired on them earlier did.

One of the aliens looked at Toq. "I understood you! But you're an alien!" Two of the creature's arms started vibrating in a manner that frankly made Toq nauseous.

"Yes." Toq saw no reason to reveal the existence of the translator. "You have two seconds to tell me why I shouldn't kill you."

"We came here to rescue you. But we thought you were trapped in the government sphere."

Toq was confused. "You came to rescue *Klingons?*"

A noise came from the hole in the ground. Toq looked down to see other Elabrej trying to clamber out of it. "They're coming for us! Mal Sanchit, we have to go *now!* We cannot afford for the oligarchs to have *any* of us in custody!"

"The military will kill us all if we do not leave now," the alien said to Toq.

Belying those words, Toq heard a muffled order from below to take the separatists alive.

Quickly, Toq weighed his options. Retreat had not been an option in part because they had nowhere to go. Now they had found people who were called "separatists" by the same military that had taken the warriors of the *Kravokh* prisoner and fired on Toq and his people. And they still had not heard from the *Gorkon*.

We have somewhere to go now.

"You have a method of transporting us?" Toq asked the alien.

The creature's arms vibrated even more now, to the point where Toq had to look away. "We have a conveyance hidden nearby. It was intended to carry however many of your kind were imprisoned by the oligarchs, so it can fit you. But we must go *now.*"

Toq made his decision. "*QaS DevwI'*, gather the remaining troops quickly! We will go with these—separatists."

"Yes, Commander!" Klaris immediately set out to follow his orders, for which Toq was grateful. His decision was probably not the one Klaris himself would have made—indeed, Toq doubted that any of his three predecessors as first officer would have made it—but he had been raised with both Romulans and Klingons, and also spent time as the adopted child of a top I.I. agent. As glorious as a suicide attack on the government complex might have been, going with these separatists offered the better chance for victory in the long run.

Toq shared few philosophies with the Jem'Hadar, but, though he gloried in battle, he also believed as the Dominion's genetically engineered soldiers did that victory was life.

A flash caught Toq's eye, and he looked down to see one of the separatist aliens struck by weapons fire. Toq immediately fired in the direction of the weapon's source, though he could see no specific target.

He then looked over to see Klaris running toward him, Ensign Kallo alongside him, the surviving troops behind them.

"We need covering fire," Toq said to the *QaS DevwI'*.

Klaris nodded, and said, "Twenty-ninth and Thirtieth Squads, cover!"

Only four troops responded to that order; Toq realized after a moment that the remaining six must have been among the twenty-one cut down.

To the alien, he said, "I am Toq, of the House of Lorgh, commander in the Klingon Defense Force, and first officer of the *I.K.S. Gorkon*."

"I am Imparter Mal Sanchit, and you must follow me."

"I place the lives of my crew in your—" He hesitated. "—hands." He just now noticed that the Elabrej had ten fingers on each of six hands at the ends of their limbs. "If you betray that trust, I will not hesitate to kill all of you."

Now four of the arms vibrated. "Understood, Toq. Follow, please."

They ran down the hill. Kallo positioned herself alongside Toq. "Commander, is this wise? We cannot trust—"

Toq cut the tiresome ensign off, taking great pleasure in interrupting *her* for a change. "My orders are given, Ensign. You will follow them or you will be put to death, is that *clear?*"

"Of—of course, sir."

CHAPTER SEVEN

Klag stood atop a hill, his head pounding so hard he thought his brain would explode out through his crest. He looked down at the remains of his ship.

No, not remains. The hull is intact, more or less.

Somehow, Leskit had managed to regain enough helm control for the *Gorkon* to land in a marsh that cushioned the impact.

That was an hour ago. Lokor and the *QaS DevwI'* who had survived were overseeing the troops, setting up a perimeter. Klag went to this hill to await Rodek's report from the crew. With Toq likely dead, Rodek was now first officer, and the situation report was his to gather.

Rodek arrived with that report in due course. The lieutenant still bore the scars of the head injury he'd sustained at San-Tarah. However, since that injury, Rodek had been much more than he was. True, he still came across as subdued, but he no longer was as passionless as he had been when the *Gorkon* first left the shipyard.

"Seven hundred and twenty-two died in the crash," Rodek said without preamble. "Many more are injured, and are being treated by Dr. B'Oraq and Nurse Gaj."

Klag nodded. Between those casualties and the ones on the Elabrej homeworld, that left them with less than two thousand crew.

"The doctor also reports that the magnetic fields on this planet may provoke headaches."

Klag smiled. "No 'may' about it, Rodek. Does B'Oraq have a prescription?"

Nodding, Rodek said, "She will dispense remedies once the injured are cared for."

"Good."

"Lieutenant Lokor reports that the *QaS DevwI'* have set up a perimeter. Since this marsh is surrounded by higher ground on all sides, it will be easy to defend." Rodek grinned, an expression that surprised and pleased Klag. "It seems Leskit chose his crash site well."

Klag threw his head back and laughed. "Indeed he did. Ship's status?"

"Engines are intact and repairable. We have replacements for most of what was damaged in the attack, and the hull breaches can also be repaired."

"When can we be spaceworthy?"

Rodek hesitated. "According to Kurak, never."

At that, Klag snarled. *Every time I think I have convinced Kurak to actually do her duty as my chief engineer, and every time I am proven wrong by that recalcitrant cow. You would think I would learn that lesson.*

"Anything else?"

"Quartermaster died in the crash, but the assistant quartermaster says that most of the supplies are intact, and we are properly provisioned for several months, even if the replicators are not brought back online. That is all, sir."

"Very well. Bring her to me."

Rodek frowned. "Sir?"

"Kurak."

"Of course, sir."

As Rodek moved down the hill, Klag turned to view the surrounding area. The marsh was a sunken area in the midst of a humid grassland. Rodek had been correct in that it was defensible. Looking around, he saw sentries posted at regular intervals. *Lokor does his work well.*

Speaking of whom, the security chief was approaching from the opposite direction, accompanied by *QaS Devwl'* Vok and Grotek. Klag recalled that Grotek was the *QaS Devwl'* to whom Lokor had sent most of the transfers from the *Kreltek.*

"You have a report for me, Lokor?"

"Yes, sir," Lokor said. "Or, rather, *QaS Devwl'* Grotek does."

Grotek stood at attention. "Sir, Lieutenant Lokor told me to be on the lookout for mutinous tendencies among the *Kreltek* transfers."

"You've found some?" Klag asked.

"I believe so, sir. I also have a suggestion for weeding them out."

Klag wondered why this was even being brought to his attention. "Has Lokor approved the plan?"

Grotek shot a look at the lieutenant. "Yes, sir."

Lokor said, "I thought you should be made aware of the plan, sir. With all of us on this planet for an indefinite time, the situation is harder to control than it would be on-ship. I thought it best to gain your direct approval before proceeding."

Better Lokor err on the side of caution than the other way around in this case. "Tell me your plan, *QaS DevwI'*."

"We send the one-seventy-first through one-eightieth on a foraging mission. All the *Kreltek* transfers are in those ten companies, including the leader of the one-seventy-first, and there are other malcontents in those squads—as is *Bekk* Moq."

"I assume," Klag said dryly, "that this Moq would be your eyes and ears?"

"Yes, sir." Grotek allowed himself a small smile. "He is a ward of my House, and he will do as I ask. In this case, sir, I will ask him to report on what the troops say to each other. Isolated from the rest of the crew, it will present them with a perfect opportunity."

Lokor added, "There is a risk, sir. They already know I suspect them, and they may rightly interpret this assignment as a ruse to draw them out. If that is so, they will say nothing."

Klag considered Lokor's words. "The worst outcome of this will be that the ten squads go on a successful foraging mission."

"True." Lokor bared his teeth.

Then Vok spoke up. "Sir, I believe there should be more."

"In what way, Vok?" Klag asked.

Vok turned to Grotek. "I assume you will equip Moq with a listening device?"

"Of course—assuming it will work in this planet's magnetic air," he added with annoyance.

Turning back to Klag, Vok said, "Then we should have twenty squads on standby, sir—to be prepared to deal with any mutineers when they return to base."

Angrily, Lokor said, "We cannot spare twenty squads in addition to the ten we will be sending out. With our casualties, we will not have enough left to fortify the perimeter. We *are* in enemy territory."

"We're six thousand *qell'qams* from any life signs," Vok said. "We can spare—"

"Enough!" Klag silenced them with the word. Their arguing was only making his headache worse. "*Ten* squads will be sent to destroy any traitors. Vok, you will select them." He looked at Lokor. "I did not take up arms against my fellow Klingons just to have my command destroyed from within." Gazing down at the *Gorkon*, half-sunk in the muck, he added, "The Elabrej have done enough to destroy us from without."

Hearing footsteps, Klag looked down the hill to see Rodek returning, Kurak limping behind him. B'Oraq had, of course, cured the broken leg, and had apparently given her something to deal with her "alcohol poisoning." Whatever it was, it made Kurak far paler than normal.

"Proceed with your plans," Klag said. "Report your progress to either myself or Lieutenant Rodek. *Qapla'*."

All three returned the salutation, and departed.

Rodek smiled as he said, "Commander Kurak, reporting as ordered, sir."

"Captain," Kurak said, and Klag noted that her voice had very little of its usual arrogant, angry timbre, "I know what you are about to say. But there is no way for the *Gorkon* to lift off."

"Why?"

Gripping her left wrist with her right arm, Kurak said, "Because the Chancellor-class ships were not designed to take off from a planet's surface. And even if they were, the *Gorkon* couldn't do it with the hull and the structural integrity field in the shape they're in."

"I do not believe that. Surely, *Commander*, there are ways to make the ship work beyond what it is designed to do!"

"Captain—"

Klag started to pace the top of the hill. "During the war I encountered several Starfleet ships. Have you ever worked with Starfleet engineers, Kurak? They are marvels. Give them a pile of rocks, a magnospanner, and a self-sealing stembolt, and they can make a working replicator that also fires phaser beams. I find it impossible to believe that the engineer who designed the *Negh'Var*, who was able to get disruptors to function within the field of subspace eddies surrounding San-Tarah, who was able to modify the ship's probes into mines, who was able to dump holodeck power into the engines—" Then Klag turned and faced Kurak. "Oh, wait—that was *Vall* who did that, was it not?"

Kurak said nothing, though she was seething. To

Klag's amusement, Rodek was grinning as widely as Klag had ever seen him do.

"You say, Commander, that the *Gorkon* cannot achieve escape velocity in a gravity well."

Snidely, Kurak said, "I was not aware that such as you knew any engineering jargon, Captain. Yes, that's true."

Klag let the insult pass. "Yet we were able to escape the gravity well of a sun when we fought the Kinshaya months ago."

"We were already in motion, and not confined by the friction of an atmosphere. We also hadn't sustained hull damage. I can fix the structural integrity field—I might even be able to strengthen it—but the ship cannot handle the stresses of taking off—"

Angrily, Klag said, "That is absurd! You cannot convince me that the stresses of faster-than-light travel are *less* than that of escaping a planet's gravity well."

"So much for your understanding of engineering. When we go to warp, we're protected by a subspace field."

Rodek asked, "Can we not protect ourselves with a subspace field when we take off from the planet?"

That brought Kurak up short, which in turn prompted Klag to laugh. "Well said, Rodek. Well, Chief Engineer, is it possible?"

"Not without considerable risk of damage to the planet."

"I can assure you, Commander, that my concern for the welfare of the planet of an enemy of the empire is minimal."

Kurak nodded, conceding the point. Klag noticed that she was even paler than when the conversation started. "Very well, then—it can be done. But it will take time. Several systems need to be repaired, and re-configuring the engines to do what you require will take several days. If that is not acceptable to you . . ."

"Several days will be more than sufficient, Kurak." Klag grinned. "It is a great improvement over 'never' as a departure time. Get to work immediately. Use any personnel you need who are not required to maintain perimeter efficiency."

"Yes, sir."

Then Kurak threw up all over the ground in front of her—as well as Klag's boots.

Still bent over, Kurak said in a weak voice, "With the captain's permission, I will see Dr. B'Oraq first."

Rubbing the front of his boot on the soft ground, Klag said, "Permission granted."

"Sir," Rodek put in, "I have a report *from* B'Oraq. She has developed a medicine that will keep us from succumbing to the magnetic fields of this planet. Prolonged exposure will result in permanent brain damage without the medicine."

"Good. Have her distribute it—after she has seen to Kurak."

"Yes, sir."

It took all of Sanchit's willpower to keep from running away screaming.

Nonetheless, she stood fast alongside the alien creature who was called Toq and calmly discussed with him what the separatists were all about as they flew through the skies of the First World in their stealth conveyance.

The conveyance was perhaps the most valuable physical asset the seps had. It was a prototype of a new conveyance the military was developing that was invisible to standard scans. Sanchit had no idea how Jammit managed to get her hands on it, but it allowed them to move freely without being detected.

But Sanchit could not get over how revoltingly strange Toq and his fellow Klingons looked. Only four legs—no forelegs, midlegs that didn't seem to be used for ambulation, and hindlegs that didn't seem to be used for any manual purpose, especially given that they wore coverings on the hindleg hands. Most peculiar of all was the odd appendage that extended upward from the torso. Their mouths were there instead of center mass like a sensible being's, and that appendage seemed to move about freely and alter its shape constantly. They only seemed to use their four legs for simple physical functions. While they sat in the conveyance, Toq's hindlegs never moved, and his midlegs only a little. Sanchit found it very difficult to carry on a conversation with someone so unexpressive.

Soon they arrived back at the home sphere of Viralas. One of the wealthiest members of the separatist movement—indeed, one of the wealthiest people on the Four Worlds—Vor Viralas's support had been another of their greatest assets. He was exactly the type of person against whom the seps fought, and his taking their side was a huge risk to him.

He also had the largest home sphere, so that was where they'd intended to take the alien prisoners.

When they arrived at Viralas's home sphere, Gansett was waiting for them in the underground conveyance storage sphere. "Did you *get* them, did you—" Then all of Gansett's legs—even the ones he was standing on—started waving with excitement. "Doane's limbs! They're real! They're really real!"

After all that, and he didn't even believe it. Then again, Sanchit thought somberly, *neither did I. Until I actually saw the aliens, I didn't completely believe it. A big part of me wanted Yannak to be right, that this was all a plot by the oligarchs—better that than to believe that the clergy had lied to us all this time. Or worse, were mistaken . . .*

"These aren't the prisoners," she said to Gansett. "These are some other aliens—they're called Klingons."

"I am Toq," the first alien said. "We were sent to rescue our fellow warriors from their prison—one way or the other."

Sanchit waved her midlegs in confusion. "That's the second time you've said that. What does it mean?"

"It means that we would either take them back to the *Gorkon* with us—or kill them."

All the Elabrej present waved their forelegs in revulsion. "You would *murder* them?"

Another of the aliens spoke, the one Toq called Ensign Kallo. "No Klingon warrior *ever* allows himself to be taken prisoner. If they are not permitted to die, then they are denied *Sto-Vo-Kor.*"

Sanchit had no idea what that meant. "I don't see

how you can—can *kill* like that. It's an offense against Doane."

"I do not know what *that* means," Toq said.

Sanchit almost laughed at that. "There is much about you we do not understand." She led them out of the storage sphere into the large central sphere that dominated Viralas's home. It was decorated with an assortment of hammocks and statuary, as well as bowls containing food and drink. "I do not know if our food will be edible to you, but—"

"You *idiot!*"

The interruption came from Viralas himself, who came into the central sphere through another entrance. "Vor Viralas, we—"

"How could you bring them *here!?* You've compromised *everything* this movement stands for!"

Stunned into silence, Sanchit found herself unable to reply, but Jammit spoke in her defense. "Don't be an idiot, Viralas, we're—"

But Viralas, whose forelegs were waving with great annoyance, kept going. "Have any of you seen the news? Seen what they have been saying about us?"

"What does *that* matter?" Toq asked. "Do you truly allow yourselves to be influenced by such irrelevancies as reportings of news?"

At Toq's words, Viralas's legs stopped moving altogether. "You—you speak our language?"

"Not quite." Toq's mouth spread wide, revealing several sharp incisors. "Our communications devices come equipped with translators. It allows us to communicate with any alien we meet."

"Any alien?" Bantrak—who had come in with Viralas— let his legs go limp at that. "There are *other* species besides you?"

Toq made a sound that Sanchit supposed, given the context, was a laugh for Klingons, though she found it a grating sound that made her entire body want to shrivel up. Then the Klingon said, "There are *thousands* of different species just in this part of the galaxy, and we've only explored a small portion of it."

"This is all very interesting," Viralas said, "but it doesn't change the fact that you should *not* have brought these people here." He walked to one of the tables in the room, which had an activator. Lifting the device, he pushed a button, causing a section of the wall to light up with a news broadcast.

"As seen in these images taken just moments ago, it has now been proven beyond a doubt that the separatist movement is responsible for the attack of these alien monsters."

Even as the newscaster spoke, the view changed from him to images of Toq and his people's attack, followed by ones of Toq and Sanchit talking.

Doane's limbs, no. Sanchit felt all her limbs shrivel. *They have images of me. They can identify me. I'm an idiot—I should never have suggested so public an attack. My career—it's over now.*

The newscaster continued as the image changed to the same one shown during Vor Jorg's address to the hegemony. *"The despicable creatures, having already murdered Shipmaster Vor Ellis and her conveyance while on their historic mission—"* Now the image was that of several military conveyances fighting Toq's fellow Klingons in the skies. "—*are now fighting against the brave and noble hegemony military in the outer reaches of Elabrej sky.*"

"This is insane," Jammit said. "They can't possibly—"

"It gets worse," Viralas said.

The image came back to the newscaster. "*But even as our valiant forces have been nobly fighting against this vile alien filth that has polluted our fine hegemony, the despicable seps have been leading these demons straight to the heart of our hegemony with a cowardly attack on the government sphere, in which more brave soldiers were mercilessly killed.*"

Now the image switched to several Klingons whom Sanchit did not recognize attacking soldiers inside the government sphere. They did indeed kill several soldiers—and, Sanchit noticed, some civilians. *Doane's limbs,* she thought, *this is disastrous.*

"*First Oligarch Vor Jorg has spoken, saying that this cowardly attack demonstrates once and for all that the separatists are a plague that needs to be eliminated from our fine hegemony, and he promised that the oligarchs would not rest until the seps and the alien filth were removed from our society permanently.*"

With that, the image went dark.

"Of course they don't mention that it was a rescue mission," Yannak said. "That would force them to admit that they have alien prisoners."

Toq's upper appendage swiveled toward Sanchit. "Your people will believe these lies?"

Sanchit barely registered Toq's words. She was still

in shock from seeing her own face on the news images.

Gansett answered the question for her. "Yes, they *definitely* will."

"Your people are fools."

Bantrak let out a puff of air. "Impressive. He's only been in the hegemony a few *atgrets*, and he's already learned that."

Sanchit finally found her voice. "Who were those others?"

"What?" Toq asked.

"The others who were inside the government sphere."

"Ah. Ours was simply a holding action. The warriors inside the—the government sphere were endeavoring to free the prisoners. Unfortunately, our ship left orbit and has not returned."

Altran spoke up, then. "You had a conveyance in orbit of the First World?"

"Yes. But it was engaged by several of your military ships."

Letting out a puff of air, Altran said, "They're not *my* military, believe me. And I'm afraid I have bad news. The news report right after the one Vor Viralas just showed us was about an alien conveyance that was discovered trying to hide in orbit. It destroyed nine of our conveyances, but then plunged to its destruction on the Tenth Moon."

Sanchit noticed that Toq's midleg hands clenched into a ball. "Don't be so sure that Toq's conveyance was destroyed, Altran." To Toq, Sanchit said, "The Tenth

Moon is where several of our fellow seps hide, in part because the planet has a strong magnetic field that makes scanning difficult."

Toq's appendage bobbed up and down. "And your news reporters have already proven themselves to be honorless liars, so I will choose to believe that Captain Klag is alive until I see proof of his death. And if he *is* dead"—now his appendage swiveled in the direction of Kallo and the others—"then at least he took the enemy with him."

Viralas's midlegs waved in annoyance. "They've linked us to you, and you've gone and destroyed over a dozen conveyances, not to mention the people *inside* the government sphere. Some of those were civilians, and you just *killed* them!"

"They are our enemy."

Sanchit was not sure if she was impressed or depressed with the simplicity of Toq's attitude.

"This changes *everything*," Viralas said.

"What, precisely, does it change?" Toq asked.

Rather than answer the question, Viralas posed one of his own: "Why did you come here, alien?"

Toq moved toward Viralas. Several of his fellow Klingons—who, Sanchit had noticed, had stayed quiet, letting Toq speak for him—moved forward with him. One or two of them unsheathed their weapons.

"You *dare* to ask us that, Elabrej? One of *your* vessels fired on the *Kravokh*. Then *your* vessels engaged the *Kravokh* when they came to investigate, destroyed it, and took its surviving crew prisoner. We were attempting to free them from their captivity. Now we learn that our captain and the rest of our crew may be dead, and you have the temerity to ask me *why we came here?*" Toq's voice increased in volume with each word.

Letting out a huge puff of air, Viralas said, "You do not understand."

"Then enlighten me." Now Toq folded his midlegs in front of him. His fellows kept their weapons out.

"For many *ungrets* we have tried to convince the government that their way of ruling the hegemony was destroying our people. More hegemons live in poverty now than at any time in the history of our nation. Children are starving to death, people cannot get *food* regularly, medical benefits that are freely available to any stratad individual are unavailable to those non-strata who actually *need* it. Work has become more and more scarce as the wealth of our people is concentrated into the highest stratas—less than one percent of our population. Our natural resources dwindle with every passing *ungret,* and our leaders do *nothing.*" Viralas's midlegs indicated the other seps gathered in the sphere. "We all gathered together because we have said, 'Enough.' We have said that the oligarchs can no longer treat us in this manner and expect the hegemony to continue. And now, when we have finally started to make some inroads, along come you—you—you *creatures* to give the oligarchs something with which to discredit us, and by which they can continue the abuses that led to our rise in the first place."

His speech finished, silence descended on the sphere. Toq's midlegs were still folded in front of him.

Then, at last, the Klingon spoke. "Our people were

once as you. We had stripped our world of many of its resources, and so we expanded outward. For many turns, we conquered everything in our path, giving little thought to anything besides our desire to bring more planets into our empire, because without them, our people would starve. We were so focused on conquest that we did not realize what we were doing to ourselves."

Toq had been pacing among the various separatists, and Sanchit couldn't help but be impressed with his oratory. She found herself prompting him. "Something changed. You said you were once as us—so something must have changed."

Again, Toq's appendage bobbed up and down. "One of our moons, the source of much of our power generation, was destroyed. We found ourselves weakened. Help came from our greatest enemy. Even though they had been our foe for many turns, they offered the hand of friendship. In the decades that followed, we flourished. No one in our empire starves now. We are warriors—we do take glory in battle—but we do not do so by sacrificing our own people."

Bantrak waved his left midleg. "That was a very pretty speech, alien, but it does not help us."

"Tell me," Toq said, "how have you done battle against your enemy?"

"What do you mean?" Viralas asked.

"What have you done to effect these changes you so desire among your people?"

Viralas's hindlegs waved slightly. "We are responsible for a variety of publications that have spoken out against the oligarchs. Occasionally, we are able to intrude upon the government broadcasts with ones of our own that speak out against the oligarchs. We—"

Toq was making some kind of noise through his mouth, as were many other Klingons. "This is all you do?"

"That is what *we* do—those of us you see here." Viralas's hindlegs waved more frantically now.

Sanchit said, "We also raid medical supply houses in order to provide for those who need it. We've stolen money from members of the Vor strata and given it to non-stratas. And we've broken into jails and released political prisoners. Those operations are generally *not* performed by us—we have a group headquartered on the Tenth Moon for the more physical aspects of our movement."

For the first time since arriving at Viralas's sphere, Kallo spoke. "You said the Tenth Moon was where the *Gorkon* crashed."

Assuming that "the *Gorkon*" referred to the alien conveyance, Sanchit said, "Yes."

"Then—if you have people there—you can contact that moon." Her appendage swiveled toward Toq. "We can find out if the captain is alive!"

Bantrak let out a puff of air. "I'm afraid not. Since the war with your people started, communications have become even more tightly secured. It is impossible to get a signal there."

"A pity," Altran added. "If we could have consulted them, we might have had a better plan for attacking the government sphere to release the prisoners."

"What was your plan?" Toq asked.

Viralas waved his forelegs dismissively. "Does it matter?"

"Yes, *alien*, it does. It is obvious that, as noble as your cause may be, you are *not* warriors, and you were unwise to try to act like you were." With one of his midlegs, Toq indicated the dozens of Klingons standing behind him. "We *are* warriors. All the Klingons standing before you live for the sole purpose of giving their lives in battle to serve the empire. One of the many species we have encountered are called humans, and they have a saying: 'The enemy of my enemy is my friend.'" His appendage swiveled around the sphere. "We share a common enemy—we share a common goal." Then the appendage settled in the direction of Viralas. "You say we have changed everything, and we have—but it is not in the way you think. If your enemy wishes you destroyed, then that enemy would use *any* means to eliminate you. Had we not come along, they would have found something else. But only a fool worries about what might have been, and I do not believe that you are fools. Let us take on our common enemy together—and we can start by examining your plan to free our fellow Klingons, and see how we can improve on it."

Viralas let out a puff of air. "You talk very prettily for so repugnant a creature, alien, but what possible reason do we have to agree to this? The sanctuary of my sphere is all that stands between you and death at the hands of the military."

"Perhaps I was wrong." Toq moved closer to Viralas again. "Perhaps you *are* a fool."

Sanchit realized that she needed to contribute. "Vor Viralas, I believe that Toq is correct. We are not fighters, and we—"

"Freeing these hideous creatures was *your* idea, Imparter," Bantrak said testily, "and it has only served to make matters worse."

Altran said, "Yes, but Toq was right. If it wasn't that, it would've been something else. Even if we hadn't been seen together, do you really think Vor Jorg would have passed up the opportunity to blame us for the alien invasion?"

"Besides which," Jammit added, "the damage has already been done. They are here, and I saw them in action. They have skills that put even our military to shame, and they are *offering* to help us. The seps on the Tenth Moon are unavailable to us, so let us make use of what we have."

Gansett's right foreleg and midleg waved in revulsion. "We cannot work with *these* things! They're hideous."

Again, Toq's mouth widened. "I was thinking the same of you."

That made Gansett's legs wave faster.

Viralas stood very still for almost a full *engret.* Finally: "Very well. Let us see what we can accomplish."

Sanchit let out a long puff of air in relief. The body language of the Klingons changed as well, though Sanchit was not sure how to interpret it.

I hope it's in a way that bodes well for us, because I fear that this movement may soon be a forgotten dream of an even more brutal hegemony. . . .

*   *   *

"You will no longer be part of the House of Varnak."

Eral's father made the pronouncement in the sitting room of the House Varnak estates, the last time she would ever see this room. He crossed his wrists in front of his face and clenched his fists.

"E—Eral?"

Wol, as Eral, daughter of B'Etakk, now called herself, stood over the body of the soldier she'd stabbed in the back with her mek'leth on San-Tarah, not realizing until too late that he had her eyes, had her crest, and was the same age as the son she'd been forced to abandon.

"I do not care about what's proper—I love you, Eral, and I want to be with you always."

Kylor said those words as he took her into his arms. She knew that it was foolish, knew that Kylor was not a worthy match for a daughter of the House of Varnak, but all she cared about when she was with him was being with him.

"You will run faster, you filthy petaQ, or you will die at the end of my blade!"

QaS DevwI' Skragg drove her hard during her training on Ty'Gokor, but she came out of it a good soldier, finding a fulfillment as Wol that she never expected to find when she was denied the ability to remain as Eral.

"The child is not mine!"

Eral could not believe that Vranx had the gall to be surprised by this. She had never taken him to her bed, not having the stomachs for it. Did he think her to have conceived by parthenogenesis?

"Did you hear? Martok's back in the chancellor's chair. They took care of Morjod on Boreth."

Wol pretended not to be moved by her fellow bekk's *words, but she knew that the House of Varnak had supported Morjod in his attempt to remove Martok from the leadership of the High Council. She soon learned that House Varnak was dissolved, and wondered if she truly was the only member of the once-noble House left alive—a bitter irony.*

"I don't care what Krantor says, we have to attack the depot at dawn, not the hill at midday."

With those words, Wol officially disobeyed her commander in battle; the rest of the troops were with her, recognizing Krantor's ineptitude, and the following day, their battle against Dominion forces was won. Best of all, Krantor died, and her insubordination died with him, since the other warriors stood by her.

"Good-bye."

Even as Eral turned to leave her home for the last time, surrounded by all her family members—including the cousin who would raise her only son—she noticed that one person broke the circle, one person did not cross her wrists: Mother. B'Etakk instead whispered a farewell to her daughter, whom she would never see again.

"Don't think I'm doing you a favor here. You'll have to earn the title of Leader, and if I think you haven't, you'll be sent to the three hundredth without a moment's hesitation."

QaS DevwI' Vok's words echoed in Wol's ears, but they did not concern her, as the threat in his words was overwhelmed by the pride she felt in being promoted to leader, and of one of the squads in First Company!

"And then—and then—the petaQ fell on top of my tik'leth!"

*Wol was more drunk than she'd been since the early days
of her discommendation, in those dark days before she realized that the Defense Force was an option. But this time she
was drunk in the company of her troops. Her troops. The
fifteenth was hers, and tonight she brought them back together.*

"But it's all a lie, isn't it?"

What?

"You're not a leader."

Father, what are you doing here?

"You're just a fool of a girl, who was too stupid to mate
with Vranx like you were supposed to."

You're dead, Father!

"Instead, you let your girlish passions lure you into the
arms of that toDSaH Kylor."

Stop it, Father.

"Now Kylor's dead, I'm dead, your mother's dead, and
your son is dead—at your own hand!"

Stop it, Father!

"You're a failure, Eral—or Wol, or whatever name
you've taken on."

STOP IT, FATHER!

"Interesting."

Something pressed against Wol's chest and legs, preventing her from sitting up as her eyes shot open. Only
when she relaxed in response to that sensation did she
realize that she was lying down—and that she was now
awake. *Dreaming—I was dreaming. . . .*

The room she was in was, of course, spherical—
rounded walls curved upward from the floor, uniting at
the top, providing neither walls nor a ceiling—and

filled with all manner of equipment that Wol couldn't begin to recognize.

Wol lay in the center of the room. The restraints allowed her to swivel her head—they held only her torso, thighs, and ankles down—so she was able to see the two Elabrej in the room with her. One was armed and decorated in the same manner as those who fired on them in the complex—Wol assumed him to be a soldier of some sort.

The other was the one who had said, "Interesting." He—Wol had no way to distinguish gender among the Elabrej, if indeed they even *had* genders, but she defaulted to the male until proven otherwise—was not decorated with the markings, and he had a device of some sort in three of his ten-fingered hands.

"I actually understood the alien's words when she awakened. 'Stop it, Father.' I wonder what that means in this context. Obviously, my hypothesis was correct in that these creatures have something on this protective covering they wear that enables their words to be translated in both directions. It's amazing technology."

Wol assumed he was dictating notes, since she couldn't imagine that his words were for the benefit of either her or the soldier. *And he has deduced the translator capability of our wrist communicators. Obviously he is a scientist of some kind.*

She tried to think back on what happened. The last thing she remembered clearly was leading the attack into the Elabrej stronghold. She remembered Trant dying in the initial attack—then nothing. *What happened to us?* Then, mentally rebuking herself, she thought, *It's obvious what happened to us—we failed. They took us—however many of us survived—prisoner along with the* Kravokh *crew.*

"I have to say," the scientist droned on, "I've been eagerly awaiting the opportunity to talk to these creatures, but I never imagined I'd actually get the chance."

Wol decided to speak. "I have nothing to say to you, Elabrej."

The scientist dropped one of his devices, apparently surprised. He bent over to pick it up with one of his middle hands, his upper hands resting on the floor. Then he stood upright on those upper hands and turned around. "So you can understand me? You have language concepts?"

"Do not turn your back on me, Elabrej! I am a Klingon warrior, and I am here to tell you that I will do everything in my power to escape you—any way I can."

Without turning back around, the alien said, " 'Turn your back on me'? I'm afraid I don't understand. What does that—?" Then four of his arms vibrated. "Oh, of course! You can only see in a limited direction—in the small area on one side of your brain pouch. So naturally, you would place some cultural significance on someone who was not directly in your line of vision. Fascinating, most fascinating."

Images started to come back to Wol. Fighting the Elabrej. Troops dropping all around her. Many Elabrej dropping, but there were so many *more* of them.

Goran killed the most, of course. Twice the size of any Klingon, and three times the size of these headless beings, he tore through them with his hands and his ancient disruptor.

But eventually, even he was brought down. The Elabrej weapons didn't kill him, she remembered that much at least.

And she remembered something else. "Take them alive," someone had said. "Take the rest of them alive."

She could not remember if any of the fifteenth—besides Trant—had died. *If they did, at least they are in Sto-Vo-Kor instead of being poked and prodded by this monster.*

"Tell me, creature—do lower beings like you have a name?"

Wol said nothing. She had said everything she intended to say to the alien scientist. Instead, she tested her bonds.

"It is as I suspected. These are just simple animal creatures, no doubt the slaves for a properly evolved species."

Controlling her reaction, Wol instead continued to strain at her bonds. *Let this bloodworm believe that we are weak. I will take pleasure in cutting him open to show him the error of his ways.*

"It's obviously something on the armor that does it. We'll sedate her and then remove the armor so we can study her more closely." As he spoke, the scientist moved closer to her and used his upper arms to place something on her neck. She tried to angle her head away from him, but the bonds held her too tight. More and more she struggled, but the room started to grow hazy and indistinct, and the words that came out of the scientist's mouth were so much gibberish, and her thoughts started to fragment. . . .

Images—her father rebuking her in the House Varnak estate's sitting room—Goran killing several Elabrej—Kylor kissing her in the woods behind the estate—Skragg training her on Ty'Gokor—her son dead at her feet by her own hands in the village of Val-Goral—B'Oraq treating her wounds in the medical bay—G'joth discussing his abortive writing projects in the mess hall—Krevor dying at the hands of the Children of San-Tarah—Trant's arm being blown off on Elabrej—Krantor giving orders that would get them all killed on Mempa IX—Vok telling her she was leader of the fifteenth on the *Gorkon*—

Then she was awake again. She had no idea how much time had passed, but her uniform had been removed, and the straps adjusted so that they would restrain her naked body. Again, she strained against those bonds, shaking her head back and forth—

—then she stopped, noticing something amiss.

It was impossible to be sure, but Wol was fairly certain that this alien *petaQ* shaved off her hair!

The *petaQ* in question continued to make observations, but with her communicator—and everything else—removed, Wol couldn't understand a word he said. Instead, she continued to push against her bonds, even though they cut into her flesh, and also looked more closely at her surroundings. She noticed that the items in the room were all focused on the center, with nothing up against the walls. Thinking back, she remembered that the other rooms were decorated like that as well.

Her struggles were fruitless. Whatever the bonds were made of, it was something she could not rend, especially not with bare skin. It appeared to be flexible to a point, probably to allow for the different sizes and shapes of people it was used to restrain. Finally, she stopped struggling and relaxed.

The bonds, which had been conforming to her shape, did not snap back to tighten against her body. *They've slackened.*

Wol grinned. No doubt the straps were designed for the smaller Elabrej. Holding a much larger Klingon was obviously straining their tensile strength.

Eventually, the scientist finished his endless droning, and then touched a control on one of the devices he was holding.

Pain sliced through every cell in Wol's body. A scream ripped from her throat as agonizing pain that seemed to come from no particular source tore through her.

Just as quickly, the pain stopped, though Wol thought she would feel its aftereffects for some time.

While she lay on the table trying to keep herself conscious, the scientist started to babble again. Then he touched another stud.

As bad as the pain was the first time, it was several orders of magnitude worse the second. Wol felt as if she was being torn limb from limb, muscle from muscle, cell by cell. It was as if every atom that comprised her form was being individually stabbed with a rusty blade and then twisted.

Then, again, it stopped, prompting the scientist to drone on some more.

Wol's breathing was heavy and labored, and she could barely focus her thoughts, but she knew that the restraints were still slackened.

The alien scientist walked over to her and moved to once again place the sedative on her neck.

Wol bit his hand.

Screaming, the scientist moved quickly away from her, cradling his bitten hand with one of the other ones. He summoned the soldier over and pointed at Wol with a third hand, giving some kind of instruction.

As soon as the soldier was close enough, Wol slipped her right leg out from under the strap and kicked the soldier at center mass. She had no idea where the Elabrej were vulnerable physically, but she assumed a hard enough kick would hurt.

In that, she was correct. The soldier stumbled backward for a moment, then lunged for her.

This time she was able to slip her arm out and grab the weapon out of the creature's surprised hands. *At least, I think he's surprised. Damn difficult to read a species with no faces. . . .*

Wol saw that the weapon had a single button on it, though it was unclear which end it fired from. Holding it up so that one end faced the soldier and the other whatever was behind her, she pushed the button.

The energy beam left the soldier dead a moment later by his own weapon.

She then turned the weapon on the alien scientist. Unlike the soldier, the scientist screamed as he died. The screams didn't last as long as Wol's did when he tried his little pain test on her, but Wol took heart in the fact that she lasted longer than he did. Her only regret was that she could only kill him the once.

I have to move quickly, she thought, *before someone notices when the soldier doesn't check in or the scientist doesn't make his report on time.* She wriggled out of the restraints and moved toward the door, naked, hairless, and unarmed but for the Elabrej weapon.

It will have to be enough.

After all, she still had a mission to fulfill. And if she couldn't get the prisoners out, she now at least had the means to give them an honorable death. . . .

CHAPTER EIGHT

Leader Kylag of the one-seventy-first was about ready to put his *d'k tahg* through *Bekk* Goz's throat. Goz was a good warrior, a fine soldier, and the very first person you'd want covering your back, but he simply would never shut up. And right now, as they worked their way through the humid grasslands of this forsaken moon in the middle of hostile territory, Goz would *not* shut up.

Kylag and Goz had joined up together during the war, fighting on the *Paklor* and then later the *Kreltek*. On the latter ship, Kylag was promoted to leader, and he always made sure to keep Goz in his squad. After San-Tarah, they came over to the *Gorkon*, a move that disheartened both of them.

But Kylag had kept his dismay to himself. Goz never kept anything to himself.

"I'm telling you, Kylag, they *know*."

"If they knew," Kylag said for the dozenth time,

"we would all be dead. Lokor may serve an honorless slime devil, but he is no fool, nor is he to be trifled with."

They were walking ahead of the rest of the detail so their words could not be overheard. Plenty of their fellow transfers—and some of the *Gorkon* crew—felt as they did that Klag was not worthy of his rank and that something should be done about it. Kylag would have preferred not to speak of it at all, but that was a lost cause where Goz was concerned.

"Then why did they put us all in the same company?"

"As I told you the last several times you asked that, for the same reason why officers do anything—to keep themselves busy in order to justify their position. This is no more unusual than when we went to the *Kreltek*. Remember, they bunched all the transfers there, too."

"This *isn't* the same thing!"

Before Kylag could tell Goz to shut up, one of the *bekk*s from the one-seventy-seventh approached. "Leader, we have found some wood that might be useful."

Goz snorted. "As if there could be any usable wood in this sauna."

Kylag glared at Goz, then turned to the *bekk*—whose name, he finally recalled, was Moq. "Good. Have Leaders Agkil, Grumal, and Pu'kor investigate further—the rest of us will stand fast."

"Yes, Leader—and Leader?"

"What?"

Moq hesitated. "I could not help but overhear the

end of your conversation—and I can assure you that the troops are rotated constantly, and not in ways that always make sense. During the campaign at San-Tarah, two decorated troops were transferred from the seventh to the fifteenth for no discernible reason."

With that, Moq moved off to tell the leaders of the one-seventy-second, one-seventy-third, and one-seventy-fourth to gather wood. Kylag chortled. "Perhaps I was wrong—perhaps Lokor *is* a fool. Moving troops *downward* makes no sense."

"*Nothing* on this ship makes sense. Why did we come behind the lines like this, only to be almost destroyed on this moon? We should be with the rest of the fleet engaging the enemy, not hiding in the shadows like a *kuvrek*."

"Because we were ordered to." As Kylag spoke, several troops came to a stop; some of them were walking toward Kylag and Goz. Most were *Kreltek* transfers, and all of them were sympathetic to the concerns of Kylag and others about the command structure of the *Gorkon* and its need to change.

Goz snarled. "Captain Klag was also ordered to conquer San-Tarah. Does he only follow stupid orders?"

One of the troops, *Bekk* Kam of the one-eightieth, said as he approached, "Is there such a thing as an order that *isn't* stupid?"

Several of the soldiers laughed at that.

"This," said Zurlkint, leader of the one-seventy-ninth, "is a bad day to die—and a bad *way* to die."

"We're not going to die here," another soldier said.

Kam said, "I think now would be the time to set our plan in motion. We have K'Nir and the rest of the sec—"

Kylag hissed in annoyance. "Be *silent*, you fool! Now is *not* the time to discuss this!"

"What better time?" Goz asked. "We are away from the ship and among—"

"We are among potential spies for Lokor. I do not wish—"

"You yourself said he was a fool." Goz chuckled. "Besides, if he was unwise enough to put us together—"

I am surrounded by imbeciles. "Then he may be smart enough to put a spy here so we may incriminate ourselves."

"If that's the case," Kam said, "the damage is done."

Kylag found he could not argue that point.

"Either way," Goz said, "I do not believe you are correct, Kam. Now is *not* the time to strike. Yes, we *think* we have the second-shift bridge crew, but we do not have Kurak, and—"

Kam frowned. "Zaloq said Kurak was in."

"No." Goz shook his head. "When Gaj gave me my shot earlier, she told me that she talked to Kurak, but she refused to join us."

"But Zaloq said Kurak hates Klag."

One of the soldiers who had not come over from the *Kreltek* said, "That was a mistake. Trust me, I've served on this garbage scow since it left the shipyard, and I can assure you that Kurak was never going to be interested in something like this. Yes, she hates Klag, but only because she hates *everyone* and everything.

The only thing we can count on from her is contempt."

"Then she can die with the rest of them," Zurlkint said.

Goz laughed. "I thought today was a *bad* day to die."

Even as others laughed at Goz's words, Tarmeth, another of Kylag's troops of the one-seventy-first, said, "Are we sure this is wise?"

Kylag, having surrendered to the inevitability that this was going to be discussed, asked, "What do you mean?"

"We keep saying that Klag's actions at San-Tarah were dishonorable—but Chancellor Martok gave those actions his blessing."

"So?" Goz practically sneered the word. "Some highborn *toDSaH* does something despicable and some other highborn *toDSaH* gives it credence. What of it?"

"Martok is no 'highborn *toDSaH*,' " Kam said defensively. "He is a commoner like us."

"Don't be absurd."

"No," Zurlkint said, "he's right. Martok was born in the Ketha Lowlands. He was a soldier like us, and he rose to power—"

"Where he became a politician." Goz spit onto the ground. "Where he was born is irrelevant—the House of Martok is a noble House like any other. That makes him as despicable as the rest of them."

Another soldier said, "Goz is right. Martok is highborn in all but birth."

Tarmeth growled. "You are truly a fool. You cannot

be highborn if you were not born to it—that's what the word *means*."

While Kylag was garnering no small amusement from the discussion, it was a sidetrack. "If we're going to discuss supplanting Klag, let us discuss it, not semantic minutiae about the chancellor. We need to—"

Kylag cut himself off when he heard the sounds of battle.

All the other warriors turned in the direction—the same direction that the one-seventy-second, one-seventy-third, and one-seventy-fourth had gone only minutes earlier.

"Warriors, to arms!" Kylag cried as he unholstered his disruptor and ran in the direction of the battle.

For the moment, at least, the problems with Klag were set aside. Whatever Kylag's opinion of his commanding officer, he was still a soldier of the empire, and he would not ignore the call of battle, nor would he allow his fellow warriors to face a foe alone.

Plowing through the tall grass, Kylag led the remaining troops toward the battle. Unfamiliar scents permeated the air, so much so that Kylag could barely make out his fellow Klingons, much less differentiate among the others. He doubted he could tell the difference between the flora and the fauna on this world, much less different species within those categories.

When he came in sight of the fifteen warriors he'd sent to gather wood, he found them fighting against the strangest creatures Kylag had ever seen.

Many different species served as *jeghpu'wI'* within the Klingon Empire, and Kylag had encountered several of them. Indeed, a number of them served in menial positions aboard the *Gorkon*. But not even the many-tentacled, multiple-eyestalked Phebens were as peculiar-looking as the beings who now did battle with the warriors of the *Gorkon*.

They had six legs, distributed evenly about their bodies, and—based on the way they were leaping around—could stand on any of them, giving them phenomenal agility. They were dodging disruptor blasts with appalling ease, as if they had eyes in the backs of their heads.

Or rather, the backs of their bodies, for that was what shocked Kylag most of all: These beings had no heads.

Trying to keep his stomachs from regurgitating the *jInjoq* bread he'd had that morning, Kylag yelled, "Fire!"

Disruptor fire sizzled through the air, combined with energy discharges from the tube-shaped weapons the Elabrej—for Kylag assumed these to be the beings against whom the empire was now apparently at war.

Blood roared in Kylag's veins. *This is what we should be doing—fighting the enemy, not skulking behind our cloak or foraging for supplies. Klag is a fool for leading us to this.*

"Stop! In Doane's name, *stop!*"

Kylag whirled around at the voice, which did not belong to any Klingon. He saw one of the Elabrej, whose weapon was stowed in a pouch on his person. His upper legs were vibrating so quickly that watching it made the *jInjoq* bread start to burble up again.

"We surrender," the Elabrej cried. "Separatists, *lay down your arms!* These creatures are *not* our enemy!"

Sure enough, most of the thirty or so Elabrej who had attacked them stopped fighting—at least, those still alive, as three were dead when Kylag arrived, and he and the remaining warriors had killed five more.

"Cease fighting." Kylag looked right at the apparent leader of these Elabrej. "For now. Who are you?"

"My name is Jeyri. We are the strong forelegs of the separatists. You must be the aliens who are making war on our government."

"We are Klingon warriors, and you are our enemy. Give me one reason why I should not order these soldiers to cut you down where you stand."

"Because," Jeyri said, "we are *not* your enemy. We have dedicated ourselves to the cause of overthrowing the very government who ordered your conveyance destroyed and who now fight you in the skies."

"Leader," Goz said, "three of our warriors are dead."

"And they died well," Kylag snapped, refusing to rise to the bait Goz was dangling. *This*, he thought quickly, *is over my head. If I do not report this immediately to the QaS DevwI', I will only be leader of the waste-extraction details. Better to follow procedure, and keep my position secure for when we finally do remove Klag.* He activated his communicator. "Kylag to Grotek."

"*Grotek.*"

"*QaS DevwI'*, we have encountered a group of natives who claim to be rebels against the Elabrej government. They have surrendered to us, and offered themselves as allies to our fight."

"Have they, now? Bring them back to the Gorkon, *Leader."*

"Yes, sir."

"And Leader? Well done."

"Thank you, QaS DevwI'*."* Kylag closed the communication and smiled. *Good—if Grotek thinks me a good and loyal soldier, it can only help.*

Kylag looked around to see that Leader Agkil was among the dead, as were two *bekks*, neither from his own squad. He knelt down and pried Agkil's eyes open. The two *bekks'* squad leaders did likewise to them.

Then, as one, the surviving warriors all screamed to the heavens, warning the Black Fleet that three more warriors were on their way across the River of Blood to *Sto-Vo-Kor.*

Leskit entered the main engineering section of the *Gorkon* to a scene of absolute chaos. Usually the place was dead quiet—nobody dared speak out of turn for fear of incurring Kurak's wrath. Often, the only voice that could be heard was that of the chief engineer, usually ripping into one of her subordinates—or, as she generally put it, one of her inferiors—for doing something incredibly stupid. As far as Kurak was concerned, that applied to any activity they performed, starting with breathing.

Of late, Kurak's mode of operation had changed. She was generally too drunk and/or too hungover to keep up a constant stream of yelling, so she saved it for several concentrated outbursts throughout the shift. So far, she hadn't killed any of her engineers, but Leskit assumed that it was only a matter of time.

Now, however, a wall of sound assaulted Leskit's ears as he entered engineering. The place was a teeming mass of activity: *bekks* dashing from place to place; ensigns bellowing out readouts from their consoles to lieutenants who then claimed that that wasn't high enough or fast enough or efficient enough; other lieutenants arguing over which method to employ.

In a corner, sitting staring at a padd, was Kurak.

"How unusual," Leskit said.

Kurak looked up at him. Her eyes were bloodshot, and she was as pale as a Borg. "What is unusual, Leskit?"

"Usually you're the only one talking in this area— often at a volume sufficient to shatter glass. Now you're the only one quiet."

"I'm adapting." Kurak made no effort to hide the bitterness in her voice.

"So I've heard." Leskit took a seat on the table perpendicular to Kurak, looking down at her over his left shoulder. "The captain asked me to get a report on your progress."

She looked up at him. "We're progressing. Tell Klag that the speed at which I accomplish the goal he has set for me will depend entirely upon how often he insists on interrupting me needlessly."

Laughing, Leskit said, "I will tell him those very words."

"Good." Kurak looked down at her padd again. "Now go away and let me work."

Leskit, however, did not move. "I didn't come to your cabin last night."

Kurak did not look up. "I noticed. It was the most pleasant night I've had in months."

"Really? If you were so miserable during my previous visits, why did you not kick me out?"

"Would you have gone?"

"Yes," Leskit said honestly. "If you ever once told me with conviction that you wanted me to leave your cabin, I would have disappeared faster than an Organian. But you never asked me to."

"I asked you to every night."

Grinning, Leskit said, "But not with conviction."

Now, finally, Kurak looked back up at him. "You can gauge my conviction, can you?"

"My dear, I can read you as clearly as the sensor readings on my helm console. Ever since your enforced enrollment in the Defense Force at the start of the war, you have been bound and determined to make the absolute worst of it."

She looked back down at her padd. "Leskit, I don't have time—"

Leskit snatched the padd out of her hand. "You'll make the time, Kurak. I've been propping you up for two months now."

"Don't be absurd, and give me my padd back."

"Not until I'm through, and I'm not at all absurd." Then he chuckled. "Actually, I'm absurd fairly often, but not about this. Klag would have put you to death a month ago if not for me getting you out of your cabin every morning. So you will listen to me now when I tell you that I know why you haven't turned me away."

"Oh really?" Kurak asked with a sneer.

"Yes, really. You see, Kurak, even though you insist on trying to make the worst of it, there is a part of you—a small part, but it *is* there, I see it at least once a night when we share a bunk—that knows that making the worst of it is incredibly stupid." Leskit grinned, fingering the neckbones. "You are many things, Kurak, but stupid is not one of them. Why do this to yourself? Why do everything you can to irritate everyone around you? Why risk your life and your well-being just for the sake of being unhappy?"

"Perhaps I prefer unhappiness."

"Nobody prefers unhappiness, Kurak—they simply take refuge in it because they don't believe happiness is possible."

"You know from where I derived happiness? Wind boat riding. But the Defense Force took even *that* from me."

"The Defense Force doesn't take anything, Kurak. It simply is. The only thing that matters is what you bring to it." He slid off the table and handed Kurak her padd back. "I will see you tonight."

Taking the proffered padd, Kurak said, "Unless I kick you out of my cabin—*with* conviction this time."

Grinning, Leskit said, "We'll see, won't we? But I'm willing to bet all the neckbones I'm wearing against all the *warnog* you haven't gotten around to drinking yet that you won't."

With that, Leskit turned and left engineering in order to give his report to the captain.

*　　*　　*

223

QaS DevwI' Grotek stood at the top of the hill that was closest to where the foraging detail had gone. Lokor stood next to him, his massive arms folded over his equally massive chest. Grotek was a combat veteran of several decades' standing. He'd faced Romulans, Kinshaya, Tholians, Jem'Hadar, Cardassians, Breen, and more in his time. He didn't intimidate easily—but Lokor standing with his arms folded, his hard face framed by his waist-length, intricately braided black hair, was a sight that always made Grotek grateful that the security chief was on *his* side.

"You heard what Moq transmitted," the *QaS DevwI'* said. "They're definitely mutineers—and they've corrupted others."

"Yes, but we don't know all of them yet." Lokor bared his teeth, which only served to make him look more intimidating. "Besides, they have Elabrej prisoners, and the captain will wish to have words with them."

"No doubt. Still, they named K'Nir and Gaj and—"

Lokor unfolded his arms and stared at Grotek. "Do not be a fool, Grotek—or do you *truly* believe that I would allow someone to command the second shift on the bridge who harbored mutinous thoughts?"

Grotek frowned—then smiled as realization dawned. The *QaS DevwI'* knew that Lokor had many on board who served as his eyes and ears, and thinking about it, was not at all surprised to learn that K'Nir was one of them.

"As for Gaj, B'Oraq can deal with her. No, I'm more concerned with who else is part of this little conspiracy.

Let Kylag bring in his prisoners and go about their business. Goz as well—it's Tarmeth who I believe I will need to have a chat with later tonight."

"An entertaining chat I'm sure it will be," Grotek said with a grin. "I will tell Vok to call off his dogs for the time being, then."

"Do so now," Lokor said. "I will deal with Kylag's prize myself."

Nodding, Grotek moved back down the hill toward the airlock that would provide access to the *Gorkon's* interior. He hoped that whatever Lokor had planned for the mutineers, he put it into action soon. On the one hand, Grotek was flattered that Lokor trusted him enough to put the honorless cowards in his unit for "safekeeping." On the other hand, he preferred to have troops in his company whom he himself could trust. He looked forward to the day, soon, when Kylag, Goz, and their conspirators would be put to death like the Lubbockian slime devils they were, and Grotek could go back to leading honorable troops into battle.

He found Vok in the *QaS DevwI'*'s office, a cramped room on deck fourteen. Just as Grotek entered, he saw Vok putting out a large candle with his *d'k tahg*. None of the other eighteen *QaS DevwI'* were present; Klaris, of course, was back on the Elabrej's homeworld, and the remaining seventeen were elsewhere on the ship or guarding the perimeter.

"A remembrance?" Grotek asked.

Vok looked up. The *QaS DevwI'* of First Company generally carried a jovial air, but now his eyes seemed heavy, his mouth curled downward for once. "After a fashion. I fear that the fifteenth is lost to us. Without the *Gorkon* to extract them . . ."

Grotek frowned. "I thought it was Second Company who went on that mission."

"They did. But the fifteenth went as well, for—for reasons I cannot explain." Vok twirled his *d'k tahg* absently. "Wol is the best leader in my company—even better than Morr. She has good instincts, a warrior's strength and courage, and the troops respond to her. I thought she'd be a *QaS DevwI'* by the time we finished in the Kavrot Sector. Instead, it seems she is dying here."

Grotek walked over to Vok. "Warriors die all the time, Vok. I don't see why you're making a fuss over this one."

A chuckle, and the real Vok started to poke through the melancholy. "To be honest, Grotek, I do not, either. But there is something about Wol, something—special. The fifteenth performed brilliantly at San-Tarah. Her loss will be keenly felt."

"If you say so." Grotek was unconvinced. Warriors were, after all, quite common within the empire. They always died, and they were always replaced. It was the way of things, and Grotek saw no need to get overly sentimental about one particular leader. "In any case, Kylag is returning with some Elabrej prisoners. For that reason—and others—Lokor has ordered them to be left alone for the time being."

Now anger clouded Vok's round face. "Lokor's plans sometimes are too clever for their own good. There is much to be said for simply carving out the diseased portion of the body rather than waiting to see what other parts it has infected."

Grotek snorted. "You want to tell him that?"

The grin that Vok gave in reply to that reassured Grotek that the melancholy was definitely a temporary condition. "When I die, it will be in battle against the empire's enemies, Grotek, not at the hands of one of Lokor's assassins."

CHAPTER NINE

The aircar—the Elabrej called it a "conveyance"—brought Toq, Kallo, Klaris, and the remaining troops to the shoreline. Sanchit herself was piloting the conveyance, mainly because no one else among the separatists would do it.

"This was your insane notion, Sanchit," Viralas had said. "You may implement it."

To Toq's mind, it was the first sane thing he'd encountered since arriving on this mad planet.

With great reluctance, Viralas was willing to show Toq and Kallo the full schematics for the government sphere. *If we'd had this,* he had thought, *we would have been able to plan the assault better.*

The first thing Toq realized was that the sphere was damn near impenetrable. Sanchit had said that the reason why assaults on the sphere were so rare was because it was so hard to get at it. Their targets, she had said, were generally secondary.

Kallo's comment was that they were tertiary, which seemed to confuse Sanchit. Toq told her Kallo didn't know what she was talking about and silenced her with a look.

Now, Sanchit wished them well, and told them again that they were insane. "I hope this works, Toq, but I am not hopeful."

"It is preferable to your own methods." Toq could not keep the contempt out of his voice. "You pick at the fingers, but do not strike at the heart. A great Klingon poet once said, 'Fortune favors the bold.' You separatists have not been bold."

"Perhaps." Sanchit's middle legs vibrated. "But boldness leads to death."

"*Everything* leads to death. What matters is the path you take to it." Toq smiled. "If a cause is not worth dying for, it is not worth having."

"That same poet?" Sanchit asked.

"No, Kahless. If we survive this day, I will tell you about Kahless."

Sanchit departed with the conveyance, leaving the Klingons standing on a rock outcropping over a calm body of water. Toq took in the smell of salt water, which was a relief after the antiseptic feel all the Elabrej structures had. They did not use wood or stonework for their spheres: it was all metal. In space, Toq understood the need for being enclosed in the firm coldness of metal, but on a planet, Toq found the practice unnatural.

While Klaris checked the area with his hand scanner, Kallo approached Toq and spoke for the first time since they left. "Why did you not rebuke her when I criticized their targets?"

"Because it is unseemly to criticize the methods of those who give you shelter."

"They did *not* give us shelter—they interfered with our battle and called us monsters!"

"By their lights, we are," Toq said. "And our battle was over—they gave us a viable retreat so we could re-group."

Kallo threw up her hands. "If they truly wished to help us—if they truly wished to overthrow their government—they would not limit themselves to petty thievery and publications. And they would aid us in this battle."

"Of course. But our words will not convince them of that. We are alien to them, as they are to us. It is our *actions* that will show them the error of their ways. All that we tell them will be lost in their revulsion for what we are."

Kallo snorted. "They have no reason to be repulsed by *us*. *They* are the monsters, with their headless bodies."

Toq rolled his eyes. *The woman is a genius, but I will kill her if she does not stop being a fool.* "As I said, Ensign, to them, we are the strange ones."

"That's ridiculous."

"No, it is not. Look at it from their perspective."

"Why would I wish to do that?" Kallo sounded genuinely confused.

Finally, Toq gave up. The young man was proud to be a Klingon, and numbered the day that Ambassador

Worf—then a Starfleet lieutenant—found the compound on Carraya where he was raised and took him, and several others, away to live in the empire as one of the greatest of his life. Before Worf came, Carraya was a haven where Klingons and Romulans lived in peace away from "the war," an event whose specifics were never stated, but was spoken of in whispers as a horrible state of affairs to be avoided at all costs. It was Worf who revealed the truth: that Carraya was a prison camp set up after a Romulan attack on the Klingon planet Khitomer. The Klingon prisoners were not allowed to die, but could not return in disgrace to the empire. A Romulan centurion named Tokath—one of the officers on the scene at Khitomer—quit his military post to oversee the prison camp. Against all odds, Klingon and Romulan lived in harmony; Tokath even took a Klingon woman to be his wife, and they had a daughter, Ba'el.

But the Klingons knew nothing of their heritage, of their birthright, of their *stories*—until Worf came and gave that to them. He taught Toq how to hunt, told all of them stories of Kahless, and finally, eventually, was permitted to leave along with all who would go with him. Toq was the first to accept the offer. He came alive for the first time when Worf took him on the hunt, and he had no regrets about leaving Carraya behind him.

However, there were some elements of Klingon life that mystified him—their resistance to proper medical treatment, for one, and Toq was eternally grateful to be serving on the same ship as B'Oraq, who had done more to advance Klingon medicine than anyone in empire history—and one such element was Klingon intolerance for anyone or anything that was not Klingon. He wondered what would happen if any of his crewmates met Ba'el, and how they would react to her pointed ears.

"Sir, I have something else to say." Kallo's statement dragged Toq out of his reverie.

"Yes?"

"While we were—interred at the Elabrej's home, I was able to determine the frequencies that the news reports broadcast on. I have adjusted my hand scanner to jam them, so the Elabrej will not have any visual records of our attack. They will no longer be able to use us for propaganda purposes."

Again, Toq had to resist the urge to strangle the ensign. "Why did you not mention this sooner?"

Looking abashed, Kallo said, "I—"

"Never mind." Toq waved her off. *I'll deal with her more firmly if and when we're back on the* Gorkon. *Right now, we need all the able-bodied warriors we can get—even the irritating ones.*

Klaris called over from a few meters away. "Sir! We have found the entrance! As they predicted, it is sealed."

What had grabbed Toq's attention when he saw the specifications of the government sphere was a tube that extended out to the ocean. Few of the separatists even knew its true purpose—only Sanchit, Bantrak, and Viralas were aware of its history. "It was used during the days before the hegemony was incorporated," Sanchit had said, "when the Elabrej Union was the largest power on the planet. Battles were fought under the sea then."

"My grandsire told me of those days," Bantrak had said. "It was obscene—actually going underwater in conveyances that were held together with rusted bolts."

Viralas had added, "We left behind such barbarity when the Elabrej unified the world."

"Conquered the world, you mean," Sanchit had said.

Toq had been forced to interrupt this reminiscing. "What is that tube?"

"It allowed the military's underwater conveyances ingress and egress to the government sphere."

"Does anyone use them now?"

Viralas's upper legs started vibrating so much that Toq couldn't look at him. "Why would they? The very idea is—"

"Obscene, yes, so you said. Why do you people have such an aversion to water?"

"Are you mad?" All of Viralas's arms vibrated then. "The ocean provides nothing. Its water cannot be drunk, it cannot be breathed, and nothing grows in it. All the ocean provides is death."

Now Toq looked down into the water that he and the others were about to dive into. It was green and brackish. Stepping closer to it, Toq could smell the filth. *No wonder Viralas thought of the ocean as a dead place—they have polluted it so much. . . .*

Klaris walked up to him and Kallo. "Disruptors have been retuned to fire underwater. That sealed tunnel entrance won't stand for long."

"Good. Are the troops prepared?"

"Yes, Commander."

"Then let us waste no more time. There are Klingons imprisoned in the government sphere, and I am loath to leave them there." The Klingons on Carraya were there only in order to spare their families the dishonor of their being captured—which meant a lifetime of those families believing them to be dead. If Toq could spare Captain Wirrk and the others that, he would.

Toq's plan was simplicity itself—dive into the water near the tube, and infiltrate the government sphere from there. Long-abandoned as it was, security there was minimal, and even if they were detected, it would take the military time to investigate—time Toq had no intention of giving them.

Weighed down enough by their armor to counteract the sea's buoyancy, the Klingons were able to sink through the brackish waters. Toq found himself relying more on his own hand scanner than on his eyes, as he could barely see the nose in front of his face in the slime-caked depths. Using the solid rock of the coastline as their guide, he and the others pushed their way downward. Toq found he had to navigate by touch more than sight, as he could barely see the faceted rock out of which, a dozen meters down, the access tube had been carved.

Based on the specifications he'd seen, combined with his own knowledge of the considerable Klingon capacity to hold one's breath, Toq had faith that they would reach the entrance before any of them suffered any of the effects of oxygen deprivation or carbon-dioxide buildup. Sanchit had also assured him that there were no natural predators in the water. Swimming in this polluted filth, Toq understood why: Nothing living could survive, much less thrive, in this. This entire planet set Toq's hunter's instincts on edge as a violation of the natural order of things. He knew that the empire had its moments of ecological irresponsibility in its history—most spectacularly, the operation on Praxis that led to that moon's destruction—but nothing on this scale. Klingons were too good at hunting to ever upset the balance that allowed the hunt to continue.

However, the Elabrej had not learned that lesson, to the point that Toq was starting to come around to their phobia of the sea. So entrenched was the pollution in the waters through which they swam that the swimming itself was slower going, and required far more effort for far less reward than anticipated. Movements that should have brought Toq down at least two meters only advanced him one.

Spots formed in front of Toq's eyes as the carbon dioxide accumulated in his cells. His arms felt like lead as they pinwheeled through the thick liquid. His hand scanner told him that the tube entrance was still several meters away.

I will not give in to this. I am a Klingon warrior, and I will not die in the filthy sea of an alien planet!

Then, just as the spots threatened to overcome his vision completely, he caught site of the entrance. Like every other piece of architecture on this planet, the entrance was circular, in this case a perfectly round piece of metal wedged in the midst of the stone. It had no features, no handles, no controls, nothing.

So leaden did Toq's body feel that he did not trust himself to swivel his head to ascertain who of the others had actually made it. Instead, he focused all of his dwindling energy on pulling his disruptor out of its holster, gripping it in his right hand, and firing it. He did not want to even waste energy taking aim, figuring the target was large enough.

To his great relief, several other disruptor beams followed his in slicing through the water. A damp smokiness competed with the odors of the garbage in Toq's nose as the weapons fire burned through the muck.

Seconds later, Toq felt himself pulled toward the tube, as the water dutifully obeyed the law of physics that stated that an object moved from an area of greater concentration to an area of lesser concentration. The disruptor fire had blown the covering to the tube apart.

Letting his body go limp, he let the water carry him. As planned, the destruction of the entrance would result in the tube's being flooded. Also as planned, his armored uniform protected him as he was tossed against the curved walls. The onrush of water bounced him all around, only occasionally allowing his head to rise above the water.

Those occasions, however, were enough. The air in the tube was stale and musty and tinged with dust and mold, but it was the sweetest air Toq had ever breathed. Despite his precarious situation, he felt the fatigue drain from his limbs as he was thrown through the tube.

Just another few seconds . . .

Sanchit's words came back to him in the eternally long seconds after being thrust into the tube: "We don't know what they might have done to the tube. Yes, it's supposed to empty into a large hangar area, but for all we know, they sealed it off. They probably sealed off the main entrance as well. Even if you get in the sea entrance, there may be a large wall at the end of the access tube—against which you'll be smashed like so much flotsam."

His head poked out from the water long enough to see that the tube emptied out into a larger room. *That's the hangar, and they* haven't *sealed it!*

With glee, Toq felt himself be dumped into the larger area, which was also circular, but a massive sphere. The water was still flowing in, but not accumulating so much. Toq found himself quickly able to tread water. He caught sight of several troops, and Klaris—no sign of Kallo yet.

"Sound off!" Klaris cried.

Within a few minutes, only one warrior did not respond: Kallo. All the troops were accounted for.

Then a small head burst through the water, gasping loudly for breath: Kallo.

The *QaS DevwI'* turned to Toq. "All present and accounted for, Commander."

Toq grinned. After all that, his entire detail survived. He started to appreciate Klingon arrogance just a bit more.

"Let's move."

Once, Jeyri had been a highly decorated defensor. He swore a vow to defend the hegemony against its enemies. Now, facing the impossibly tall leader of the aliens, with the strange growth where his forelegs should have been, he found himself frightened for the first time in his life.

It wasn't until after he met Vor Viralas and Mal Sanchit that Jeyri had realized that the hegemony's enemies were the people in charge of it. It wasn't until they showed him the parts of the large cities never seen on the news broadcasts, or the economic forecasts done not by those on the oligarchs' payroll but by independent experts whose findings were quickly silenced by the oligarchy, that Jeyri realized that the best way to fulfill his vow was to join the separatists.

Naturally, it was the end of his military career. But the years of training the defensors had given him proved useful. For one thing, it was with the military that he learned of the Tenth Moon and its magnetic field that made it hard to scan—and also impossible to live on. The defense base that had been constructed on the moon had to be abandoned when all the personnel assigned there suffered brain damage from prolonged exposure to the fields.

But the separatists had a physician who was sympathetic to their cause who provided them with an antidote to the exposure. This physician refused to publish her findings, concerned that the government would simply abuse her research.

So Jeyri had set up a base here from which he coordinated the tasks that Vor Viralas or Mal Sanchit or Yer Bantrak or the other separatists needed him and his handpicked team of soldiers to complete.

When he saw that a conveyance crash-landed in

the grasslands, he immediately set out to investigate. If it was the Elabrej military, he and his people would capture as many as possible and interrogate them. If it was the aliens who were now fighting the hegemony, he would learn what he could and pledge to aid them.

He had been taken to their leader, who sat in a strange, squared-off room inside his conveyance. Jeyri found the construction of the aliens' conveyance to be maddening—so many angles and flat surfaces. It violated Jeyri's sense of order, as if whoever built the conveyance threw various flat pieces of metal together and hoped for the best. Jeyri couldn't imagine how anyone could survive in such harsh environs.

The leader, who called himself Captain Klag, stood tall over Jeyri. Near the door to the room, another of the aliens stood; he was named Lieutenant Rodek. The alien who brought him here, Leader Kylag, was nowhere to be found. An alien named Lieutenant Lokor had brought Jeyri here, and then was told by Captain Klag to oversee Jeyri's people.

Jeyri had no idea how it was that he could understand what the aliens said, and vice versa.

"Give me one reason, Jeyri of the Elabrej, why I should not kill you and all your followers for attacking my troops."

Jeyri let out a puff of air. "Your soldier—Leader Kylag—asked the same thing. I will tell you what I told him: We are not your enemy. We are the strong forelegs of the separatist movement that has been trying to bring down the oligarchy that rules the hegemony, and it is my wish that we join forces with you against our common foe."

" 'Strong forelegs'? What does that mean, precisely?"

Since these aliens didn't seem to *have* forelegs, it was, Jeyri thought, a reasonable question. "It means we commit the acts the separatists require of us. We obtain medical supplies for those who need it but cannot afford it, we release political prisoners from their incarceration, we liberate currency from the undeserving Vor strata and give it to needy non-stratad, we—"

"And you do it from this moon?" Captain Klag asked.

Jeyri waved his midlegs in annoyance at being interrupted. "Yes."

"Why do you do these things?"

"I—" Jeyri hesitated. "I am not sure I can convey to you the entire recent history of the Elabrej Hegemony, Captain Klag. Suffice it to say that the oligarchy that rules us is decadent and corrupt. They exploit our people for their gain and give the people nothing in return for their hard work save poverty and sickness. And now they are using the discovery of your people as an excuse to divert more resources to the military and away from the people—and also as a tool to use against our movement."

Captain Klag did not speak for the better part of an *engret*. Then: "What weapons do you employ in your movement?"

"Several dozen small conveyances that are invisible to our scanning technology. They can be seen, but the naked eye is of little use in the vastness of the sky."

The features on Captain Klag's growth changed shape. "That is certainly true."

"We also have several military-issue hand weapons that we use to defend ourselves when it becomes necessary."

Captain Klag folded his midlegs in front of his torso. "Your—conveyances do not have weaponry?"

"No."

"And you do not strike at military targets?"

This question confused Jeyri. "We do not strike targets—if we did that, we might murder some of our fellow hegemons. Our goal is not to kill, but to effect change."

"Change does not come easily, Jeyri, and if you are not willing to make sacrifices, then your entire cause is pointless." Captain Klag went to the other side of the desk in the office. Jeyri found it impossible to determine what the alien was thinking, as his body language was impenetrable. His legs barely ever moved. "You say your object is to remove your government? Then you need to *hurt* your government. Helping those whom the government does not help is an honorable task, but it will not accomplish your goal. Your military is fighting a war against us, and they have done significant damage to two of our vessels that we *know* of. As long as we are trapped on this planet, we cannot contact our fleet to see if they are winning or not."

"I wish I could say," Jeyri said truthfully. "Since hostilities with your people began, we have lost all contact with the First World."

"A pity." Captain Klag rested his arms on his desk.

"My point, Jeyri, is that you are fighting a war as well, but you are fighting it very poorly."

Jeyri waved his forelegs in anger. "We have succeeded in *every* mission!"

"Yes, you have won battles—tiny, inconsequential battles! You claim to be warriors, leading the charge against your hegemony, but you have no taste for warfare!"

Revulsed, Jeyri said, "What you suggest would mean possibly killing some of our kind."

"Of course it would—that's what happens in a war. If you do not have the stomachs for that, Jeyri, then I suggest you remain on this moon until you die of old age—weak and infirm—because if you do not do what it truly takes, then you will not win the day. There will be no glory—there will be no victory."

Jeyri was unable to keep the contempt out of his voice. "Do not presume to speak to me of victory, alien."

Captain Klag's growth levered backward, and a strange sound emitted from it. Then he said, "Very amusing, Jeyri. You attack my troops, you then beg me to ally with you, and you speak to *me* of being presumptuous?"

His forelegs waving in contriteness, Jeyri said, "My apologies, Captain Klag, but—"

"But nothing." Captain Klag rose from behind the desk. "I will make you an offer, Jeyri. My—conveyance, as you call it, is under repair and will not be spaceworthy for several days. My mission is to help the Klingon Empire defeat the Elabrej Hegemony. I will work with you separatists in order to accomplish that goal—which will give us both what we want."

Jeyri liked the sound of that—but not the implications. "You wish to use our resources to murder innocent hegemons." He deliberately did not phrase it as a question.

"We will endeavor only to strike military targets, but yes, some innocents may die. Does that sicken you?"

"Yes," Jeyri said honestly.

"It sickens me as well. I prefer to face an honorable foe—battle should be done between warriors. But the universe is not so permissive, and the reality is that your hegemony has attacked my empire. I am sworn to defend my empire, and I will do so by whatever means are necessary. You say your government is corrupt, that your oligarchs are destroying your people. Those same oligarchs have ordered the death of my people, and imprisoned others against their will. If you will not do what is necessary, then I will instruct Lieutenant Lokor to lead the thousand or so troops at my disposal to your headquarters and take what we need in order to accomplish our goal."

For a full *engret*, Jeyri stood in the room with Captain Klag and the ever-silent Lieutenant Rodek. Jeyri had no idea what the other alien's function was—a bodyguard? aide? Regardless, he had not participated in the conversation. From his time as a defensor, Jeyri did not find that unusual. Subordinates only spoke when spoken to, after all.

He waved his midlegs briefly. "Your conveyance did battle with hegemony military, did it not?"

"Yes," Captain Klag said.

"How many?"

"Seven ships altogether."

"Did any of them survive?"

"No."

"And you crash-landed?"

"Yes."

"Yet your conveyance will be spaceworthy in only a few *digrets*." Jeyri let out a puff of air. "And somehow you are able to speak our language and make us understand yours."

Again, Captain Klag's growth's features shifted. "And what conclusion do you draw from all of this?"

Another puff of air escaped from Jeyri, as he wished to Doane that he could figure out what Captain Klag was thinking. But these aliens remained wholly inscrutable. "That I would be a fool if I allowed you to become my enemy when you have offered us the leg of friendship. Especially since you could easily take what you want *without* asking." After a moment, Jeyri allowed himself to say the words he had stopped himself from saying during so many conversations with Mal Sanchit and with Vor Viralas and with Yer Brantak and with his own subordinates. "And especially because your words are correct. We are losing our war, and the only thing to do under those circumstances is to change tactics. I will take you to our redoubt, Captain Klag, and we will fight our mutual enemy together."

"Grotek to Tarmeth."

Tarmeth let out an annoyed sigh and stopped the

playback on his padd. He was curled up in his bunk with the latest episode of *Battlecruiser Vengeance*—or, rather, what he chose to think of as the latest. In truth, the last installment of the serial was produced over a hundred years ago, but Tarmeth had recently obtained the entire run, and he was going through them one night at a time.

Grotek's call interrupted Captain Koth of the *Vengeance* as he was about to repel a Federation boarding party. The episode was produced during the height of tensions between the empire and the Federation, and the party consisted of computer-generated images of what were supposed to be an Andorian (with skin more green than blue and overlong antennae), a Vulcan (with ears far too pointed), a Tellarite (who looked more like a *targ* than the alien in question), a Betazoid (with fully blacked-out eyes instead of the simple dark irises common in that species), a human (with eyes too large and mouths too small), a Trill (with spots covering her entire body), and a Denobulan (with the ridges misplaced). To Tarmeth's mind, the inaccuracy just added to the joy of it. These over-the-top old-fashioned productions were so much more enjoyable than the staid operas and leaden dramas that littered the empire's modern-day performance landscape. Nobody was making anything that was as much *fun* as *Battlecruiser Vengeance*. Goz always teased him about the inane predictability, but that very predictability was the appeal to Tarmeth. After all, everyone knew what Kahless said in the Story of the Promise, but that didn't make hearing the story any less compelling—so what was wrong with the thrill Tarmeth knew was coming as soon as Koth drove back the Federation invaders, strode onto their bridge, and declared, "I am Koth— Koth of the *Vengeance*—and this ship is my prize," as he did in every installment?

Activating the communicator on his wrist, the *bekk* said, "Tarmeth."

"Report to me in Lieutenant Lokor's office, Bekk."

"Yes, sir."

Tarmeth stuffed the padd into his duffel. *I'll have to finish the episode tonight before sleeping.* Goz's incessant harping on the inanity of *Vengeance* had led Tarmeth to skip the evening meal and watch the latest episode in his bunk while the rest of the one-seventy-first ate in the mess hall.

Climbing down the ladder to the deck, Tarmeth wondered what this was about. Usually the squad leaders dealt with the troops, not the *QaS DevwI'*. *Of course, Kylag could be in Lokor's office with Grotek.*

He hoped that it was a simple mission—perhaps bodyguarding duty or covering the armory. Tarmeth was in no rush to die. He didn't believe in an afterlife, thinking it just a bunch of nonsense told to gullible Klingons so they wouldn't mind dying for the empire so much. As far as Tarmeth was concerned, *Sto-Vo-Kor* was as fictional as *Battlecruiser Vengeance*.

Once, he made the mistake of bringing that up over a meal. The resultant argument was another reason why he avoided the mess hall these days. Kylag wanted to know why Tarmeth joined the Defense Force if he was so afraid of dying. Tarmeth replied,

"I'm not *afraid* of dying, I'm just not in a rush to do it, is all."

What he didn't tell them was the real reason why he joined the Defense Force: He was unfit to do anything else. His parents were servants in the House of Pagax—in fact, they were the *only* servants, as the House of Pagax was a minor House indeed. Father had hoped to train Tarmeth to become skilled in cooking or house-work or one of the other menial tasks he and Mother performed for Pagax and his family, but Tarmeth was terrible at all of them. Pagax refused to allow the boy to serve his House. The one thing Tarmeth had always been good at was fighting; he got into many brawls as a youth, primarily due to other children teasing him about his family and who they worked for, and he always won.

So he joined the Defense Force.

Mostly, Tarmeth was happy with his service—as he generally avoided coming anywhere near officers and other highborn *yIntaghpu'*. The *bekk* had little use for the upper class and their tiresome notions of honor; it was why he was willing to go along with Leader Kylag's desires to overthrow the captain. Klag drew over a dozen ships into an absurd conflict just because he wouldn't go back on his word to a bunch of furry aliens. The very notion appalled Tarmeth. As far as he was concerned, the sooner the universe was rid of Klag the better.

He arrived at the office of the chief of security, a small, cramped space occupied by a desk piled with padds and two Klingons. One was the office's occu-

pant, Lokor, who was sitting at the desk. The other was
Grotek, standing near the door. *No Kylag—interesting.*
Behind the desk was a door. Nobody knew what was on
the other side of the door. Many a mess-hall conversation had centered on what it was Lokor kept back
there—everything from torture devices to a harem—
but Tarmeth's considered opinion was that the door
was a fake that didn't actually lead anywhere, and he
kept it there as an intimidation tactic. *One that won't
work on me.*

"*Bekk* Tarmeth, reporting as ordered." He stood at attention as he spoke the words.

Lokor looked at Grotek. "That will be all, *QaS
DevwI'.*"

Without hesitation, Grotek said, "Yes, sir," and left
the office without even giving Tarmeth a look.

What in Kahless's name is going on here?

Rising from behind the desk, Lokor fixed an intense
gaze upon Tarmeth. Until now, the *bekk* had never realized how pitiless the lieutenant's brown eyes were.

"You transferred over from the *Kreltek* after San-
Tarah, did you not?"

"Yes, sir."

"How did you feel about that?"

I hated it. But Tarmeth was too well trained to say
that aloud to an officer. "I had no feelings on the subject, sir. I am a soldier of the empire, and I go where I
am told."

Lokor nodded, his long intricately braided hair
bouncing slightly. "That is the answer I would expect
from a good and loyal *bekk*." He walked around the

desk to stand next to Tarmeth who, for his part, continued looking straight ahead. "But you are not a good and loyal *bekk*, are you, Tarmeth?"

"I—I don't know what you mean, sir."

Suddenly, Lokor grabbed Tarmeth by the left shoulder and pushed him against the bulkhead to the *bekk*'s right. The impact slammed into his side. Before he could recover his wits or his breath, Lokor shoved his massive right arm in the space between Tarmeth's chin and chest, pressing up against his neck. Tarmeth's breaths came more slowly.

"I know what is happening, Tarmeth. I know that Leader Kylag is part of a conspiracy to overthrow Captain Klag. I know that you have the ship's nurse and the second-shift bridge crew loyal to your cause."

His voice straining to be heard through the pressure Lokor was putting on his throat, Tarmeth said, "That— that's not true!"

"Are you calling me a liar?"

"No! No, sir—merely that you—you are mistaken!"

Lokor laughed long and hard at that. "You have not served on this ship long, young fool, so let me tell you what an absurd notion that is. I know everything that happens on this ship. I know that *Bekk*s Yojagh and Moq are having sexual relations in secret. I know that three of the squad leaders in First and Second Company are no longer using the names they were born with. I know that Ensign Kallo would rather be a painter than an officer, but that she is dreadfully bad at painting. I know that Leader Ryjjan has borrowed storage in the cargo bay from two officers in order to store barrels of bloodwine. I know that Commander Kurak has a nephew who will enter Defense Force officer training in less than a year, at which point she will resign her commission. I know that Leader Hovoq is impotent. I know that Lieutenant Yaklan writes fiction under an assumed name. I know that Leader Wol accidentally killed her own son at San-Tarah. I know that *Bekk* J'nfod cheats when he plays *grinnak*. I know that most of the neckbones that Lieutenant Leskit wears were not taken in battle as he claims. I know that Leader Zurlkint has a fondness for a Terran fruit called *sutawberIs* and he had a box of them smuggled in when we left Ty'Gokor. I know that Leader Kylag has two different mates on two different planets in the empire. I know that you received those recordings of *Battlecruiser Vengeance* you're so fond of in exchange for a set of coins that, should your father ever find out you traded them, he would kill you. And I know, Tarmeth, son of Morgoth, failed servant of the *pitiful* House of Pagax, that you are part of a conspiracy to overthrow Captain Klag, and you will tell me *everyone* who is a part of that conspiracy."

Tarmeth's mouth had gone dry. He of course had no idea if most of Lokor's claims were true—indeed, he seriously doubted what he said about Yojagh and Moq, since Moq had a mate back on Qo'noS—but the last three things he said were absolutely true. Tarmeth had tasted some of Zurlkint's human fruit— he found it vile—Kylag had indeed taken on two separate mates, the second after accidentally impregnating her, and Tarmeth had traded Father's hideous collection of useless coins for the *Vengeance* recordings. For that matter, Hovoq being impotent explained a great deal.

Even as Lokor's arm pressed more tightly against his neck, a thought penetrated the panic that was threatening to overwhelm Tarmeth: *Why is he asking me this if he knows everything?*

His voice croaking now, he asked, "Why—do you—need—me?"

"I don't *need* you, Tarmeth. You are simply the most expedient method I have for making sure that *all* the conspirators are dealt with."

"You mean—killed." Tarmeth wondered why Lokor bothered with the euphemism.

"Eventually, yes. I understand that you have no wish to die—that you fear death like some kind of human."

Tarmeth did not respond to the statement. "Why— why should I tell you—anything? You're going to—to kill me anyhow." As soon as Lokor started reciting the secrets of half the *Gorkon* crew complement, Tarmeth knew he was never going to leave this room alive. *Which is a pity—I wanted to see Koth take that Federation ship. . . .*

Lokor's mouth spread into a wide grin. "Oh, I rather hope you *don't* tell me anything."

Now Tarmeth was even more confused.

Indicating the door with his head, Lokor said, "Do you know what I keep behind that door?"

"N-No."

"Oh come now, I'm sure you've speculated. A storage place for my sexual playthings, a stash of bloodwine, a special armory, a bank of surveillance equipment from which I watch the entire ship—you've thought all those things, have you not?"

Thinking that telling the truth just at the moment would only make a bad situation worse, Tarmeth did not answer the question.

"As it happens, the reason why I keep the contents of that room secret is because what is in there is quite illegal. Are you familiar with the mind scanner?"

Tarmeth's stomachs started to churn. The *klongat* leg he'd grabbed to eat before retiring to his bunk started to burble back up his throat. What he knew about the mind scanner mostly came from old episodes of *Vengeance*. But when he was younger, he had gone through a phase where he wanted to learn about history, and he had studied the Khitomer Accords, and one thing he remembered was that one of the terms of the accords was the banning of such technologies as subspace weaponry—and mind scanners.

Unbidden, an installment of *Vengeance* came back to him. Captain Koth had taken a Nausicaan pirate prisoner. When he refused to talk, Koth used the mind scanner on him. By the time Koth was done with him and had learned who was financing the pirates, the Nausicaan—not much of a specimen to begin with—was a mindless vegetable.

"How—how can you have one?"

Again, Lokor laughed. "The only people who learn of it are soon thereafter in no position to discuss it." He pushed his arm tighter onto Tarmeth's neck, causing the *bekk* to cough. "You see, there are worse fates than death, Tarmeth. Shall we proceed to the back room?"

"No!" Tarmeth had no desire to die, but he had far less desire to live out his life like that Nausicaan on *Vengeance.*

Lokor pulled his arm back, allowing Tarmeth to breathe more easily. "A pity. I was looking forward to learning why a cowardly *petaQ* such as you would enter the Defense Force, would choose to serve the cause of honor when you have no conception of what the word means. The mind scanner may have provided those answers."

"I had nowhere else to go," Tarmeth muttered.

"What was that?" Lokor asked.

"I joined the Defense Force because I had nowhere else to go—sir."

Lokor grinned again. "Nowhere is precisely where you have left *to* go, Tarmeth. If you reveal the names of all the conspirators, I will grant you *Mauk-to'Vor,* and you will go to *Sto-Vo-Kor,* having redeemed your honor by exposing the cowards among us. The alternative . . ."

Tarmeth nodded emphatically.

Briefly, the *bekk* entertained the notion that Lokor was bluffing, but he discarded it for two reasons. One was that Lokor was a prototypical highborn officer: full of imbecilic notions of honor and duty that precluded telling so blatant a lie. The other was more fundamental: Tarmeth had no desire to find out the hard way that Lokor was telling the truth.

Besides, even if Tarmeth did call Lokor's bluff, the only possible result of that would be Lokor making Tarmeth's death very long, very slow, and very very painful.

Tarmeth didn't care much about *Mauk-to'Vor*. Lokor could shoot him in the head for all the difference it made. *Dead is dead—it doesn't matter how you get there.* Tarmeth had been hoping not to get there for some time yet, but he knew that was a forlorn hope in the Defense Force.

As he began to give Lokor a list of names, Tarmeth's only regret was that he'd never find out how, exactly, Captain Koth would take the Federation ship.

Wol was really starting to like the feel of the Elabrej weapon.

She had killed several of the aliens as she worked her way through the circular tubes and spherical rooms of the government complex. The first two had only been wounded by the blasts, as she had yet to master the nuances of the firing control. Eventually, she reasoned that the length of time she held down the activator button—which was the only feature on the tube-shaped weapon—determined the power level of the blast it emitted.

Unfortunately, she had no idea where she was going. She did not have Trant's homing beacon to use as a guide to the prisoners, and they had been unable to determine the layout of the complex from the *Gorkon*. All she could do was keep moving through tubes and spheres until she found what she was looking for, killing anyone who got in her way.

This was made more complicated by the fact that she kept seeing images in her mind of Klingons— ones whom she knew couldn't possibly be present, like

Skragg, who was probably back on Ty'Gokor making some new collection of would-be *bekks* miserable, or Krantor, who was dead, or Vok, who was back on the *Gorkon*.

Making her legs move forward was not always the easiest task in the world. The alien scientist's experiment left her central nervous system in a state of disarray. Every fiber of her being cried out to relax, to lie down, to let the pain pass.

But Wol was a warrior. Such weak thoughts might have been appropriate for a daughter of the House of Varnak, but she was a squad leader in the Defense Force. She would not succumb to this.

She worked her way through a tube, stumbling awkwardly on the rounded floors. Fatigue started to overwhelm her, so she stopped moving.

Her vision swam, and suddenly Skragg was standing before her. *"Do not simply stand there like a Regulan bloodworm—move!"*

Wol moved.

A closed and locked door stood before her.

It wasn't the first one she'd encountered since escaping the alien scientist—*and how glorious it was to see him die in agony*—but she found she could no longer remember how she got through the others.

Yojagh. If he was here, he could get it open.

But Yojagh was not here. He was one of the ones Wol had to free—if he was still alive.

Krantor appeared this time. *"I don't care how you do it, Bekk, but get through the door!"*

She aimed the circular Elabrej weapon at the circular door panel next to the circular door and fired by pressing the circular button.

Overfond of circles, are these Elabrej. I should kill them for that.

The door opened to reveal about a dozen Elabrej, who all looked surprised at the appearance of a hairless, naked Klingon woman aiming a weapon at them.

Though not nearly as surprised as they were when she fired that weapon.

Only four of them were armed and decorated like soldiers, so Wol fired on them first. As she did so, Father appeared before her. *"I will only kill Kylor because I have to. I cannot—will not—kill my only daughter."*

Which is funny, Father, Wol thought as she killed the remaining Elabrej in the room, *because I killed my only son, whose existence caused you to kick me out. If I didn't know you were already dead, I would hunt you down and kill you for putting me in a position where I would do that.*

Wol enjoyed hearing the screams of the eight who died after the soldiers. The soldiers, of course, didn't scream. The squad leader she served under on her first assignment, a woman named Tarnax, appeared before her now. *"Soldiers are trained in how to die well. Civilians, on the other hand, usually die very badly."*

The prisoners were not in this room, so Wol left it, and the twelve corpses, behind—after pausing to pick up a second weapon from one of the soldiers. *One for each hand.*

She had yet to hear any alarms. She wondered why that was.

Then she did hear an alarm. No longer equipped with a translator, she could not understand the announcement that accompanied it.

Not that she cared overmuch.

When she entered the adjoining sphere, three soldiers were aiming a weapon at her; the one in the center was spouting gibberish—*as if I know or care what you alien filth are saying.* Wol fell and rolled on the floor, firing both weapons at once. The shots the soldiers fired at her all went over her head.

The shots she fired killed all three soldiers. They didn't scream.

Wol liked it better when they screamed.

This most recent sphere was a smaller one, and it led to a bigger one in which she found herself confronted by four more soldiers—

—and a sphere within the sphere containing about a dozen Klingons. Eight were as naked as she was, and in terrible shape. Their hair was unkempt and filthy—and in some cases, infested—and their bodies were covered with dirt, waste product, and infected sores. The others were in stripped-down versions of their uniforms, the same as Wol was when the alien scientist—*may he rot in Gre'thor*—took her to his laboratory. One of the latter group was Goran, who was unmistakable, towering as he did over everyone else. She wondered if G'joth and Kagak also survived.

"Leader? Is that you?"

Wol knew that voice. It was G'joth. *He did survive. Good.*

On the other side of the sphere was another door,

and it was blasted open just as Wol started firing on the soldiers. Two of them died without screaming.

Commander Toq, Ensign Kallo, *QaS DevwI'* Klaris, and several troops came through the other door. The Elabrej soldiers did not change position, but flawlessly fired behind them.

Then Wol remembered the alien scientist's words before he sedated her—*and before I killed him*—that indicated that the Elabrej had three-hundred-and-sixty-degree vision.

Klaris and one of the troops killed the other soldier.

Cheers came from the holding cell—*holding sphere?* Wol wondered, then decided it didn't matter—as the soldiers fell and the remaining troops entered the sphere.

Toq, however, was looking at Wol with a certain amount of confusion.

She stood at attention. "Leader Wol reporting for duty, sir. I have come to free the prisoners."

Glancing up and down her naked body, Toq then grinned. "You're out of uniform, Leader."

"Not my doing, sir—none of it," she added, looking up briefly.

"Nor is it ours," said one of the naked Klingons. "I am Captain Wirrk. Who are you?"

Turning toward the holding sphere, Toq said, "I am Commander Toq, first officer of the *Gorkon*. We have come to take you from this place." Then he looked back at Wol. "Though it seems our efforts were unnecessary."

It took Wol a moment to realize that Toq was expecting a report. Skragg appeared next to the commander. *"Do not simply stand there like a Regulan blood-worm—speak!"*

She spoke. "We were overwhelmed by Elabrej forces, Commander." Wol's words seemed to echo hollowly in her own ears. "Those of us who did not die in battle were sedated. I was taken to a laboratory. The aliens—experimented on me."

Toq nodded. "That explains why your tresses have been shorn."

"Yes, sir. However, I was able to escape. I have killed many of the enemy, sir, including the scientist who did this to me."

"Well done." He turned to Kallo. "Ensign?"

Only then did Wol realize that Kallo and one of the other troops were inspecting the locking mechanism. As they did so, she looked around the cell. She saw Goran, of course, and G'joth. Standing between them was Kagak, and next to G'joth on the other side was Zabyk. Of Yojagh, there was no sign. *He must have been killed. Moq will be devastated.* Wol was one of the few on board who knew about those two. *I shudder to think what would happen if Lokor found out.*

But it didn't matter, because Yojagh was dead.

And it also didn't matter because the fifteenth survived. *Except for Trant, of course, but he barely counts.*

After a few moments, Kallo got the door open.

Toq said, "We can arm some of you. Those of you we cannot, stand by someone who is. We have a method of escape—"

"No."

That, Wol saw, was Wirrk. Despite being shorn of

uniform and weapons, despite being covered in muck and barely being able to stand upright, the fury in the captain's face was a sight to see.

"Sir, I believe—"

"I am the ranking officer here, Commander, and I say we will not escape this place. After what they did to me, to my ship—to my *crew*—I will not rest until this entire structure is razed to the ground!"

Wol found she couldn't argue with the sentiment.

Yet it was Krantor, the man she disobeyed during the Dominion War, whose image she saw now standing next to Wirrk. *"This one makes a lot of sense, Wol. You should listen to him."*

CHAPTER TEN

Leskit hadn't had this much fun since that time during the Dominion War when he'd led two Cardassian skimmers into an aerial chase through the rain-spattered skies of Nramia, eventually getting them to crash into a mountain that Leskit himself had avoided hitting with his *Jakvi*-class strike ship by a mere eighth of a *qell'qam*.

Now he was wending his way through the turbulent atmosphere of the Elabrej's First Planet—*and how unpoetic can you get when it comes to nomenclature,* the old Klingon thought, *it is to weep*—in one of the separatists' conveyances. His was one of eighteen that entered the planet's atmosphere, using the cover of a weather system over one of the smaller continents—which, Leskit was disgusted to learn during the briefing, was called the Fifth Continent—to mask their entry.

Only eighteen people left on the *Gorkon* were rated to pilot aircraft, which meant they could not use all twenty-five conveyances the separatists had available.

The separatists themselves refused to participate in the mission.

Their leader, Jeyri, had argued passionately on the Klingons' side, but all that did was convince the others to let the conveyances be used to attack sites on the First World.

"The tactics of subtlety will no longer suffice," Jeyri had said to his people. Most of them, Leskit noted, were paying less attention to Jeyri's words than they were to Leskit and his fellow Klingons. *Then again*, Leskit thought with amusement, *most of us were staring at them, too. They are strange-looking beings, the Elabrej.*

The conveyance started to bounce as an updraft hit it. Leskit struggled to compensate. Behind him, he heard the sound of *Bekk* Lojar throwing up. Lojar was there to provide weapons fire, using both a hand disruptor and an Elabrej weapon, which he would fire out one of the portholes once they came near the targets. All the conveyances were using that method, except for Captain Klag's. They had been able to mount one of the Gorkon's rotating disruptor cannons onto Klag's ship.

Between heaves, Lojar said, "You'll get us both killed, you blind old *toDSaH!*"

"If you think *this* is bad, you should try it when there's really bad weather."

"This isn't bad weath—" Lojar's words were cut off by another heave.

Luckily for Leskit's nose, which was offended by the contents of Lojar's stomachs that now occupied the deck, it was a dry heave. *At least it won't get any worse.*

"It isn't bad weather by comparison to Nramia." He grinned. "If we live, I'll tell you all about *that.*"

Done heaving, Lojar said, "If we live, I will kill you for this."

Leskit laughed.

One of the Elabrej had a reply for Jeyri's comment about changing tactics: "If we do alter our methods, if we do start doing physical harm to spheres and people—how, then, do we position ourselves as being better than the oligarchs? We call them uncaring, we call them murderers, we call them destructive—yet if we do as you suggest, how are we better than them? How can we say that we are providing something better if we do what they do?"

Checking the heads-up display while trying to keep the conveyance on course was not easy for Leskit. The consoles were designed for a species that could use all six limbs while sitting in a large cushion tethered to the controls. (The cushion itself was necessary to keep the occupants secure during acceleration, since the Elabrej had yet to master artificial gravity or inertial dampers.) A Klingon could barely fit in the cushion that was built for a much smaller Elabrej, and had a difficult time operating a console meant for someone whose notions of ergonomic efficiency were quite literally alien.

Leskit, of course, had mastered the controls inside of five minutes. There wasn't a flying machine in the galaxy that the old lieutenant couldn't fly—or if there was, he hadn't found it yet.

If only the other seventeen pilots could say the same. Or, rather, sixteen, since one of the conveyances had exploded en route, killing both its occupants. No one was sure what happened, though, having flown one of these things from the Tenth Moon here for the past several hours, Leskit could think of half a dozen possible reasons off the top of his head. The engines on these things were not the best maintained in the galaxy, nor the most efficient even if they *were* maintained.

Leskit checked the altimeter, again cursing the Elabrej for their lack of proper sensor technology. The lieutenant hated having to depend on estimated measurements and the limits of visuals for his flying. *Give me a good sensor reading any day. Then again, with their ability to see all around them, the Elabrej probably trust their sight a lot more.*

He activated his communicator. To do so, he had to take one hand off the controls for a moment, which caused the conveyance to buck and weave a bit. Leskit quickly got the craft under control, but not before Lojar went into the dry heaves again.

"Something amuses you, Leskit?"

Not realizing he'd been laughing at Lojar out loud until Klag's comment, Leskit quickly said, "Only *Bekk* Lojar's bad taste in lunch choices. I'm getting a first-hand look at those choices on the deck of our conveyance. We're about to leave cloud cover, sir."

Even as Leskit said those words, the clear window that went all the way around the spherical conveyance became useful again, as the clouds dissipated. The wind shear decreased, but now they were being rained on. Looking around quickly, Leskit counted the number of conveyances that broke cloud cover with him.

To his irritation, he counted only fourteen besides himself.

"Sir, I'm only seeing fifteen breaking cover."

"*All vessels, sound off,*" Klag said without hesitation.

Paying only partial attention to the counting off of each ship, Leskit instead noticed that one of the conveyances didn't look right. Based on the markings, it was Ensign Go'mat, and based on the way it was descending, nobody was at the controls. Nonpilots probably couldn't tell the difference between the two, given how subtle that difference was, but Leskit knew instantly what had happened.

Ensign Go'mat did not count off; neither did *Bekk*-Jamok or Lieutenant Kass, which accounted for the conveyances Leskit did not see. *We must have lost them in the stratosphere somewhere.*

"Sir," Leskit said, "I believe that Ensign Go'mat is dead—his ship is going into free fall."

"*Then let us hope that it crashes on a viable target.*"

Leskit chuckled. "I'm sure that will annoy the separatists no end, sir."

When Jeyri's arguments had fallen on deaf ears—*if the Elabrej even have ears, though I suppose they must hear with something*—Klag had stepped to the fore. "You asked how attacks on military targets, how damage to important structures, how loss of life would make you better than your enemy. To that, I only have one answer: It is the only way you *can* be better than your enemy. You sit here on your moon, protected by the magnetic field, and hope that you will not gain the notice of your foe. You are like a *chuSwI'* beast, tunneling under the ground to avoid predators, occasionally poking your head aboveground just long enough to make a few annoying noises, then scurrying back to your hiding place before anyone can step on you.

"The process of separation is a violent one. If you truly wish to separate from your hegemony, then you must also commit to the violence that will be necessary to achieve it. To gain victory, *you must fight*. If you are not willing to make sacrifices, if you are not willing to face your foe across the battlefield, if you are not willing to commit to the battle—then your cause is a sham."

Leskit had the feeling that Klag's words would have been more moving coming out of a mouth that was located on his chest instead of on a strange thing on top of his body where his upper arms should have been. The Elabrej's instinctive reaction to the Klingons was so extreme that Kahless himself probably would not have been able to move them.

Still, he mused as one of the Elabrej cities came into view, *at least it was enough to get us the ships.* Though Leskit had to wonder if it was Klag's words, or simply the fact that they were scared of the Klingons. *Not that it matters much—the result is the same.*

Leskit was starting to grow fascinated with the Elabrej's obsession with the circle. Every piece of architecture, every piece of equipment, every marking he saw was circular in nature. It was as if the entire concept of the corner just passed them by. *Along with the concept of a head.*

With only fourteen ships left, Leskit wondered

which targets would be eliminated. The plan had been for each conveyance to take one of eighteen targets, including several military supply storage facilities, an important financial center, the military's main headquarters and training grounds, and the homes of each of the seven oligarchs. That last had been Jeyri's idea. "They will not be there, of course," the separatist had said, "and most people won't understand the significance of those targets, since the oligarchs' places of residence are not public knowledge. I only know them from my time as a defensor. But it will send an unmistakable signal to the oligarchs themselves."

As if reading Leskit's mind, Klag now spoke. *"We will only attack the first five military supply depots. We will not be attacking the military training grounds."* Leskit frowned as Klag reassigned the conveyances to their new targets. They had lost four, yet Klag had removed five targets. Then the captain said, *"Leskit, you are to accompany me to the commerce sphere."*

"Yes, sir," Leskit said, wondering why that was necessary. The captain had a disruptor cannon, after all—that was why he was taking the much larger commerce sphere.

"Meet back at orbital position wa'maH vagh *in two hours. Qapla'!"*

Twenty-seven warriors, including Leskit, all returned Klag's salutation; then the ships all separated in different directions.

The wind shear increased as Leskit and Klag both traveled farther east toward the commerce sphere. Leskit couldn't help but notice a lack of air traffic, which struck him as odd. *Perhaps they are limiting flights in times of war.* This was a problem, insofar as it made them stand out. *Let us hope that the stealth technology the Elabrej use is as good as they claim it is.* Given how poorly several of the conveyances did function, Leskit had his doubts.

Switching to a short-range frequency, Leskit said, "Captain, although I'm honored to be asked to come along with you at the expense of destroying the training grounds, I'm surprised you don't have more confidence in the ship's disruptor cannons."

"I have plenty of confidence in the ship's disruptor cannons, Leskit—it is the ship's engineers I am less sanguine about."

Leskit sighed. "Sir, I'm sure Kurak—"

Klag chuckled. *"For once, Leskit, Kurak is not the problem—which, I have to say, is a relief."*

"I can imagine, sir."

"No, Kurak delegated this task to Lieutenant Yaklan, something I was not told until after the modifications were complete."

Confused, Leskit asked, "What's wrong with Lieutenant Yaklan?"

"More than you might imagine. Suffice it to say, the disruptor cannon is no longer an option."

Leskit interpreted that to mean that whatever was wrong with Yaklan was not something Klag was about to share on an open communications line. "Understood, sir."

"Kurak actually seems to be doing her job of late. It is a welcome change. If she is any danger of changing back,

Leskit, you will be the first to know—I trust you to make sure that I am the second."

"Of course, sir." Not that Leskit expected it to matter all that much. Kurak would go her own way regardless. Leskit was just happy to have her way include letting Leskit into her cabin every night—which she had continued to do, her threats notwithstanding. *And who knows? Perhaps she will actually listen to my advice. Or perhaps not. As long as she keeps letting me bed her, what do I care? Perhaps tonight I'll bring the meyvaQ again—she really enjoyed that the last time.*

Another city coming over the horizon caught Leskit's eye, and he put thoughts of Kurak on the receiving end of his *meyvaQ* to the back of his mind. The commerce sphere was the centerpiece of this city, based on Jeyri's intelligence.

Once, Leskit had the misfortune to visit Ferenginar. In the capital city of that dreary, humid world, the architectural centerpiece was the Tower of Commerce. There was little about the Ferengi that Leskit admired, but they did make impressive structures. Climbing toward the cloud-ridden skies of Ferenginar, the latinum-encrusted Tower of Commerce was a monument to capitalism.

In contrast, the Elabrej's equivalent structure was just a big sphere in the middle of a bunch of smaller spheres. *No poetry to their architecture, either,* Leskit thought. *If we do conquer these people, we'll have to teach them about artistry.*

Lojar then spoke in a shaky voice. "Lieutenant,

there's a ship approaching—it has what those aliens claimed were military markings."

Smiling, Leskit said, "Come now, *Bekk*, the Elabrej wouldn't lie to the people they gave their conveyances to."

The *bekk* just sneered.

"Ready weapons." Leskit prepared for the onslaught of wind and sound that accompanied Lojar opening one of the portholes wide enough for the muzzle of his disruptor. His ears popped at the change in pressure, even as the sound of the howling wind filled his ears.

A voice came over the speakers. *"Unidentified conveyance, you are violating hegemony airspace. Prepare to—"*

Leskit was wholly uninterested in preparing for anything at the Elabrej's behest. "Fire!"

Lojar's disruptor fire struck the military ship dead-on; a moment later, so did a similar beam from Klag's conveyance. Leskit was grateful that the captain had the foresight to have backup in case the disruptor cannon didn't work.

The weapons did their jobs well. Smoke belched from two new holes in the Elabrej ship, and it started to tumble—if a spherical vessel could truly tumble—toward the ground.

"Well done, Leskit. Now let us complete our task—let the Elabrej know that they faced warriors this day."

"Glad to, sir." Leskit grinned as he angled the ship toward the commerce sphere.

Today, he thought, *is a good day to fly. . . .*

Vor Brannik was not looking forward to this meeting of the oligarchy. The second oligarch knew that Vor

Jorg would react badly to the news he was about to impart.

It was bad enough that they had to move to the second sphere, the secret, secure sphere located on Twelfth Island in the Second Sea. Only two dozen people in the entire hegemony besides the seven oligarchs even knew that this place existed. At Brannik's insistence, with the third through seventh oligarchs' support, and over the strenuous objections of the first oligarch, the seven of them along with their aides (who comprised seven of the twenty-four others who knew about the second sphere) retreated here after the government sphere was secured following the combined alien/separatist attack. The risk to the oligarchs' lives was too great, and the attack came frighteningly close to succeeding.

Brannik entered the meeting sphere. All save Vor Markus were present in their hammocks already, and the sixth oligarch walked in a moment later, apologizing for her tardiness.

"It's all right," Brannik said as he clambered into his hammock, "I just got here myself." He held the report in his right midleg. "I'm afraid the news isn't good. The commerce sphere, five different supply spheres for the military, Defensor Headquarters, and the home spheres of each and every one of us have been attacked."

"They found Defensor Headquarters?" Markus said agitatedly.

"No," Brannik said, "they attacked the old one. Vor Ralla is still safe at the new location on the Ninth Continent." Just as the oligarchs had retreated to a secret location, the first defensor had done likewise with the military headquarters.

"The aliens?" Jorg prompted.

"Not exactly, First Oligarch." Brannik spoke reluctantly. "By conveyances belonging to the separatists—but piloted by the aliens, yes."

"You mean to tell me that the aliens really *are* working with the seps?" Seventh Oligarch Yer Gosnot asked incredulously.

"Looks like it, yes," Brannik said. "And that's not the only bad news."

"How could there be worse news?" Fourth Oligarch Vor Mitol's forelegs were vibrating with anxiety. "The seps have never attacked us like *this* before."

"Their conveyances don't even have weaponry," Fifth Oligarch Yer Blos said. "How *did* they attack?"

Brannik let out a puff of air. "Their conveyances *do* have windows. The aliens fired with hand weapons."

"Where did these aliens even come from, anyhow? Are they the same ones who attacked the government sphere yesterday?"

"No." Brannik waved his forelegs in annoyance. "We think these are the survivors of the conveyance that crashed on the Tenth Moon and they met up with the seps there. We've always considered the possibility that the seps have a base there."

Mitol said, "That's not possible. No one can survive on the Tenth Moon."

"As rarely as I might ever say this, Mitol's right," Jorg said. "*You've* considered the possibility, Brannik, but the rest of us know better."

"Either way, it wasn't the same ones." Brannik tried to get the conversation back in the right direction. "And the reason why I know this is the next piece of bad news. There has been a second attack on the government sphere. The aliens came in through the old sea tube."

"The what? What are you talking about?" Third Oligarch Vor Anset asked.

"By Doane's limbs." Now all of Mitol's legs were vibrating with anxiety. "How did they find out about the sea tube?"

"What is he talking about?" Anset asked again.

Vor Jorg angrily said, "The sea tube, Anset, is an old access port to the sea. We used it hundreds of *ungrets* ago when seafaring conveyances were common."

"Why in the name of either Demiurge would we construct seafaring conveyances?" Markus asked.

"Why doesn't matter," Brannik said before the conversation derailed further. "The point is, the tube is there, the aliens found out about it, and at last report were storming the government sphere. Dozens are dead, including Protector Yer Terris and Mal Donal, and the prisoners are probably free."

Jorg let out a puff of air. "We have to send reinforcements."

"From where?" Blos asked. "Brannik, I assume that all our planet-based units are dealing with the sep attacks."

Brannik waved his hindlegs in acknowledgment. "And we lost several of them to the aliens in their attacks."

Jorg was undeterred. "Fine, then get a unit or two down from space."

Waving his right foreleg, Brannik said, "We can't do that, First Oligarch."

"Why not? There are, what, a hundred conveyances up there? Surely we can spare one or two to defend the government sphere."

Brannik was looking forward to this part even less. "We *sent* one hundred and forty-seven conveyances against the aliens." He hesitated. "There are only thirty-nine left, and most of those are badly damaged."

"What about the alien forces?" Anset asked.

"Of the fourteen alien conveyances, only six have been destroyed."

"How is this possible?" Mitol asked. "How is it possible that we could lose one hundred and eight conveyances to a group of brainless alien monsters?"

"Because they're neither brainless nor monsters," Blos said in a tight voice. "I said nothing before because I knew you trusted Mal Donal, Brannik, but the man is obviously an imbecile. These aliens are *not* fools, they are not mindless slaves following the orders of another species. In fact, I'm starting to think they might be cleverer than we are."

"That's absurd," Mitol said. "First Oligarch, I see no reason to listen to the blatherings of this Yer. The biggest mistake we ever made was letting non-Vor into the oligarchy."

Gosnot, the other Yer in the room, waved his midlegs in annoyance. "Wait an *engret*, Mitol—"

Brannik waved his forelegs. "Enough, both of you, we—"

But Blos was not done with Mitol. "They are cleverer, you legless fool, and you know how I know this? Because it was not until *after* we accused them of working with the seps that they started *actually* working with the seps. How do you think they learned of the sea tube? Or gained access to sep conveyances?"

Nobody said anything in response. Brannik felt his legs shrivel as he realized the truth of the fifth oligarch's words.

Jorg's own legs did not move. "She's right, isn't she?" he asked Brannik.

"I think she might be, First Oligarch. Accusing them of collaborating may have hurt the seps in the public eye, but it helped the aliens learn of the seps' existence. We *gave* them a resource to use against us that they could not have known about otherwise."

Mitol let out a puff of air. "They're not a 'resource,' they're a bunch of malcontents with a predilection for meaningless gestures."

"Not anymore," Anset said quietly. "I'd say today's gestures had meaning. It will take *sogrets* to repair the damage the seps did today, and leave us vulnerable to further attacks by the aliens."

Another silence descended upon the meeting sphere.

Finally, Brannik spoke to their leader. "First Oligarch, I think we have to start thinking in terms of surrender."

"No."

"First Oligarch—"

"I said, *no!* We are the rulers of this hegemony, and I

will not let some alien filth take it from us! Divert *all* resources—*all resources*—to stopping this threat! Enlist every able-bodied hegemon to aid in the war effort. This is our biggest priority—to eliminate this alien plague once and for all! Are we agreed?"

Three of the oligarchs, Mitol, Makrus, and Gosnot, said, "Yes," immediately. With Jorg, that meant four of the seven oligarchs approved of this course of action, which meant the entire oligarchy was bound by it.

Waving his midlegs in satisfaction, Jorg said, "Make it happen, Brannik. I want those aliens gone!"

"Yes, First Oligarch."

But Brannik knew that this was a fool's errand, and that the hegemony that they had spent so long building and making great was about to collapse under the weight of a group of aliens that no one even believed in half an *ungret* ago.

Toq stared at the naked, filthy, unarmed form of Captain Wirrk and tried very hard not to laugh.

In truth, that was horribly unfair to the captain and what he had endured. His honor was tarnished with every moment that passed in this spherical cell, being denied an honorable death while alien *petaQpu'* poked and prodded him.

However, neither Toq's amusement nor Wirrk's dishonor was relevant now. As strong as their forces were, as well as they had done to get from the access tube to where Wirrk and the others were being held, the fact was that they were lucky, and that luck was going to run out soon. They had to get back to the tube, and thence back to Viralas's home before they were overrun by the forces arrayed against them in this complex.

Toq suspected, however, that Wirrk would not see it that way. Still, he had to try. "Captain, we must escape, *now*. We cannot raze this structure with the forces we have here."

"You call yourself a Klingon?" Wirrk asked with a sneer. "Do you think so little of your fellow warriors that—"

"I do *not* think little of *any* of you," Toq said. "But there is a larger—"

"Enough! I am your superior, boy, and I say we destroy this vile place! Honor must be restored, and it cannot be until this affront to the empire is ashes on the ground!"

Toq closed his eyes for a moment. "Sir, you are not speaking rationally—"

A woman, also naked, stepped forward. "Captain, he is correct. We cannot—"

"Do not *dare* speak out of turn, B'Etloj!"

"Do not *dare* speak to me that way, *Captain*—or need I remind you that it is only because of me that we are not still trapped here?"

Toq stared at the woman, recognizing the name from the briefing. "You are the I.I. agent who contacted Trant."

B'Etloj turned to Toq. "Assuming Trant is the agent who informed you of our location, yes." Looking back at Wirrk, she said, "This is an I.I. operation, Captain, and you have no authority—"

"I have *every* authority, you spineless bloodworm!

My ship has been destroyed, my surviving crew humiliated! I will have my vengeance."

"We will have our vengeance," Toq said. "I promise you that, sir. But we must go, *now*."

"I will go nowhere with you, boy."

"Commander."

Toq turned at the sound of Wol's voice. The naked, shorn warrior was standing near one of the doors, along with G'joth and Kagak, both members of her squad, who were hunched over the door's controls. "Yes, Leader?"

"There are Elabrej coming. We're deactivating the door, but that will only hold them back for a few minutes. We must go."

Wirrk snarled. "No. We stay and fight them!"

B'Etloj started, "I am ordering you to accompany the commander to—"

"Never! You I.I. *petaQpu'* may be cowards, but—"

"They're coming!" Wol cried. "Form a skirmish line, quickly!"

Even as the troops moved to defend the room, Toq looked at B'Etloj. The woman's eyes were unreadable. *Typical I.I.*, Toq thought, having far more experience with that agency than he was entirely comfortable with.

Normally, the only way out of this would be a challenge. Wirrk was behaving irrationally, and Toq had every right to fight Wirrk for leadership of this mission. But there was simply no time.

Besides, he thought, *he does deserve the chance to regain his honor.*

He then looked at B'Etloj and said a word. It was a word he learned from his adoptive father, a man named Lorgh. If Lorgh knew Toq was aware of the word's existence, much less its significance, Lorgh would probably do things to Toq that would make slow torture seem like a pleasure. But he needed a quick solution to the problem facing him, and this would do it.

For her part, B'Etloj knew the word's significance also, and, in a credit to her I.I. training, responded immediately. "I cede command to you, Commander."

Pretty much everyone else in the room looked at Toq in shock—even Wirrk. "Captain, you will remain here along with whoever wishes to stay and fight." He cast his gaze around the room. "Those of you with more than one weapon, give one to those who are unarmed. Anyone who wishes to join Captain Wirrk in regaining the honor of the *Kravokh* may do so. The rest of you will come with me to the access tube, where we will rendezvous with the separatists and plan our next attack."

The sound of weapons fire on the door drew Toq's attention.

"They'll be through in less than a minute, sir," Wol said.

Wirrk gave Toq a look. "You're Klag's first officer, boy?"

"Yes, sir."

"Tell him to enjoy the bloodwine—he'll know what I mean."

The weapons exchange went quickly—save for B'Etloj, all those from the *Kravokh* stayed behind, as did five of the *Gorkon* troops, leaving the remaining *Gorkon* crew to go with Toq.

G'joth walked up to Wirrk and handed him a *qut-luch*. "Captain, this belonged to *Bekk* Davok—he was my best friend, and he died in battle at San-Tarah. It is a fine blade—I can think of no better cause for it to be used in."

Grinning, Wirrk took the offered blade. "Thank you, *Bekk*—I will do honor to your friend."

"Let us go!" Toq yelled. "Ensign Kallo, take point with the fifteenth."

Wol nodded her appreciation at Toq for that honor. Toq nodded right back. Based not only on what she said, but the reports Toq heard over the speakers in the complex since their invasion started, the swath Wol cut through the Elabrej probably had as much to do with their safely freeing the prisoners as Toq's own surprise entrance.

As his troops moved out, Toq gave Wirrk a final look, his own group forming their own skirmish line. "*Qapla'*, Captain."

"It is a good day to die, Commander. *Qapla'*."

CHAPTER ELEVEN

Lokor entered his cabin to find that K'Nir was already there, and had already removed all her clothing.

He struck her hard in the jaw with the back of his hand. A thrill passed through his body as she crumpled to the floor, blood dripping from her mouth.

"I told you, *I* want to be the one to undress you!"

"I'm sorry."

Lokor raised his hand.

"I'm sorry, *master,*" she amended quickly.

"Better." He lowered his hand and then started to remove his own uniform. "You did well."

"Thank you, master."

"I chose Tarmeth to be the informant. He was already weak."

"An excellent choice, master. May I get up now?"

"No." Lokor took off the rest of his uniform, and stood naked over K'Nir. Then he kicked her in the ribs.

Her voice more strained, K'Nir said, "I'm sorry for presuming, master."

"You should be." He kicked her again, the mild pain of his foot's impact with her stomach giving him another thrill. Seeing the bruising that was already starting to form on her enticing flesh almost gave him goose bumps. "Each of the conspirators will be dead by the end of the primary shift tomorrow, and before they die, they will know that Tarmeth betrayed them."

Now K'Nir sounded pathetic. "No one will know that I betrayed them?"

"Unless I decide to tell them." He crouched down next to her. "Perhaps I will tell one of them. Kylag, perhaps—or Zaloq."

K'Nir whimpered. She drew her arms close to her chest, covering her breasts.

"Yes, I think I will do that. I will describe your treachery—and then I will let that one go to find you. What do you think that Zaloq—or Yaklan, or Gaj— will do to you when they find out that you led them on, that you lied to them, that you told them that you were on their side, that you are truthfully loyal to Captain Klag, so much so that you lied to your fellow warriors and betrayed their trust by telling Lieutenant Lokor of their conspiracy? What will they do if I tell them that?"

Again K'Nir whimpered.

"I did not hear you. Speak louder."

"Please don't."

"Please don't what?"

"Please don't tell them."

He crouched down next to her and put his hand on her throat. Tightening his grip, he said in a very low, very dangerous voice, "Please don't *what?*"

Gasping for breaths that would not come, she croaked, "Please don't, master!"

Letting go of her throat, he stood back up. "Give me a reason why I should not go tell Yaklan right now that you are a traitor to their cause."

"What reason would you like me to give you, master?"

Throwing his head back, Lokor laughed heartily toward the ceiling. Then he swiveled his head back down toward her, the ends of his braids tickling against the small of his back. "Very good, K'Nir! *Very* good! You may stand up now."

Slowly, unsteadily, K'Nir rose to her feet, still whimpering. However, she let her arms fall to her side so Lokor could see her in her glorious nudity—including the bruises that he had inflicted upon her.

"You have one hour until your shift commences," Lokor said. "You have that long to use whatever means are at your disposal to persuade me not to tell anyone of your betrayal."

K'Nir smiled. "Because you are an honorable man and you would not lie to fellow warriors?" Gone was the whimpering.

Lokor smiled right back. "Do you truly think I care about behaving honorably toward those who would murder the captain?" Then he smacked her again. This time, she fell to the bunk, smashing her jaw on the corner of the metal surface.

She struggled to her feet. Lokor could smell the blood that now pooled beneath her nose and in her mouth.

Smiling, she leapt at him and began in earnest her convincing.

Half an hour before the primary shift was to end, Kurak entered the bridge. This surprised Rodek, as he could not recall a single time in the nine months since the *Gorkon* left the shipyards for its shakedown cruise that the chief engineer had set foot on the bridge.

"The *Gorkon* is ready to leave the surface."

Rodek blinked. "I thought we would not be prepared for another two days."

In all the years that Rodek had known the chief engineer—they also served together on the *Lallek* during the war—the gunner had never seen Kurak smile until now. "So did I. It seems that I'm better than I thought I was."

Snorting, Rodek said, "Nobody's as good as *you* think you are, Kurak."

Rodek's jaw fell open at the second unfamiliar gesture from Kurak in a row: a laugh. "Perhaps not—in that case, I am better than Captain Klag thought I was. In any event, we can get under way immediately."

"Lieutenant!"

Turning at the sound of Kal's voice from the operations console, Rodek said, "What is it, Ensign?"

"Sir, I have been able to penetrate the magnetic field. We can now send and receive communications from off-planet."

"Well done, Ensign. Contact the captain."

Nodding, Kal said, "Yes, sir."

Moments later, Leskit's voice could be heard over the speakers, albeit laden with static. "*—skit to* Gorkon, *we are taking heavy fire from the enemy. Survivors have achieved escape velocity, but we do not have sufficient power to make it back to the Tenth Moon. If you can hear us, for Kahless's sake, get out here and help us. Talk to Jeyri, do something!*"

Rodek shook his head. *Leave it to that old razorbeast to survive an attack.* "Leskit, this is Rodek."

"*It's about time somebody answered. I assumed that with Toq and Kallo off-ship, you'd be useless.*"

"What is the captain's status?"

"*He's alive, but the communications in his conveyance are down, so he's left the futile gesture to me.*"

"Not so futile, my friend," Rodek said with a grin, "and we need not involve ourselves with the Elabrej. Kurak has repaired the *Gorkon*, and we can get under way immediately."

A pause.

"*I will inform the captain. And I will ravage that woman like she's never been ravaged before when I get back.*"

Kurak smiled again. "Such confidence, Leskit. What makes you think I want you anywhere near me?"

A longer pause. Laughter started to spread throughout the bridge.

"*Rodek, my good friend, next time, please tell me when Kurak can hear me when I'm talking about her.*"

"What would the fun be in that, my good friend?"

"*I will kill both of you when I'm back on board. Speaking of which, how soon can you get here?*"

Rodek looked at Kurak, who shrugged. "Two hours—perhaps one and a half if the checklist goes faster than expected."

"*We'll be here. I have to sign off to inform the captain—I can speak with him on his personal communicator, but if I use this frequency, I'll blow it out.*"

"I take it your mission was successful?" Rodek asked.

"*Oh, most definitely. We lost about ten ships, but we did considerable damage to the Elabrej.*"

"Sir," Kal put in, "I'm receiving news broadcasts—as well as one of the pirate broadcasts from the separatists. Whatever the captain did, it created quite a stir." The young ensign grinned. "The Elabrej are running scared, sir."

"Of course they are, Ensign," Rodek said with a grin of his own. "That is how all enemies of the empire wind up."

"The most devastating blow was to the government sphere," Kal added.

"*Wait a moment,*" Leskit said, "*the government sphere wasn't one of our targets.*"

Rodek blinked. "The separatists?"

Snorting, Leskit said, "*Please—they could barely be talked into lending us these firetraps.*" Then, suddenly, Leskit burst out laughing. "*You know, we left Toq attacking the government sphere. You don't think—?*"

"That he didn't get that glorious death he promised us in the mess hall just yet?" Rodek shook his head. "It would seem not."

"*Since we have two hours, I'll see if we can raise him. See you soon, Rodek. Out.*"

Chuckling, Rodek retook the first officer's chair. "Commander Kurak, if you'd be so kind as to get us under way."

"Of course," Kurak said in as respectful a tone as she was ever likely to use, before heading toward the turbo-lift.

"Ensign Kal, tell the *QaS DevwI'* to bring the troops back on board."

"Yes, sir."

The door rumbled aside to let Kurak enter the lift, but there were three occupants already: Lieutenant Yaklan, Ensign Zaloq, and Ensign Krat. Yaklan had no reason to be on the bridge, especially with Kurak already here—*who*, Rodek wondered, *is watching engineering?*—and Zaloq and Krat's shift—they staffed the gunnery and communications consoles during the second shift—did not start for twenty more minutes.

Rodek was about to ask them what they were doing here when they each unholstered disruptors and fired.

Ducking to avoid the blast, Rodek pulled out his own weapon. *Lokor told us this had been dealt with!* he thought angrily as he fired, the shot taking Krat out.

He could see Kurak struggling with Yaklan, which unfortunately spoiled his shot, so he aimed for Zaloq.

The world suddenly went white around Rodek as a

disruptor blast struck him directly in the face. Agony coursed through his crest and features as he fell to the deck.

To Rodek's complete confusion, his last thought as he mercifully fell into a coma was: *You did this to me, Worf. . . .*

CHAPTER TWELVE

Toq sat on the shoreline, waiting for Mal Sanchit to return. After he and his team had emerged from the access tubes and swum to the surface, Toq activated the signal that would tell Sanchit to return with her conveyance to take them back to Vor Viralas's home sphere.

The commander had expected—or at least had hoped—to return with roughly the same number of warriors as he left with, possibly more. Instead, he had considerably fewer, a state of affairs he had only anticipated if they failed.

But we did not fail. Wirrk and his crew will die in battle, not on the table of some Elabrej laboratory.

That prompted him to look at Leader Wol. Unburdened by a uniform, she had had the easiest time swimming to the surface during their escape. After they emerged from the water, G'joth had lent her the top of his uniform. Still, she looked peculiar with her head shaved. Her eyes were haunted, as if she were possessed by *jatyIn*. She was standing alone, staring out at the water. The rest of her squad—G'joth, Goran, and Kagak—stood in a cluster nearby. Toq smiled in admiration. *A show of support, that they are nearby, but not interfering.*

He got up and walked over to where she stood. It might not have been proper for the others of the fifteenth to speak to Wol without her permission, but Toq was the first officer.

At his approach, Wol stood at attention. "Yes, Commander?"

"Stand easy," Toq said with a wave of his hand. "You did *very* well today, Leader. Your distracting the Elabrej forces probably helped us gain access to the prisoners as easily as we did. You served your ship and your empire with distinction." Then he looked up at her smooth crown. "And made quite a sacrifice as well."

At that, Wol laughed, running a hand over her shaved head. "Indeed, sir." She stared back over the ocean. "The Elabrej scientist who—who did this to me seemed amazed that Klingons had any concept of language. I think he believed us to be thralls—mindless savages who fight at the command of some greater master." She shook her head. "I wonder if that is how all Elabrej see us."

"Most do not see us at all," Toq said. "They see only the foe they have to face. I had the opportunity to see several of their news reports—they view us only as a monstrous enemy."

"They do not greet their foe face-to-face," Wol said.

"It was a pleasure to kill them." She lifted her arm, and Toq saw that she still held the Elabrej weapon she'd taken. She tossed it in the air and caught it unerringly as it came back down.

Toq smiled. "I see you have a trophy."

"Whatever the other flaws of the Elabrej, they do create fine weapons. I will keep this as a memento of my—of our victory today."

"Your head is not enough of one?" Toq asked with a laugh.

"Several years ago, circumstances—" She hesitated. "I was forced to cut my hair down to the scalp. It grew quite long within a matter of days. So this memento will not last long."

"Good." Toq put a hand on her shoulder. "You are a fine warrior, Leader. You handled the entire mission—starting with the revelation that you had an I.I. traitor in your midst—with honor. I consider it a privilege to serve on the same vessel as you."

"Thank you, Commander." Wol looked over at G'joth, Goran, and Kagak.

Toq followed her gaze. G'joth looked concerned, oddly enough; Goran was large and impassive as always, and Kagak looked as concerned as G'joth. *Concern for their commander—it speaks well of Wol's leadership. . . .*

"If you'll excuse me, sir," Wol said, "I have something I need to say to my squad."

"Of course."

As Wol moved away, Toq heard a whine start to build in the air. Looking up, he saw that Sanchit was coming back.

Then his communicator activated, and he heard words he had all but given up hope of hearing: *"Klag to Toq."*

"Captain!"

Several of the warriors around him perked up at that. Kallo ran over to him. "Is that the captain?"

Ignoring the idiotic question, Toq said, "Where are you, sir?"

"In orbit. I confess, Toq, I had feared you lost until I learned that the government sphere had been attacked again."

"You gave us a mission, sir," Toq said matter-of-factly.

"Indeed, I did. We have been busy as well."

Quickly, Klag filled Toq in about meeting a group of separatists on the Tenth Moon. Toq interrupted that with a laugh, prompting him to tell of his own encounter with the separatists, and how they had lost contact with the Tenth Moon contingent.

"It seems, Toq, that we've joined forces without even realizing it."

"Yes, sir. Where is the *Gorkon?"*

"According to our last contact with them, they will be here within two hours. However, our own ships are deteriorating. I assume that loud noise I hear is a ship landing?"

"Yes, sir—Mal Sanchit, one of the separatists, is bringing us to one of their headquarters."

"Excellent. Provide the coordinates for that place, and we will join you until the Gorkon *arrives."*

"Yes, sir! I will have to get them from Sanchit. Wait one moment."

Toq ran toward Sanchit's conveyance, a song blossoming in his heart. In truth, his words to the separatists notwithstanding, he feared that the *Gorkon* had been destroyed in battle, and that he, Kallo, Klaris, and the others would be trapped on this misbegotten planet for the rest of their lives. He was quite relieved to learn that this would not be the case.

First Defensor Vor Ralla had no idea who the aide was who ran into his office sphere yelling at the top of her lungs, but whoever she was, he fully intended to have her shot. This had been one of the worst days in Ralla's long career as head of the Elabrej military. Reports from the sky were that the aliens were routing their forces. The plasma weapons did their job even better than anticipated—which was good, as the missiles were wholly useless against their defenses—but the Elabrej conveyances had absolutely no defense against the aliens' odd energy weapons. And then there were the ground assaults, from the commerce sphere to the residences of the oligarchs to the government sphere itself.

They also attacked the ostensible military headquarters, but since the first encounter with the aliens, Ralla had moved Defensor HQ to a secret location on the Ninth Continent.

It was the government sphere attack that had Ralla the most concerned; the sphere had gone quiet with no new information coming out of there for over an *atgret*. When he'd been appointed to the job of first defensor so many *ungrets* ago, Ralla could not imagine a circumstance under which the hegemony would be in any danger of falling. The government was stable and prosperous, the only disaffection coming from a group of inefficient malcontents. Now, though, he was starting to think that, even if they were able to drive off the aliens—something Ralla didn't truly think his military to be capable of—the hegemony would be badly wounded, perhaps fatally.

So an aide coming in bleating at him did nothing to improve his mood.

"We found them! We found them!" All six of the aide's legs were waving so fast they were practically invisible.

"Found what?"

"The separatists, sir!"

That got Ralla's attention. "Explain."

"We intercepted a transmission made between two of the aliens. Most of it was in their gibberish, but they spoke with an Elabrej, who revealed the location of their stronghold on this planet."

"Where?"

"That's the amazing thing, sir—it's at the estate of Vor Viralas."

Ralla thought his limbs would shrivel up and fall off his body right there. "Did you say Vor Viralas?"

"Yes, sir."

When Ralla first learned of the existence of the alien creatures, it had nearly destroyed his entire view of the world. Only his three dozen *ungrets* of military training kept him from devolving into a panic. He had covered himself well, even scoffing at the first cleric's skepticism, all the while sharing in it. It simply did not occur to Ralla that the clerics could be wrong about the

Elabrej's place in the world, and so when they were proven wrong so spectacularly, it almost destroyed Ralla.

It was probably that experience that allowed Ralla to deal with this latest intelligence with more aplomb. Once, the news that a Vor strata was involved with a tiresome group of rebels against the very system that gave the Vor their rightful place at the top of hegemony society would have been greeted with derisive laughter. Indeed, Ralla had received intelligence on more than one occasion that indicated ties between Viralas and the seps, but Ralla had always dismissed it. Such a thing was simply not possible.

But so were malformed, hideous alien beings murdering hegemons by the hundreds.

Ralla regarded the aide. "You're absolutely sure of this?"

"I can play the recording for you if you wish, sir."

Normally, Ralla would have considered such a step unnecessary—he trusted his intelligence people implicitly, or he never would have given them the jobs they had in the first place—but this was too big, and the response too outrageous to be ordered without definitive proof.

Reaching into her pouch, the aide removed a recorder and activated it.

First he heard the gibberish of the aliens. Then he heard a distinctively Elabrej voice say: "The home of Vor Viralas—it's located at the third finger of the fourth arm of the Second Continent."

His left hindleg waving in irritation, Ralla said, "It's

only been a few *digrets*, and already the seps have taught these aliens our cartographical methods."

"Yes, sir. Should I call Second Defensor Vor Bramma?"

Ralla hesitated. Ordering a military attack on the grounds owned by a fellow Vor strata was unprecedented. Then the moment of hesitation passed. *This entire war is unprecedented.*

"Yes. Have him assemble a strike team. Their target is—" He let out a puff of air. "—Vor Viralas's estate. And inform the oligarchs of what we are doing and why, including a copy of that recording. They will want an explanation."

"Yes, First Defensor."

"And may Doane grant mercy to all of us for what we do," Ralla muttered too quietly for the aide to hear.

"This is your fault!" Bantrak yelled at Sanchit as batteries assaulted Viralas's home sphere. "I knew attacking the government sphere was a mistake!"

Sanchit knew that Bantrak was right, though not for the reasons he thought. She doubted that the military—occupied as they were with fighting against the Klingons—had developed a method of detecting the separatists' stealth conveyances in the past *digret. But they are still able to intercept communications.* Sanchit hadn't concerned herself with that because the oligarchs and the military didn't have the Klingons' translation capabilities.

They could understand me just fine, though, she

thought angrily. The words had already escaped her mouth when she realized that giving away the location of Vor Viralas's home sphere on an open channel was an idiotic thing to do.

At first, Sanchit feared the sphere would be destroyed, but then Toq's superior arrived, along with a dozen or so conveyances that Sanchit recognized as belonging to Jeyri's group on the Tenth Moon. This would not have given them much of an advantage on the face of it, but then she saw the same kind of weapons that Toq's people used being fired out the portholes of the conveyances.

These Klingons are clever—and adaptable. We are less so, and it may destroy the hegemony. Then again, isn't that truly our goal?

The floor shook, and Sanchit fell to the floor, preventing injury only by bracing herself with her forelegs.

"Where is Viralas?" she asked Bantrak.

However, the old man was not finished berating her. "*You* suggested this! *You* were the one who took those demons in, and look what it's brought down on us!"

Angrily, Sanchit said, "It's brought us closer to victory than we've gotten in all the *ungrets* since we started this movement, Bantrak!"

A piece of the sphere broke off and almost hit Bantrak. "You call *this* victory?"

"Yes I do, Bantrak, because I've spent my life studying history, and I've learned two truths. One is that governments always fall and the other is that they do so because they believe they cannot possibly fall. This is victory for us because the oligarchs are running scared.

This is victory because they consider us enough of a threat to attack us like this."

"If it hadn't been—"

"Bantrak, do you *truly* believe that Vor Ralla couldn't have figured out where we were if he actually put any effort into it?"

Unlike the other separatists, Bantrak knew Ralla, which was why she asked him the question. After letting out a puff of air, Bantrak said, "No. To be honest, I always assumed that he received intelligence that Viralas was involved and dismissed it—indeed, that that was the only thing saving us."

"If he's acting on it now, it's because he thinks we're worth responding to—which we weren't until the Klingons came."

"And what do you think they will leave in their wake, Imparter?"

Before Sanchit could answer that question, Toq ran into the room along with the strange-looking Klingon who did not have the same fuzz on her head that the other Klingons had. She also wore less of the strange armor.

"We have to abandon this sphere," Toq said. "Your military has landed ground troops—they'll be taking the outer spheres soon. We need to form a defense inside while Captain Klag attacks from the outside."

"Ground troops?" Bantrak's forelegs waved with shock. "Doane's limbs, are we an ancient castle being harried by arrow-firing defensors?"

"Apparently we are," Sanchit said. "Let us go."

The strange-looking Klingon gestured to the door. "This way."

Then the world exploded.

Sanchit cried out in pain as she felt something slice into one of her hindlegs, and she fell to the floor.

Three soldiers stood in a very large hole where part of the sphere used to be. One of them—the highest-ranking one, based on his markings—said, "You have one *engret* to surrender, or we wi—"

Energy from Toq's weapon and the other Klingon's Elabrej weapon—taken off a soldier in the government sphere, apparently—interrupted, and all three of the soldiers were dead moments later.

Bantrak's forelegs waved in anger. "They were giving terms of surrender!"

Toq lowered his weapon. "And I just gave them our answer. We must move before more come in."

Sanchit struggled to rise up on her forelegs. She found it difficult to focus on her surroundings, so overwhelming was the pain.

"Are you all right?" Bantrak asked.

"I'm fine, just a small cut." Sanchit was lying. She was amazed that she was still conscious.

"We will help you when we get to a safe part of the sphere." Toq and the other Klingon moved toward the doorway as the sphere shook again. *This place will collapse in a few* engrets, Sanchit thought as she struggled to join them.

Then she noticed another soldier in the hole in the wall, aiming his weapon.

Toq did not move.

Sanchit remembered that the Klingons had appallingly limited vision. She had wondered if that was why they were so much cleverer—they could not see all around them like normal people, so they had to compensate. But it also meant that Toq and the other Klingon had no idea they were about to die.

They cannot die—they're our only hope.

With what little strength she had remaining, Imparter Mal Sanchit leapt into the path of the weapon that was about to kill Toq.

Toq heard Sanchit's scream and the weapons fire from behind him at the same time. He whirled around to see that another Elabrej stood in the hole in the curved wall. He and Wol had both fired their weapons and killed the soldier before it completely registered with Toq that Sanchit had leapt into a blast that was meant for him.

Those honorless bloodworms would have shot me in the back—and Sanchit saved me.

Toq knelt down over her singed, bleeding body. He blinked, then looked over at Bantrak, whose legs were vibrating. "I cannot tell if she is alive or dead."

"Keep—fighting—" Sanchit's voice was terribly weak.

"What?"

"You—only—hope—for—Elabrej—keep—fighting . . ."

A final puff of air came from her. Toq had seen many beings from many worlds die before, and even on so alien a creature as the Elabrej, he recognized when death arrived.

Bantrak's arms were still vibrating. "Her death is on your head, alien."

Wol aimed her disruptor at Bantrak. "She died saving the commander's life—it was a warrior's death!"

"What possible difference could that make?" Bantrak asked.

"Every difference." Toq pointed at Sanchit's corpse. "And she, at least, understood that."

He looked down at her body. The Elabrej did not have eyes that could be pried open, so Toq skipped that part of the ritual. Instead he simply threw his head back and screamed to the ceiling.

Sanchit risked much to save Toq and his team, and was the only one of these passionless creatures who understood the way of the universe. *There is a new warrior in Sto-Vo-Kor tonight—for if any of these Elabrej deserve to cross the River of Blood, it is she.*

Wol, to her credit, joined in the scream.

When they were done, Bantrak said, "You are insane. You will destroy our entire way of your life with your savagery."

Toq stared in shock at Bantrak, but it was Wol who responded: "Isn't that what you want?"

"Don't be ridiculous, of course I don't."

"Then why do you do what you do? You are called separatists—do you not want to destroy your entire way of life in favor of a new one?"

Rising to his feet, Toq said, "We do not have time to discuss this. More of these soldiers will be coming." Without another word, he led Wol and Bantrak out through the doorway to the better-protected inner spheres of Viralas's estate.

*   *   *

"The systems are failing, sir!"

Klag ground his teeth at the report from Jaketh. "I'm aware of that already, *Bekk*. Continuous fire."

"I'm trying, sir." Jaketh aimed his disruptor through the porthole, but was unable to hit anything.

As he struggled to keep the increasingly unaerodynamic Elabrej craft from crashing into the estate that housed the separatist movement, Klag started to worry that the battle would be lost. The Elabrej military had taken the perimeter of the estate and were moving in. *Plus*, Klag thought angrily as he stabbed at the recalcitrant controls, which were all placed in ridiculous locations, *their ships are actually in good working order, which is more than can be said for these useless metal balls the separatists gave us.*

He glanced around to see how the other ships were doing, cursing the Elabrej for not having proper sensor technology. The only ship that was doing serious damage to the Elabrej was Leskit's—which did not entirely surprise Klag. *That old razorbeast could fly a bird-of-prey with its engine removed.*

The battle would have gone much better if the disruptor cannon worked. Right now all it was doing was providing extra drag on the craft as Klag struggled to keep it aloft in the turbulent atmosphere of Elabrej's First World. He would not be around to do that much, had Lokor not warned him that Yaklan was one of the potential mutineers on board the *Gorkon*. By the time he learned that Yaklan installed the cannon, they were already en route to the First World. A scan revealed the explosive device Yaklan had installed that would kill

Klag and Jaketh, and destroy any other ship that was within a quarter of a *qell'qam* of them, if the cannon was activated.

Klag hoped that Lokor had spoken true when he said the conspiracy would "no longer be a factor" by the time Klag reported back to his ship.

An Elabrej blast took out one of the ships piloted by *Bekk* Gan, leaving Klag's forces down to four of the separatist conveyances. For their part, they had destroyed only three of the dozen ships the Elabrej sent.

"Klag to Toq."

"We're holding the line, sir, and I believe we can do so as long as the Elabrej ground forces remain as they are."

Snarling, the captain said, "Understood." If they landed more ground troops, Toq would likely not be able to hold the line. They would die well, at least. *I thought I lost my first officer once this mission. I will not do so again without a fight.*

He managed to coax the ship into a flight path that would take it directly toward the vessel that just destroyed Gan's ship. "Get ready to fire," he told Jaketh.

"Yes, sir."

Klag found that the controls would no longer respond. He tried to pull the craft up, but it would not follow his instructions. Jaketh fired on the Elabrej ship with his disruptor, but they were about to crash into it as well.

So be it. If we are to die today, it will be only after we send as many of these creatures to Gre'thor as we can.

"Prepare for impact." Klag was completely calm. He had no great desire to die on this world, but he also

303

knew that he had no say in the matter, only that his cause was a just one, and he would be rewarded for his efforts in *Sto-Vo-Kor*. It was the goal he had spent his life trying to achieve.

Then, much to his surprise, the Elabrej ship exploded. Klag was rocked in the cushion that kept him in place in the circular ship, and the small craft tumbled end over end toward the ground.

Struggling with the controls, he eventually managed to get the ship to hover about half a *qell'qam* off the ground—right before half those controls failed completely, providing him with a display in a language he did not know, but which he recognized from the crash course Jeyri had given them as indicating nonfunctionality.

Klag noticed that the sun, which had been shining brightly overhead, was now totally blocked by something.

Gazing out the window, Klag felt his blood roar, and the beginnings of a song forming in his heart.

It was the *Gorkon*.

Klag's ship moved through the air with all the grace and beauty of a *lotlhmoq* bird, its disruptor cannons all—save the one sitting uselessly atop Klag's conveyance—firing on the Elabrej ships, blowing them to pieces. It was less the explosion than the displacement of the massive Chancellor-class vessel as it plowed through the atmosphere that caused Klag's ship to tumble through the air.

Minutes later, it was over. The *Gorkon* swooped into the air, heading toward orbit.

"Gorkon to Klag. This is Commander Kurak in command."

Klag almost swallowed his own tongue. "Kurak?"

"Yes, sir—I'm sorry, but Lieutenant Rodek was incapacitated during a failed mutiny led by my petaQ of an assistant. Dr. B'Oraq is caring for him." A pause. "Ensign Kal reports that your ship's engines are about to implode. Shall I have you beamed aboard?"

It took a moment for Klag to find his voice. "Yes—yes, beam all Klingons in the area to the Gorkon immediately."

And then I will find out who this impostor is who is pretending to be my recalcitrant chief engineer. . . .

CHAPTER THIRTEEN

First Oligarch Vor Jorg wasn't sure when it was that he lost control. *It had all seemed so reasonable—these alien creatures could be used to rally the hegemons and gave us the excuse to unleash the new weapons. We should have won!*

Brannik came into his private sphere in the secret redoubt. "I've got bad news."

"Do you ever have anything else, Second Oligarch?" Jorg snapped. "Must you always enter my presence with yet *another* piece of bad news? Is it my lot in life now to be inundated with report after report after report of the sheer incompetence of our military?"

"No—it's your lot in life to be given reports on how stupid we were to engage in a war with people who are a lot better at it than we are."

"What are you talking about?" Jorg had never heard Brannik talk such nonsense before. These were inferior beings, Mal Donal said so. . . .

"I mean that they've outfought us in every possible

sense. I've looked over the reports from what's left of our military forces in the skies, and they have battle-field tactics that make us look like amateurs. Plus they can defend against our weapons—not forever, but they can, which is more than can be said for us against theirs. And now the latest." Brannik walked over to the hammock where Jorg lay and handed him a recorder.

Jorg looked at its display. It told him of an attack on the estate of Vor Viralas—who, it turned out, had sepa-ratist leanings. Unfortunately, the aliens were with the separatists, and dozens of conveyances were destroyed.

"Doane's limbs," Jorg muttered. "Vor Viralas is a sep?"

"I don't think that really matters all that much, do you, First Oligarch?"

"I can't believe it. I *know* Vor Viralas. He's a high strata of the first order. How could he *possibly* put his legs in with—"

"Doane take it, Jorg, will you *listen* to me?" Brannik's midlegs were waving with more anger than Jorg had ever seen—and it was the first time Brannik had ever called him by name since they were children.

"How *dare* you speak to me in this way, Brannik! You may be the second oligarch, but that doesn't give you the right—"

"We're *losing*, Jorg! Don't you understand? Our mili-tary has been decimated, the commerce sphere has been destroyed, the government sphere has been taken."

Jorg waved his midlegs in dismissal. "Don't be ab-surd. We can't be stopped by a group of mindless savages—"

"They're *not* mindless savages, Jorg. They're a lot smarter than Mal Donal thought, and—"

"It doesn't matter." Jorg simply refused to accept what Brannik was telling him. Such notions were nonsense, and unworthy of a member of the Vor strata. "We have the greatest military in the history of the world. They will fight to the bitter end."

"That end's closer than you think—and what motivation do they have to fight?"

"What are you talking about?"

"We can't pay them, Jorg." Brannik's forelegs waved in irritation. "All the money in the commerce sphere was destroyed by the aliens."

Jorg waved his hindlegs dismissively. "We can pay them out of our own capital."

"That would be the capital that we kept in the vaults under our homes?"

"Yes, the—" Realization dawned on Jorg. "The homes the aliens destroyed. Doane's limbs, Brannik, we can't pay them?" He waved his right foreleg. "No, wait, that's ridiculous, of course we can. We'll make up credit slips. After all, we're still worth plenty—we can always raise a new tax, the people won't have any problem with supporting the military in our efforts against alien demons who have come to destroy us, and then—"

The door opened, and one of Jorg's aides—Jorg could never remember their names; they were non-stratad anyhow, so it wasn't as if their names were worth remembering—ran in. "First Oligarch! We're receiving a transmission from Fourth Defensor Mal Rennols!"

Brannik's forelegs waved with relief. "He was one of

the ones at the government sphere. Where is he?" he asked the aide.

"On his way here right now—he has a report, but he said he would only give it to the first oligarch."

Jorg couldn't believe it. At least Rennols was a Mal strata, so it wasn't as big a breach of protocol as it might have been under other circumstances, but Jorg was still appalled at Rennols's effrontery for insisting on speaking directly to the first oligarch. There were channels—he would speak to Vor Ralla, who would then speak to the oligarchy.

Still, I suppose in times of war such minutiae tend to be the first casualty. Besides, I do want to know what's going on at the government sphere.

"All right, then," Jorg said. "Put him through here."

To Jorg's surprise, he did not see the fourth defensor on the screen that formed in the sphere wall. Instead, it was one of the aliens.

"What in Doane's name—"

"*Greetings, Elabrej. I am told you are the leader of your people.*"

"I am the first oligarch," Jorg said angrily, "and I have nothing to say to you."

Brannik then spoke, annoying Jorg. "How did you gain access to this channel?"

"*The same way I gained access to this ship—or 'conveyance,' as your people refer to it—by taking it from your feeble military. Your Fourth Defensor Mal Rennols gave in very easily.*"

"I repeat," Jorg said before Brannik could act like a fool a second time, "we have nothing to say to you."

"*Then you may simply listen. I and several of my fellow warriors, including most of those whom you cruelly took prisoner, have come to take our revenge—and to strike a blow for our empire. Right now, we are piloting several dozen of your 'conveyances' toward your secret redoubt— your fourth defensor gave us the knowledge of the redoubt's location as well, when we captured him in your government headquarters. They should crash within a minute or so.*" The strange growth atop the monster's torso had a feature—Jorg could only assume it was his mouth, since it opened and closed in time with his words—that curled now into a strange rictus. "*I am Wirrk, son of Haggar, captain of the I.K.S. Kravokh, and I am here to tell you, first oligarch of the Elabrej Hegemony—that today is a good day to die.*"

Jorg felt his windpipe go dry. His limbs would not move. *They wouldn't—they couldn't—they—*

Then the world exploded around him. . . .

Klag sat in the wardroom with Toq, Kurak, Leskit, and Lokor. They all sat in silence as they listened to the transmission that Ensign Kal had intercepted during the *Gorkon's* strafing run of the separatist hideout.

"*I am Wirrk, son of Haggar, captain of the I.K.S. Kravokh, and I am here to tell you, first oligarch of the Elabrej Hegemony—that today is a good day to die.*"

Toq looked at Klag. "According to the sensor readings, twenty-four of the small ships used by the Elabrej military were piloted directly into the mountain that—apparently—housed the hidden location of the oligarchs."

Klag shook his head. "When we were at Ty'Gokor, Wirrk expressed dismay at our mission of exploration. He felt that it was not a worthy task for warriors. Today, he proved himself wrong—and died as a Klingon."

Lokor, who, like Wirrk, was of the House of Grunnil, said, "Haggar was always going on about Wirrk and how far he would go in the Defense Force. I look forward to telling the old man how his son died—it will bring him joy."

Regarding his chief engineer, Klag said, "What brought *me* joy was seeing the *Gorkon* swooping through the air of the First World like a *lotlhmoq* bird. I have to wonder how this was accomplished, especially given who was in command."

Kurak was sitting calmly in her seat. Unlike past meetings, where fury seemed to be ready to burst out at any moment, she now had an equanimity that Klag would never have believed her capable of, did he not see it with his own eyes. "You have every reason to be surprised, Captain. It was, in fact, the attempted mutiny that can perhaps be blamed."

"How do you mean?"

"When Yaklan, Krat, and Zaloq came onto the bridge, I came to a realization." She looked at the ship's pilot. "Leskit was right."

At that, Leskit laughed. "I have to say, Commander, that it is about time you realized that."

Klag also laughed. "I must confess to a certain skepticism."

"Understandable, Captain, *believe* me." To Klag's amazement, Kurak sounded amused—another emotion he wouldn't have credited her with. "But he told me recently that I was being a fool by forcing myself into unhappiness. And when Yaklan and his band of *toDSaHpu'* tried to take the bridge, I realized that I would be very unhappy if they succeeded and more happy if I made the best of my assignment here." She smiled. "Which is why I took great joy in snapping Yaklan's neck, and then taking the *Gorkon* into the atmosphere to win your battle."

Klag nodded. "Well done, Commander—and well done, Leskit."

"Thank you, Captain," Leskit said, "but I'm sure my reward will come later tonight."

Kurak grinned. "You're confident."

"*You're* the one who just told everyone how right I am."

Throwing his head back, Klag laughed heartily, as did everyone else at the table.

When he was done, Klag then looked at Lokor with a serious expression. "This brings us to the next order of business. You assured me before we left the Tenth Moon that the mutiny would be dealt with with due efficiency. I hardly call a coup attempt and my second officer in the medical bay efficient."

Lokor did not sound at all contrite, even though Klag had made it clear through his tone that an answer that displeased him would result in the lieutenant's death—as, in truth, might an answer that pleased him. "Actually, Captain, Commander Kurak can be blamed to some degree."

The old Kurak boiled to the surface. "What?" she asked with a snarl.

"Your repairs were finished ahead of schedule. Yaklan and his conspirators were planning to make their move when the *Gorkon* was spaceworthy. I had not expected that to be for another day at least, and I intended to use today's primary shift to deal with them."

Klag supposed that was reasonable. "I expect a full report on the *entire* plan and what you intended—and how what happened *did* happen, Lieutenant, am I completely understood?"

Matter-of-factly, Lokor said, "Of course, sir. You'll have it by the end of the shift."

Before Klag could continue, Ensign Kal's voice interrupted. "*Bridge to wardroom. Captain, you have a transmission from General Goluk.*"

Smiling, Klag said, "Put it on the viewer here, Ensign."

Goluk's heavily lined face, framed by his gray mane and beard, appeared on the screen. "*Captain, the enemy is in full retreat—what's left of the enemy, anyhow. Only a dozen of their ships are intact, and they're setting course back to you.*" The general let loose with a rare smile. "*Feel free to destroy them.*"

"I will, General. What were our losses?"

"*Their weapons were quite impressive—we lost the* Gowron *and the* Azetbur, *as well as four of my fleet.*"

"They died well," Klag said.

"*Of that, you can be sure. The River of Blood is crowded this day.*"

"*Bridge to wardroom.*" That was Kal's voice, and he sounded urgent. "*I do not wish to intrude, Captain, but we are receiving a transmission from someone who calls himself First Defensor Vor Ralla.*"

Toq shot Klag a look. "From what the separatists told us, that is the name of their military leader."

"Put him through here, Ensign," Klag said, "and tie General Goluk in."

The viewer went to a split-screen view, Goluk's fierce mien on the left and the unreadable form of an Elabrej—this with definite military markings—on the right.

"I am Klag, son of M'Raq, captain of the *I.K.S. Gorkon*. This is Goluk, son of Ruuv, commander of our forces."

"Then you are the ones to whom I wish to speak. I come to ask for terms of surrender."

"You speak for your government?" Klag asked.

A puff of air expelled from the alien's chest. *"We no longer have a government, thanks to you. The first cleric has claimed power, but I still control our military, and I will be the one to ask for terms."*

"There are no terms," Goluk said. *"You will surrender without condition to the Klingon Empire. Then we will determine what is to be done with you."*

Another puff of air. *"I am in no position to argue with you. I will await your representative in the military sphere."*

"We destroyed that," Klag said.

"No, Captain, with respect, you did not—you destroyed a military sphere, the one we said was our primary headquarters, but it was truly located elsewhere. It is located at the fourth finger of the ninth arm of the Seventh Continent."

"I can translate those coordinates," Toq said quickly.

"Good." Klag gave his first officer an approving nod. "Expect someone soon, First Defensor. Screen off."

The viewer returned to simply a view of Goluk. *"I will remain behind and determine whether or not we should bother to add this misbegotten hegemony to the empire."*

"Sir," Toq said, "it might not be worth the trouble to conquer these people. Their wealth is concentrated among a very few, many of whom are now dead. Their infrastructure was already razed before they came into conflict with us—they are now on the verge of collapse. If we do conquer them, they may force us to divert resources to rebuilding them—and I was under the impression that the function of our exploration of this sector was to *increase* our resources."

Goluk glowered at Toq, and Klag wondered if his first officer let his youthful enthusiasm get the better of him. On the other hand, Toq *had* spent more time among the Elabrej than any of them. *"I will take your words into consideration when I investigate the planet, Commander. The Kesh will remain behind, along with the remains of my fleet. In the meantime, I have been in touch with Chancellor Martok. His orders were to continue the campaign, but when it was finished, all the Chancellor-class ships were to report back to Qo'noS. Except for the Kesh, you, Captain Klag, and the others will follow that order."*

"Yes, General."

Goluk nodded. *"Out."* The screen went dark.

"It is good that we are returning home, Captain," Kurak said. "My repairs were sufficient to get us out of orbit, and will get us back to the Homeworld—barely. We need proper repairs in a shipyard."

Klag nodded. "Indeed. Plus we have many crew to replace. Leskit, set course for Qo'noS, and proceed immediately. I wish to be as far from this hegemony as possible as quickly as possible. Execute at warp nine?" He looked at Kurak. She shook her head. "Warp eight, then, as soon as we're clear of the system."

Getting to his feet, Leskit said, "With great pleasure, sir." He gave Kurak a smile as he rose.

"Except for Toq, you're all dismissed."

Lokor, Leskit, and Kurak departed the wardroom.

Klag regarded his first officer. "You did well, Toq. I must confess, I had given you up for dead when we were forced to abandon the First World and leave you behind. You performed brilliantly."

Toq beamed. "Thank you, sir."

"And you're also lucky Goluk didn't order me to kill you for your effrontery."

At that, Toq slumped in his chair. "I am sorry, sir, I—"

"Do not worry," Klag said, waving his arm in dismissal. "He did *not* order me to, so all is well."

"Sir, what about B'Etloj? She was the I.I. agent who informed Trant about Captain Wirrk and the others. I had a cabin assigned to her, but she has asked numerous times to see you. I informed her that you were too busy."

Klag smiled, grateful for his first officer's perspicacity. "I've had quite enough of I.I. for one mission. As I recall, she elected not to stay with her captain, instead leaving with you?"

"Yes, sir."

Snorting, Klag said, "Tell her I will remain unavailable until we reach Qo'noS. If that is unacceptable to her, she can spend the trip home in the brig instead of the cabin you gave her."

"Gladly, sir." Toq rose. "If that is all?"

"Not quite, Commander." He reached under the table, pulling out a bottle he'd placed there before the meeting began. It was a bottle of '98 bloodwine from the K'reetka vintner. "I won my bet with Wirrk, which means I get to enjoy this bloodwine. I would be honored if you, who saw him last, would share it with me, since he is not here to do it himself."

Toq grinned. "The honor would be mine, Captain." He walked over to the replicator and ordered two mugs.

"You *must* be joking."

G'joth's words were the first ones that any of the fifteenth said after Wol finished her story, and he did not speak them until after a several-second silence, during which G'joth guzzled most of his *warnog*. They sat around one of the tables in the mess hall—Goran taking up two spaces, as usual, with Kagak on one side of him and G'joth on the other. They hadn't yet been assigned a fifth to replace Trant, nor did Wol expect one until after they reported back to Qo'noS.

Wol was happy to be back in uniform, and even more happy about the auburn stubble that had already started to form on her crown. *With any luck, by the time we get home, and the* Gorkon *is repaired, I'll have at least a decent head of hair instead of looking like General Chang.*

After taking a bite of *klongat* leg, G'joth went on. "When you told us down on the Elabrej planet that you had something important to tell us, I didn't imagine it was this."

Wol shrugged and grabbed a handful of *racht*. "I felt you should know."

"Why?" Kagak asked, spitting his heart of *ghISnar* on the table as he spoke. "If your House is no longer, what difference does it make?"

Pausing to swallow her *racht*, Wol then said, "Because I argued with the officers to allow you all to know that Trant was an I.I. agent. My reason was that I did not wish to ask warriors to go into battle without knowing who they were going into battle *with*. But by that token, you all should have known that I was born Eral, daughter of B'Etakk, of the House of Varnak."

"The *defunct* House of Varnak," G'joth said. "Although I appreciate the gesture, Leader, I don't see the point. Trant was still an I.I. agent—but you are no longer Eral. That was past." He laughed. "Besides, I don't believe it. You're too good a soldier to ever have been a highborn *petaQ*."

"Don't underestimate highborn *petaQpu'*," Wol said, returning the laugh. "We have our moments."

"Pfah." G'joth chewed thoughtfully on his *klongat*. "No member of any noble House would have been able to break out of that Elabrej lab and run naked through enemy territory—and win."

"G'joth is right," Kagak said. "It is an honor to be part of your squad, Leader Wol." He held up his mug of *chech'tluth* in salute.

"It doesn't matter," Goran said.

"Why is that, Goran?" Wol asked.

"Because that was the past. In the past, I was a prison guard, but then I stopped. So it doesn't matter anymore. In the past, you were Eral, but then you stopped. So that doesn't matter anymore either. What matters is that you are our leader and we will follow you. That is what the fifteenth does."

"The big man is right," G'joth said. "It wasn't Eral, daughter of B'Etakk, of the House of Varnak who led the fifteenth to the latest in a series of victories, it was Leader Wol. And she is the one I'm proud to serve under." He raised his *warnog* mug. "To our leader."

Kagak raised his *chech'tluth*, and Goran raised his mug—Wol wasn't sure what was in it. "To our leader!" they both bellowed.

Wol smiled. "Thank you." They all drank. Wol's bloodwine was oily and wonderful as it slid slowly down her gullet, coating her tongue and throat. *Not Pelgren, but it'll do.*

"They should write songs about our squad," Kagak said.

G'joth snorted. " 'They' never will. Songs are only about officers. I, however, am seriously considering writing one of my own."

Wincing, Wol asked, "Didn't you learn your lesson from your last abortive attempt at writing, G'joth?"

"Yes—I learned that I needed time to hone my craft. It's been two months, that's time enough for me to try again. Though I may try dramatic fiction—I was able to get my hands on some copies of *Battlecruiser Vengeance.*"

"What's *Battlecruiser Vengeance?*" Kagak asked.

Sighing dramatically, G'joth looked at Wol. "The youth of the empire will amount to *nothing* if they remain unaware of the classics."

"I'm not the youth of the empire," Goran said, "and I've never heard of it, either."

"Obviously, I will have to educate you both by showing you some episodes. I think I'll start with the one where he battles the Romulans."

"He?" Kagak asked.

"Captain Koth—Koth of the *Vengeance!*" G'joth grinned. "Watching them has given me some magnificent ideas."

G'joth's grin was infectious, and Wol found herself sharing it. "I shudder to think, G'joth, what you will do with those ideas."

"As well you should, Leader, as well you should."

THE ADVENTURES OF THE
I.K.S. GORKON WILL CONTINUE. . . .

CHANCELLORS OF
THE KLINGON EMPIRE

The Chancellor-class vessels are named after the twelve who occupied the position of head of the Klingon High Council prior to the current chancellor, Martok, son of Urthog. Some of the known chancellors include:

Kesh (unknown–2292). First appeared in the novel *Star Trek: In the Name of Honor* by Dayton Ward. Methods of ascension and departure unknown.

Gorkon (2292–2293). First appeared in the feature film *Star Trek VI: The Undiscovered Country*. Method of ascension unknown. Assassinated in that film by conspirators, and replaced by Azetbur.

Azetbur (2293–2311). First appeared in *Star Trek VI*. Ascended after the death of her father, Gorkon, in that film. Assassinated by Ditagh, and replaced by Kaarg in the novel *Star Trek The Lost Era: Serpents Among the Ruins* by David R. George III.

Kaarg (2311–2323). First appeared in *Serpents Among the Ruins*. Ascended after the death of Azetbur in that novel. Died by unknown means, and replaced by Ditagh, as mentioned in the novel *Star Trek The Lost Era: The Art of the Impossible* by Keith R.A. DeCandido.

Ditagh (2323–2334). First appeared in *Serpents Among the Ruins*. Ascended after the death of Kaarg, as mentioned in *The Art of the Impossible*. Died of natural causes and replaced by Kravokh in *The Art of the Impossible*.

Kravokh (2334–2346). First appeared in *The Art of the Impossible*. Ascended after the death of Ditagh in that novel. Killed in a duel by K'mpec, who replaced him in that novel.

K'mpec (2346–2367). First appeared in the *Star Trek: The Next Generation* episode "Sins of the Father." Ascended after challenging Kravokh and winning in *The Art of the Impossible*. Died of poison, and replaced by Gowron in the *TNG* episode "Reunion."

Gowron (2367–2375). First appeared in "Reunion." Ascended after the death of K'mpec in that episode. Killed in a duel by Worf, and replaced by Martok in the *Star Trek: Deep Space Nine* episode "Tacking Into the Wind."

Martok (2375–present). First appeared in the *DS9* episode "In Purgatory's Shadow" (though a changeling impersonating him appeared in the earlier *DS9* episode "The Way of the Warrior"). Ascended after the death of Gowron in "Tacking Into the Wind."

GLOSSARY OF KLINGON TERMS

Most of the language actually being spoken in this novel is the Klingon tongue, and has been translated into English for the reader's ease. Some terms that don't have direct translations into English or are proper nouns of some kind have been left in the Klingon language. Since that language does not use the same alphabet as English, the transliterations of the Klingon terms vary depending on preference. In many cases, a more Anglicized transliteration is used instead of the *tlhIngan Hol* transliterations preferred by linguists (e.g., the more Anglicized *bat'leth* is preferred over the *tlhIngan Hol* spelling *betleH*).

Below is a glossary of the Klingon terms used. Anglicized spellings are in **boldface;** *tlhIngan Hol* transliterations are in ***bold italics.*** Please note that this glossary does not include the names of locations, people, or ships. Where applicable, episode, movie, or novel citations are given where the term first appeared. Episode citations are followed by an abbreviation indicating show: TNG=*Star Trek: The Next Generation*, DS9=*Star Trek: Deep Space Nine*.

bat'leth *(betleH)*
Curved, four-bladed, two-handed weapon. This is the most popular handheld, edged weapon used by Klingon warriors owing to its being favored by Kahless, who forged the first one. The legendary Sword of Kahless now held by Chancellor Martok is a *bat'leth*, and most Defense Force warriors are proficient in it. [First seen in "Reunion" (TNG).]

bekk *(beq)*
A rank given to enlisted personnel in the Defense Force. [First referenced in "Sons and Daughters" (DS9).]

bolmaq
An animal native to the planet Boreth that makes a bleating sound and tends to run around in circles a lot. [First referenced in *Honor Bound*.]

chech'tluth *(chechtlhutlh)*
An alcoholic beverage best served heated and steaming. The word seems to derive from the verbs meaning "to drink" and "to get drunk." [First seen in "Up the Long Ladder" (TNG).]

chuSwI'
A rodent that mostly lives underground and makes an annoying noise.

Dahar Master *(Da'ar)*
A warrior who has attained legendary status in life. [First referenced in "Blood Oath" (DS9).]

d'k tahg (*Daqtagh*)

Personal dagger. Most Defense Force warriors carry their own *d'k tahg*; higher-born Klingons often have them personalized with their name and House. [First seen in *Star Trek III: The Search for Spock*.]

gagh (*qagh*)

Food made from live serpent worms (not to be confused with *racht*). [First seen in "A Matter of Honor" (TNG).]

ghISnar cat

Small animal, apparently not a very vicious one, though with perhaps a predilection for trying to sound fiercer than it actually is. [First referenced in "The Way of the Warrior" (DS9).]

ghIntaq

A type of spear with a wooden haft and a curved, two-bladed metal point. Also the name given to a person who serves as a close and trusted advisor to a House. It is possible that the latter usage evolved from the first, with the advisor being analogized to a Househead's trusted weapon. Sometimes Anglicized as *gin'tak*. [Spear first seen in "Birthright Part 2" (TNG); advisor first referenced in "Firstborn" (TNG).]

glob fly (*ghIlab ghew*)

Small, irritating insect with no sting and which makes a slight buzzing sound. [First referenced in "The Outrageous Okona" (TNG).]

grapok sauce (*gha'poq*)

Condiment, often used to bring out the flavor in *gagh* or *racht*. [First seen in "Sons and Daughters" (DS9).]

Gre'thor *(ghe'tor)*

The afterlife for the dishonored dead—the closest Klingon equivalent to hell. Those who are unworthy spend eternity riding the Barge of the Dead to *Gre'thor*. [First mentioned in "Devil's Due" (TNG).]

grinnak *(ghInaq)*

A game. [First referenced in *Honor Bound*.]

jatyIn

According to legend, spirits of the dead that possess the living. [First mentioned in "Power Play" (TNG).]

jeghpu'wI'

Conquered people—more than slaves, less than citizens, this status is given to the natives of worlds conquered by the Klingon Empire. [First used in *Diplomatic Implausibility*.]

jInjoq

A type of bread. [First referenced in *A Time for War, a Time for Peace*.]

khest'n *(Hestlh'ng)*

Interjection with no direct translation. [First used in *The Final Reflection*.]

klin zha *(tlhInja)*

A popular board game. [First seen in *The Final Reflection*.]

klongat *(tlhonghaD)*

A beast native to Qo'noS that is much larger than a *targ* and more difficult to subdue. [First referenced in *Honor Bound*.]

kuvrek *(Quv'eq)*

An animal that prefers the shadows.

lotlhmoq
Predatory bird native to Qo'noS that swoops into the water to catch food.

Mauk-to'Vor *(ma' to'vor)*
A death ritual that allows one who has lost honor to die well and go to *Sto-Vo-Kor* by being honorably killed by a Housemate or someone equally close. [First seen in "Sons of Mogh" (DS9).]

mek'leth *(meqleH)*
A swordlike one-handed weapon about half the size of a *bat'leth*. [First seen in "Sons of Mogh" (DS9).]

meyvaQ
A sex aid.

nagh
The name of a waterfall on Qo'noS. The word literally means "stone."

petaQ
Insult with no direct translation. Sometimes anglicized as *pahtk*. [First used in "The Defector" (TNG).]

Qapla'
Ritual greeting that literally means "success." [First used in *Star Trek III: The Search for Spock*.]

QaS DevwI'
Troop commander on a Defense Force vessel, generally in charge of several dozen soldiers. Roughly analogous to a sergeant in the modern-day army. [First used in *The Brave and the Bold* Book 2.]

qell'qam
Unit of measurement roughly akin to two kilometers. Sometimes Anglicized as *kellicam*. [First used in *Star Trek III: The Search for Spock*.]

qutluch

A weapon favored by assassins, one that leaves a particularly vicious wound. [First seen in "Sins of the Father" (TNG).]

racht *(raHta')*

Food made from live serpent worms (not to be confused with *gagh*). [First seen in "Melora" (DS9).]

raktajino *(ra'taj)*

Coffee, Klingon style. [First seen in "The Passenger" (DS9).]

Sto-Vo-Kor *(Suto'vo'qor)*

The afterlife for the honored dead, where all true warriors go, crossing the River of Blood after they die to fight an eternal battle. The closest Klingon equivalent to heaven. [First mentioned by name in "Rightful Heir" (TNG).]

taknar *(taqnar)*

An animal, the gizzards of which are sometimes served as food. [First referenced in *A Good Day to Die*.]

targ *(targh)*

Animal that is popular as a pet, but the heart of which is also considered a delicacy. [First seen as a pet in "Where No One Has Gone Before" (TNG) and as a food in "A Matter of Honor" (TNG).]

tik'leth *(tIqleH)*

An edged weapon, similar to an Earth longsword. [First seen in "Reunion" (TNG).]

tIq

A river on the planet Qu'vat. The word literally means "long."

toDSaH
Insult with no direct translation. Sometimes Anglicized as *tohzah*. [First used in "The Defector" (TNG).]

trigak *(tlhIghaq)*
A predatory animal with sharp teeth that it bares before attacking. [First referenced in *Honor Bound*.]

warnog *(warnagh)*
An alcoholic beverage. [First seen in "Rightful Heir" (TNG).]

yIntagh
Epithet with no direct translation. [First used in *A Good Day to Die*.]

Glossary of Klingon Terms

KLINGON NUMBERS:

1: *wa'*
2: *cha'*
3: *wej*
4: *loS*
5: *vagh*
6: *jav*
7: *Soch*
8: *chorgh*
9: *Hut*

10: *wa'maH*
20: *cha'maH*
30: *wejmaH*
40: *loSmaH*
50: *vaghmaH*
60: *javmaH*
70: *SochmaH*
80: *chorghmaH*
90: *HutmaH*

100: *wa'vatlh*

1000: *wa'SaD*

ACKNOWLEDGMENTS

First and foremost, thanks to John J. Ordover, who was the one who, way back in 1999, said it would be nifty if I wrote the first novel featuring Worf as Federation Ambassador to the Klingon Empire following *Deep Space Nine*'s finale, and also indulged me in my desire to have most of the action take place on board a Klingon ship. After *Diplomatic Implausibility* was released in 2001 to much acclaim, John was then the one who let me bring that ship, the *I.K.S. Gorkon*, back in my "starship team-up" duology, *The Brave and the Bold*, published in 2002, and then signed me up to write standalone *Gorkon* adventures, the first two of which came out in 2003, and the third of which you're holding in your hands.

John worked on the plot for *Enemy Territory* with me before departing Pocket Books to explore some strange new worlds of his own, and the series was handed over to Marco Palmieri, an editor of magnificent skill, erudi-

Acknowledgments

tion, insight, and, most of all, patience. Some of the best work in my career to date has been under Marco's tutelage, and I'm thrilled that he's going to be the caretaker for Klag and the gang going forward.

Several of the characters herein first were brought to life on the screen, and I owe the actors who played those roles a huge debt: the late David Graf (Leskit in DS9's "Soldiers of the Empire"), J.G. Hertzler (Martok in numerous episodes of DS9), Sterling Macer Jr. (Toq in TNG's "Birthright"), Tricia O'Neill (Kurak in TNG's "Suspicions"), Tony Todd (Rodek in DS9's "Sons of Mogh"), and most especially the big man himself, Brian Thompson (Klag in TNG's "A Matter of Honor"). Thanks also to Keith Hamilton Cobb, whose portrayal of Tyr Anasazi on Gene Roddenberry's Andromeda was the inspiration for Lokor, and the late André the Giant, whose portrayal of Fezzik in The Princess Bride was the inspiration for Goran.

For aid and assistance above and beyond: Dayton Ward, whose military expertise has always been most helpful; Tammy Love Larrabee, who designed the Gorkon and its brother ships (see the specs in the back of The Brave and the Bold Book 2), not to mention the Jakvi-class ships mentioned in Chapter 10; David Mack, from whom I stole General Goluk, and who is one of the best sounding boards I know; Dr. Lawrence Schoen, head of the Klingon Language Institute, for consistent linguistic aid, and also to Dr. Marc Okrand, who created the Klingon language in the first place; John M. Ford, for The Final Reflection in general and for Battlecruiser Vengeance in particular; the rock band Jethro

Acknowledgments

Tull, in its many and varied incarnations over the last thirty-five-plus years, whose music has always been inspirational to me; and Paula M. Block and John Van Citters of Paramount Licensing, who continue to be the best licensing folk ever and whose comments and suggestions always make the book better.

The usual reference sources: *The Star Trek Encyclopedia* and *Star Trek Chronology* by the tireless Mike & Denise Okuda; *The Klingon Dictionary* by the redoubtable Dr. Okrand; *Star Charts* by Geoffrey Mandel; and the various companions for *Star Trek* (by Allan Asherman), *The Next Generation* (by Larry Nemecek), *Deep Space Nine* (by Terry J. Erdmann & Paula M. Block), and *Voyager* (by Paul Ruditis). Also the folks on the various online bulletin boards, who keep us all honest: Psi Phi (www.psiphi.org), the *Trek* Literature board on the *Trek* BBS (www.trekbbs.com), the Simon Says *Trek* Books board (www.startrekbooks.com), and the *Star Trek* Books and *DS9* Avatar Yahoo!Groups (groups.yahoo.com). Plus, the Malibu Gang, the Geek Patrol, and the Forebearance for all the usual reasons.

And finally, last but never least, Terri Osborne, who was even more helpful than usual in kicking my butt to get this book finished.

ABOUT THE AUTHOR

Keith R.A. DeCandido numbers among his accomplishments the Nobel Prize for Economics, winning three Olympic gold medals, fifteen years spent in the Peace Corps, being named an advisor to four different Presidents, doctorates in literature, psychology, and art history, and lying like a rug in the first paragraph of his author bios.

In truth, he has written many many novels, short stories, comic books, eBooks, and nonfiction books in tons of media universes. Besides the prior two *I.K.S. Gorkon* novels—*A Good Day to Die* and *Honor Bound*—he has also written the *Star Trek* novels *Diplomatic Implausibility* (which introduced the *Gorkon*), *Demons of Air and Darkness* (part of the highly successful line of post-finale *Star Trek: Deep Space Nine* novels), *The Brave and the Bold Books 1–2* (the first single story to encompass all five TV series), *The Art of the Impossible* (part of the *New York Times* best-selling *Lost Era* miniseries), *A Time for War, a Time for Peace* (the best-selling finale of the acclaimed nine-book *Star Trek: The Next Generation* miniseries), and *Ferenginar: Satisfaction Is Not Guaranteed* (half of Volume 3 of the *Worlds of Star Trek: Deep Space Nine* miniseries). His *Star Trek* short fiction has appeared in *Gateways: What Lay Beyond, Deep Space Nine: Prophecy and Change, New Frontier: No Limits*, and *Tales of the Dominion War*, and he wrote the four-issue *Next Generation* comic-book miniseries *Perchance to Dream*. He codeveloped and edits the monthly *Star Trek: S.C.E.* eBooks starring the Starfleet Corps of Engineers, and has also written nine eBooks in the series.

Forthcoming *Trek* work includes *Articles of the Federation*, a novel about politics in the *Star Trek* universe, as well as short fiction in the tenth-anniversary *Voyager* anthology, *Distant Shores*. He'll also be telling Klag's story in the *Tales from the Captain's Table* anthology, and assures all and sundry that there will be more *I.K.S. Gorkon* adventures as well (he's already hard at work on Book 4).

Keith has also written in the universes of *Gene Roddenberry's Andromeda, Farscape, Serenity, Buffy the Vampire Slayer*, Marvel Comics, *Resident Evil*, and more. His original novel *Dragon Precinct* was published in 2004, and his award-nominated anthology *Imaginings: An Anthology of Long Short Fiction* was published in 2003. He lives in New York City with his girlfriend and their two cats, Marcus and Aoki. Find out too little about Keith at his official Web site at DeCandido.net or just e-mail him directly at keith@decandido.net.

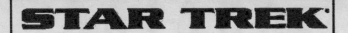

WHAT BEGAN IN
A TIME FOR WAR, A TIME FOR PEACE
AND *TITAN: TAKING WING*
CONTINUES IN

ARTICLES *of the* FEDERATION

A NOVEL BY
KEITH R.A. DeCANDIDO

A LOOK INSIDE THE HALLS OF
POWER IN THE *STAR TREK*
UNIVERSE.

STAR TREK®

ACROSS

1 Bajoran cat
5 Medic for a colony of ex-Borg in "Unity" [VGR]
9 Author Bombeck
13 Used an energy containment coil
15 Kind of energy in "Shadowplay" [DS9]
16 God-like computer in "The Apple" [TOS]
17 Arachnid with half-meter-long legs
18 Doc symbiont who succeeded Jadzia
19 Teer on Capella IV in "Friday's Child" [TOS]
21 Be a breadwinner
22 Spanish wave
24 2024 San Francisco problem
25 Science station Tango
28 PC alphanumeric: abbr.
30 Soufflé
33 Taxi
34 Like 17 Across
36 Onsoron ___ star system
39 Assault weapon
40 T'Lani government envoy in "Armageddon Game" [DS9]
43 Opposite of dep.
44 Wishes restraint
48 ___ Targ (Klingon dishes)
49 Shogun capital
49 Bajoran poet Akorem in "Accession" [DS9]
50 Elevator inventor
51 Homeworld of two assassins sent to DS9 in "Babel"
53 Leader before Leeta
55 Aldorian beverage served in Ten-Forward
56 Mass. motto word
56 ___ wing-slug
61 ___ -raves of Ne'kfat
63 Lifeform indigenous to the Orikisn homeworld
65 U. Paris apart-time heat
67 Radiate
68 Flaxxless commander who ordered Kirk away
69 Klaang escaped from one in "Broken Bow" [ENT]
70 Cape for Scotty
71 Bilaanth: Prefix

DOWN

1 Royal tasters
2 Samson friend of Jadzia Dax
3 Chess castle
4 Base where the Magellan crew put on a talent show
5 Ndelo who played Drax
6 Used a travel pod
7 Restless
8 "Enterprise" supervising producer Howard
9 Brannon on "Violations" [TNG]
10 Tarkessian imaginary friend of Guinan as a child
11 McGivers who befriends Khan in "Space Seed" [TOS]
12 Saloon leader
14 Actor Morales
18 "___ and Loss" [DS9]
20 Alpha-currant ___
25 Selver
27 Superstore shout
26 Member of Klingon Intelligence in "Visionary" [DS9]
29 Regime on Ekos in "Patterns of Force" [TOS]
30 Devotion creature Korax compared to Kirk
32 Parent of P'Chan in "Survive Instinct" [VGR]
35 Modernized

37 Deanna on "Star Trek: The Next Generation"
38 Pound sounds
41 Warp core reactor output
42 Captain of the U.S.S. Equinox also in the Delta Quadrant
45 Author LeShan
47 Tactical officer out night shift in "Rightful Heir" [TNG]
49 Bajoran grain-processing center
51 Kes is kidnapped to this planet in "Warlord" [VGR]
52 Tanandra Bay, for one
54 Show horse
56 Priestly robes
57 "Inter Arma ___ Silent Leges" [DS9]
59 Sect of the Kazon Collective
60 Miles O'Brien's coffee-cutoff hour
62 Of old
64 Gigatons: Abbr.
65 Fight thrasher

STAR TREK®

First in an all-new series!

Following the harrowing events of the *Errand of Vengeance* trilogy, tensions between the Federation and the Klingon Empire are the highest they've been...

Errand of Fury:
Book One:
Seeds of Rage

by
Kevin Ryan

Available next month wherever books are sold!